HIDDEN MAGIC

THE DARK CARNIVAL
BOOK FOUR

TRUDI JAYE

WWW.TRUDIJAYEWRITES.COM

Hi, my name's Trudi Jaye, and I've got a secret...

A secret society, that is.

Especially designed for people like you who love reading my books, the Trudi Jaye Secret Society is a place filled with magic, laughter, and most of all... free stories.

Everyone who joins the society is given access to an ancient tome full of the stories, novellas, bonus epilogues, and deleted scenes from all the different Trudi Jaye series.

Called **The Shadow Archives,** you can access it by heading to my website and joining the secret society...

Join Trudi Jaye's Secret Society... if you dare!

www.trudijayewrites.com/shadow-archives

Hidden Magic is published by Star Media Ltd

Published 15 December 2015 by Star Media Ltd

Copyright © Star Media Ltd, 2015

Cover design: PCTC Design

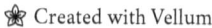 Created with Vellum

To my delightfully wonderful daughter Zoey. You are the light of my life.

CHAPTER 1

*H*enry whistled through his teeth as he gazed up at the steel and glass monstrosity in front of him.

It towered overhead, making him squint as he tried to see the top through the glare of Tampa's midday sun.

He glanced at the piece of paper again, just to make sure. Yep. It was the right place. He was going to have to put up with this for the next month.

It's just a month, Henry. And the money they're going to pay for the contract will cover a third of what we owe on the last installment to the bank.

We're relying on you.

Jack's words still ringing in his ears, Henry sighed. He didn't have much choice. He glanced back at his car, a pristine condition 1974 Dodge Charger SE parked across one and a half spaces, and considered leaving. When Rilla had said she would fly him down to Tampa from the Compound in Montana, he'd shaken his head and insisted on driving.

It had taken him a few long days, but he'd arrived in one piece, and was far calmer than if he had flown.

He still thought this was a bad idea. He didn't like spending long periods away from the Carnival and he didn't like working on projects where he wasn't the one in charge—or was related to the person in charge. Plus, ordinary people made him edgy.

But Jack had been persistent and, despite his reluctance, the Carnival was depending on him.

Heaving a big sigh, Henry took off his cowboy hat and strode into the building through the glass revolving doors. It made him tired just thinking about spending an entire month with ordinary folk. The way they thought, the way they talked —the way they judged based on how you looked, instead of who you were on the inside. It all added up to a headache.

The massive entrance area was stark and industrial, with concrete floors and steel beams visible overhead. Henry's boots struck the polished floor, and the sound echoed through the high-ceiling entranceway. Glass featured heavily in the design, as did steel bolts and rivets.

There was no signage to give any hint of what they did here, but the massive security guard standing next to the reception desk said it was something they wanted to protect. Henry nodded at the guard who had arms twice the size of Henry's and a chin that looked like it could bulldoze mountains. The man didn't even blink.

When they'd told him about the contract, Jack had muttered something about smart-room robotics and nanotechnology, but both fields were so wide, Henry still had no clue what the project might be. Not that it mattered; he could generally turn his hand to whatever was needed. He'd been doing it since he was old enough to pick up a spanner and help his father fix the thrill rides and to invent whatever they needed to grant the wish of the Carnival's Mark.

He strode up to the starchy woman at the black marble

reception desk who'd been eyeing him suspiciously ever since he'd come through the doors. Her perfect makeup was marred by the frown line in her forehead, and her dark brown hair seemed to be glued in place.

"Can I help you?" she said.

"I certainly hope so," he replied, giving her his best toothy smile.

She looked down her nose at him, her glasses perched precariously on the end. Apparently, she didn't respond to good ole carnival charm. Henry tipped his head to one side. "You know, you need a contraption to keep those glasses properly on your nose. I could do that, if you gave me a bit of time with them." He leaned in and squinted at the tiny screws on the side of the glasses.

She blinked, leaned away, and pushed the glasses up her nose. "Your name?"

Her voice was so cold Henry had to suppress the urge to shiver. "Oh sorry, I was distracted. Henry Kokkol. I'm here on assignment."

"Assignment?" She looked Henry up and down. He glanced downwards; cowboy boots, ripped jeans, and a faded David Bowie t-shirt—his usual. He'd taken his cowboy hat off as soon as he'd entered the building. His Momma had raised him properly.

He nodded. "Assignment."

"You know what we do here, Henry?"

"Design high-end smart room and nanotechnology for the international market. So I believe. I didn't have time to do much more than look you up on the internet before I was sent here."

"And you still feel you're in the right place?" Her voice was snide, but Henry was distracted from her attitude by the glasses. They'd fallen down her nose again.

Henry shrugged. "It's not the place I'd choose to be, but it's the place I've been ordered to report."

"And who are you here to see?"

Henry pulled out his piece of paper again, and checked the name. "A Dr. Callaghan, according to this piece of paper."

She sighed. "Dr. Callaghan is the owner of the company and our Chief Operating Officer. Are you sure that's the name on your piece of paper? If I call his office and you're not expected, I'm going to be annoyed with you, Henry."

Henry smiled. "You're not going to be disappointed,"—he paused, looking at her name badge—"Wanda."

Wanda narrowed her eyes, not entirely certain he could be trusted. However, she picked up the phone and dialed a number. "Deirdre, there's a Henry Kokkol here to see Dr. Callaghan?" Her voice implied she knew it was a hoax.

Henry leaned casually against the reception desk, tapping a finger on the marble, waiting patiently.

"Yes, Deidre, I'll send him right up," she said. Wanda glanced up at Henry, who grinned and winked.

Wanda shook her head. "I can see you're going to be trouble, Henry Kokkol. Dr. Callaghan will see you now. He's on level twelve. Robert will escort you to the elevators." She waved one hand toward the large security guard.

Henry smiled. "Thank you, Wanda, for your help. I appreciate it." He ambled over to the elevators in Robert's wake. The guard inserted a keycard to unlock the call button, and pressed it with one beefy finger. The elevator doors opened immediately. Henry nodded at the impassive guard and stepped into the small space. It was fancy, all done up in mirrors and industrial steel. He sighed as he pressed the button for level twelve. This was already tiresome, and he'd only been here five minutes. He vowed that he would finish this contract within the week, no matter what. He knew he could do it. The magic pulsed through his veins even this far away from the Carnival.

When the doors opened, Henry stepped out into another, very different, entranceway. This one was much friendlier, with cream walls and old 50s advertisements for toys— mostly rockets and cars—framed on the walls. A blonde receptionist with another perfect up do was waiting behind a wooden desk.

"Mr. Kokkol? Dr. Callaghan will see you now. Please follow me." The younger receptionist smiled at Henry, her blue eyes sparkling, and stood up.

Henry followed her to a set of double doors. She pushed one open, and led him into a large room, filled with strange and incredible paraphernalia. Henry looked around in wonder. Old-fashioned video games, life-size statues of movie characters, bits and pieces of machinery, cars and even boats all littered the room. There was even a Tardis.

"Hey there, Henry. It's so great to meet you!" A friendly voice emerged from the side of a strange metal contraption at one end of a large wooden table. A moment later, it was followed by the shape of a tall, gangly man who looked to be in his early twenties. "I'm Lucas Callaghan."

He took in Henry's surprised stare, and sighed. "I'm older than I look. Bad genetics mean people never believe I'm the one in charge. It's lucky I'm more intelligent than most of them, or I'd never survive." He flipped his long, brown hair out of his eyes, and grinned down at Henry.

A surprised bark of laughter escaped Henry's mouth. "It's, uh, good to meet you, Dr. Callaghan," he said, holding out his hand to the younger man. Despite himself, Henry liked him already.

"Lucas, please." He took Henry's hand in both of his and shook it vigorously. "It's great to have you here. Jack told me all about you. He said you're a genius with machines." He looked like an overgrown kid on Christmas morning.

Henry shook his head, suddenly nervous. "I hope Jack hasn't been boasting too much. I'm good with figuring out how things work, mostly." He could fix anything, and create whatever they needed for the Gift. But that was different to working in the outside world in some fancy research lab. His palms started to sweat and he wondered if he was going to get out of here in a week after all.

"That's exactly what we need. We've reached a roadblock on our latest device, and I've decided a fresh pair of eyes will help the team push through."

Henry walked forward and touched a massive engine sitting at the other end of the table from where Lucas had been working. "Is this what I think it is? A Chrysler A57 Multibank? The engine they used in the tanks in World War Two?"

"One and the same." Lucas gave a pleased smile. "I have a working model in storage. I'll let you drive it sometime." Lucas walked over to stand next to Henry beside the table, and slapped one hand on his shoulder. "I knew you were the right man for this job, as soon as Jack told me about you."

"I don't even know what it is you're doing here, Lucas."

"It's really quite simple. We're trying to take smart room technology to the next level, to have it on us at all times. Not just when we enter a certain place or room, but all the time."

Henry frowned. "At the risk of bursting your bubble, wearable technology is pretty much mainstream these days, isn't it?" he said.

Lucas grinned. "Oh, yes. I really like you. You don't hold back. That's just what this team needs." He touched the motor sitting in front of them with a reverent finger. "You're right, it's old news. Our project takes it further. At least, it was supposed to. It's a Second Skin Kinetic Intelligent Neurosystem."

"A what?" Henry struggled to imagine what that sequence of words might mean in practice. Some kind of computer that was worn on the skin?

"We call it SSKIN. Come on, it'll be easier to just show you. I'll introduce you to the team."

Lucas led Henry back out to the elevators and pressed the button, talking the whole way. "The team is small, and they're probably going to resist the idea of someone else coming in to help. But I know you're going to blow our socks off, I can feel it." Lucas rubbed his hands together and grinned. The doors to the elevators pinged open and Lucas gestured for Henry to go first.

"Research lab," said Lucas as he entered.

"Certainly, Dr. Callaghan," replied a woman's voice.

"Voice-controlled elevators?" Henry said, his eyebrows raised.

"Only for me." Lucas grinned. "Privileges of being the boss."

"Do you tinker with inventions as well, Lucas?" Henry was suddenly curious about the background of the enthusiastic man in front of him. How had he come to be the owner of a multi-million-dollar technology company?

"Yes, I'm an inventor, too. I have a PhD in nanotechnology from MIT."

"So a big time inventor, then." Henry was being sarcastic, but Lucas didn't pick up on it.

"Not so much big time as lucky. My PhD research into an alternative heating system was picked up and purchased by a rather large multinational company. Luckily, it wasn't my only idea, so I was able to take that money and set myself up here. The rest is history." Lucas swept his arms wide indicating the building around them.

Henry was impressed. Lucas really had done it all himself.

The doors opened, and they walked out into a large open floor plan area. Aside from a few desks with extensive computing systems to one side and at the back of the room, and a meeting area with a table and chairs, the area was filled with shelves and tables covered with robotics equipment—metal legs and arms, computer parts, keyboards, nuts and bolts, wires and cables, soldering devices—in all shapes and sizes.

Henry itched to start putting things in the right places. His hands even rose up of their own accord, as if to grab the closest part and get to work. He literally had to clasp them together in front of him.

He took another step into the room and stopped. He sensed a faint metallic magic floating in the air around him, whispering to him. He glanced at Lucas, and the other men who were walking toward him. It wasn't coming from any of them.

They might not know it, but someone was working magic here.

CHAPTER 2

*F*rom her cubicle on the far side of the room, Fee looked up. Something tingled down her spine; the intuition she relied on for survival. Lucas was standing in front of the lift and next to him was a golden god. Tall and broad, with blond hair and a chiseled chin. He smiled at the room in general and Fee knew she was in trouble.

She took a sip of her iced tea, wondering what to do. Something tapped on her glass, and she looked down at the little metal creature who had stowed away in her handbag this morning. He was one of her inventions, a tiny spider-like robot with multiple legs and a constant desire to swim in water. She'd been trying to create something that could test the purity of water in third world countries. Instead, she'd ended up with an annoyance. She sighed and tipped him into the glass of water she kept on her desk. She watched as he splashed around, before going back to her immediate problem.

The others generally ignored her, left her in the corner, and didn't bother her too much, only coming to her when they needed a particular bit of robotic help to grease the wheels of the project. She preferred it like that. She certainly didn't want to make friends with any of the scientists on the team.

However, her intuition was going off big time, and she knew something was about to change. Goosebumps appeared on her skin, and she rubbed her arms. What if they'd found her? What if this man was a scout sent to assess the situation? The exit sign to the far side of the elevators blinked mockingly at her. She'd never be able to make it there before this man, if he *was* here for her.

Something tickled her neck, distracting her from her dark thoughts. She grabbed at the metal creature hiding in her hair. Another damn stowaway. This one was bigger, but with five waving hands like a crab's. He moved like a crab too, but he used his arms for evil instead of good. He was one of her early attempts; but instead of a handy robot to find lost items, she'd created a kleptomaniac who loved nothing more than to steal her stuff. She pulled him off, and her gold necklace landed in her hand along with the robotic thief.

"You can't *do* that," she whispered at him. She shoved him into her top drawer and quickly shut it. Hopefully, that would keep him safe for a little while.

She looked up again to see the delightfully arrogant—yet annoyingly clueless—Dr. Pelgrim Shaw stride over to the elevators. He wore his usual perfectly groomed shirt and pants, his hair short and his face impeccably shaven. He was the political beast among them; he knew how to work the room, and who to make up to. And obviously, the boss was the perfect place to start. She watched through narrowed eyes as Pelly shook Lucas' hand, and then turned to the new man. As the big blond man smiled and shook his hand, and Lucas continued to talk, Pelly's shoulders stiffened. His voice raised a little and he let go of the golden god's hand.

Fee smiled as tension drifted across the room. It wasn't

often that Pelly was taken down a peg or two, and it was good to be a witness when it did happen. Lucas generally left them to it; he liked to give people space to be creative in their research. Unfortunately, Pelly just wanted to rule the world. And if his world happened to consist of the research and development lab at Callaghan Technologies, so be it.

The others were now drifting over, drawn by the raised voices and the promise of excitement. They were a team of five, and she was the only woman. Eugene, David, and Nolan were all excellent researchers in their own fields, but had the stereotypical shyness and introverted personalities of scientists the world over. Nolan led the way—he generally did of the three of them—his glasses reflecting off the fluorescent lights overhead. He was most used to dealing with people; he'd been a practicing doctor for several years before deciding research was his passion. Eugene was next; his retro 70s look accidental rather than purposeful. Then came David, the newest member of the team, who was so shy he looked like he might actually run if startled.

Fee watched as Lucas made the introductions, wondering what he really thought of the team, and Pelly's leadership. Their employer's real thoughts were hidden behind his outer shell of smiling enthusiasm and affability. He had one hand casually in his pocket, a smile on his face, and laugh lines around his eyes. Fee shook her head. Before meeting Lucas, she wouldn't have thought it was possible for someone to seem so outwardly open and yet be so good at hiding what they actually thought.

Pelly might bluster and scoff about it; but they were significantly behind schedule on the project, and Fee had been wondering how long Lucas would let it go on. Pelly was smart in a lot of ways, but he underestimated the sharpness in Lucas's gaze and saw only an affable, friendly—and thereby supposedly malleable—young man.

Fee started flicking the tip of a ballpoint pen off and on. Lucas was talking as each of the three researchers shook the stranger's hand, carefully watching their reactions. With each passing moment, Fee became more convinced this was a monumental moment for the team. Something was about to happen that would change everything. Was Lucas closing them down? Or perhaps putting this new man in charge? Perhaps he was here to buy them out?

Her fingers stilled on the pen. Or had the Witch Hunters finally found her?

The last thought sent a chill across her skin and she had to resist the urge to crawl under her desk. What good would that do if they *were* here for her?

Pelly glanced in her direction, and motioned with his hand. She sighed. He was right, it was time to come out of hiding and face whatever was going to happen. She'd learned to be quick on her feet over the years. She would deal with this, whatever it was, straight on.

Standing, Fee brushed at imaginary fluff on her knee-length black dress, and then pushed a strand of her long hair back behind one ear. She took a deep breath and headed over to meet their visitor.

As she neared the golden god, she realized he was enormous. He didn't top Lucas for height—no one did—but he had a breadth, a feeling of solidity that Lucas lacked. His alert gaze didn't seem to miss anything, and Fee could tell he'd summed up Pelly immediately. He smiled kindly at the other three and made conversation with them easily. They were blossoming in the sunlight of his attention.

Who was he? Why was he here? The questions thrummed in her head, making her dizzy with apprehension.

"Ah, Fee, thank you for joining us." The reprimand in Pelly's voice was unmistakable. "Fee is our robotics expert. Anything robotic, she creates it for us. Fee this is Henry. He

12

will be joining the team for a month as a...consultant." Fee was used to reading the not-so-subtle undertones in Pelly's voice, and he didn't think much of Henry and his status as consultant.

"Hi, Henry, nice to meet you," she said with a glance at Lucas, who was chatting to the others with an easy smile on his face. He seemed pleased with Henry's inclusion in their team. Their boss had subtle magic of his own, although he didn't wield it in the same purposeful way Fee did. It had helped him create his company from the ground up, and Fee trusted his instincts when he was enthusiastic over some particular path.

"I'll gather some schematics while you introduce yourselves," said Pelly, his chest puffed out like a gorilla protecting his patch. He would probably get old schematics, just to put Henry off. He walked away and, as he passed him by, Nolan caught his arm, asking him a question in an undertone, their backs to Fee.

"Fee? That's an unusual name," said Henry, holding out his hand with a smile.

Sighing, Fee prepared herself to tell him the usual lie about what it was shortened from. "So I'm told," she said. The second her hand touched his, alarm bells went off in her head. A sizzle of blue lightning streaked down her arm and up Henry's. Colors burst inside her head, exploding like Fourth of July fireworks. It was confusing, painful, and beautiful all at the same time.

Fee felt a moment of complete chaos, and then everything went black.

CHAPTER 3

*H*enry only just managed to catch Fee.

As soon as he'd touched her hand, electrical feedback had hit all his senses at once; it felt like he'd been dumped into water with an electric current running through it, while someone dragged their nails down a chalkboard, and someone else played the violin off key. Bright lights flashed in his head and pain streaked along his senses.

However, he hadn't reacted as badly as Fee, and he'd only just caught her before she hit her head on the hard concrete floor. Once the initial pain subsided, an uncomfortable buzzing vibration danced over his skin where he was touching her, sending prickly shockwaves down his body.

Glancing around, he saw the shocked faces of the other researchers. What had just happened? He didn't understand it, and his thinking was slowed by the flash of energy from Fee's initial touch. "Is there, uh, somewhere I can put her?" he asked. He wasn't sure who had seen the actual lightning, but it hadn't been natural, and they were going to have questions.

"I don't know what's wrong with her," said Pelgrim,

walking over from where he'd been talking to Nolan. "She didn't report any illness to me when she arrived this morning." His expression said he didn't want to get closer to Fee and risk contamination.

Henry figured Pelgrim hadn't seen what had happened—he was the kind of guy who would question it. Gesturing to a couch near the elevator banks, Pelgrim stayed where he was while Henry strode over and deposited her gently on the couch. As soon as he withdrew his touch, the electrical current zinging along his nerve endings stopped, and Henry stepped back, letting out a relieved breath.

He focused his attention on the unconscious woman in front of him. She was medium height, long white-blonde hair, and freckles fighting for space across her nose. He'd noticed her grey eyes just before they'd touched hands. Nothing unusual about her—except the painful feedback they'd both experienced.

Henry tried to reason it out in his head. What could cause this kind of reaction? It had felt like opposite forces hitting each other, or two magnets with the same charge, unable to be in the same space at the same time.

Had the strange reaction he'd felt affected his magic? A moment of panic had him reaching inside himself to find his connection to the Carnival. It was buzzing with heat, but otherwise unharmed. He breathed a sigh of relief.

Then what was happening? Who was this woman?

"I'm so sorry about this, Mr. Kokkol. She's normally very efficient," said Pelgrim, a tinge of embarrassment in his voice.

"She can't help fainting," interrupted Lucas, frowning down at Pelgrim.

"Oh, certainly not, Lucas. I didn't mean to imply..."

"Should we call a doctor?" one of the other men suggested.

Henry cleared his throat. "Maybe a cold cloth for her face? I'm sure she'll come around again in a moment. Then we can find out what happened." And perhaps he could convince whoever had seen it that the blue lightning was to do with something other than the raw magic he could still feel stinging the air around them.

The men all looked at each other uncomfortably. "She keeps to herself mainly. I'm not sure if she has any medical problems," said Pelgrim stiffly.

Henry looked around at the four men in front of him, all so different. According to Lucas, they had been working together for a while now, but none of them seemed to be connected. The magic inside him stirred to life, and he knew the first step he was going to take to get this project back on track.

He looked down at Fee. First, he had to figure out what had happened between them so that Fee didn't faint every time they shook hands.

Nolan had just placed a cold cloth over her forehead when Fee started to wake up. She blinked, and for a moment, just stared up at all the men hovering over her. She blinked again and this time her eyes darted around, as if she was looking for a way to escape.

"How about we all give Fee some room," suggested Lucas. As one, they shuffled back a step.

"How are you feeling Fee?" asked Pelgrim.

Fee nodded slowly. "I'm fine. I don't know what happened. I think I might need to eat," she said. She pulled herself up to sitting, although she kept the cold cloth on her forehead and leaned forward a little.

Henry examined Fee's expression as a new thought occurred to him: did she really think her fainting fit was caused by lack of food? Maybe she didn't know about the magic? Surely, she'd felt the same burst of energy he had?

"Take all the time you need," said Lucas. "The rest of us are going to sit down at the conference table and discuss where things are at with the SSKIN project. We need to get Henry up to speed as quickly as possible."

Fee glanced at Henry, and electricity sizzled down his spine. He rolled his shoulders, trying to get rid of the uncomfortable sensation.

"I'll grab my sandwich and join you in a minute," she said.

"You're quite welcome to go home, if you're not feeling well," said Lucas, his tone worried.

Fee shook her head. "I'm fine. I'll be there soon." She stood up, waving away Nolan's offer of help, and walked slowly back to her desk at the far end of the room.

Henry followed the others to the large meeting table, and sat down near the head of the table next to Lucas. Pelgrim pushed Eugene out of the way to ensure he snagged the seat across from Henry, and on the other side of Lucas. The man had a unique sense of his own importance.

He was going to be a problem.

"Pelgrim, why don't you explain SSKIN, and we can go from there?" said Lucas.

"The whole project?" said Pelgrim.

Lucas sighed gently. "Why don't you start by introducing the team?"

"We all have expertise in nanotechnology, to varying degrees," said Pelgrim. "I also have an excellent knowledge of the field of artificial intelligence. Nolan here is a medical researcher. David specializes in patterns and learning theory in computing. Fee is our robotics expert, and Eugene is an engineer. We're aiming to combine these fields to create something new and exciting."

Henry nodded. So far, so boring.

"We initially considered smart room concepts, where a room is set up to interact with individuals using an amalgamation of robotics and advanced computing, thereby providing information and assistance on multiple levels. But it was already being done by too many other researchers. So we tried to take it further. What about something on a person? An item of clothing perhaps? Again, it was already being done, so we tried to take it another step forward." Pelgrim cleared his throat and looked around the room, finishing on Lucas.

"Go on, Pelgrim," said Lucas. "Henry is part of the team now. He has to know what you're working on."

"We are trying to create a computer that is also a second skin. Something that people can wear over their real skin, for a variety of purposes. It needs to be strong and durable, to protect them, but also to survive the rough treatment most people will mete out. It needs to have the technology inside it to provide all the kinds of information people expect, like the time, their email, heart rate monitors, that kind of thing. We're also working on a skin that will help people recover from illnesses, or even catch and heal disease before they're aware they have it. It needs to have an AI portion, so that it learns information about the person, and can increasingly make their lives easier."

Henry nodded slowly. "So it's a kind of protection suit, keeping them safe from the world around them?" He couldn't think of anything worse. A freaking body suit. But despite his personal distaste, the idea created a small spark of interest.

Pelgrim gave a smug smile. "We believe we can make it so people will live longer if they wear the suit. It would be as close to immortality as anything is these days."

Henry shifted in his seat. That was a big claim. "Was there a reason you wanted to do a second skin, rather than a body suit?"

"A body suit would be obvious; everyone around them would know they were wearing it." Pelgrim paused. "We wanted to provide something subtle, that only the wearer would know about."

Again, Henry nodded. It was a worthwhile point. "You want it to be smart enough to diagnose illnesses and treat any problems?"

"Yes."

"And a person who was high profile could wear it instead of a bulletproof jacket. That's how strong you want it?"

Pelgrim nodded. "Certainly."

"And also be used for day-to-day activities? So nanocomputers inside the skin? How thick is it?" Henry's mind was already whirring with the possibilities. He'd worked on skin previously, but only because he'd wanted to provide a realistic prosthetic leg for Kara, their last Mark from the previous season. He could get Frankie involved to do a bit of global research on the topic for him. He'd have to get up to speed ASAP.

"We have it down to five millimeters, but it needs to be much thinner to work," said Nolan, the most talkative of the other three men in the group. He was short, going slightly bald on top, and wore his glasses like a protective screen.

Henry nodded. "Tell me more."

"We've struck some problems; the main one being that the heat of a person's skin brings the temperature of the second skin up to levels where it can't operate. It shorts out every time."

"Makes sense. Body heat can be a problem." When he'd designed the prosthetic leg for Kara, he'd had to tinker with heat to make sure his fake skin didn't cause her problems.

"We also haven't been able to determine the best use of the nanotechnology. We've been arguing over what to include. We have finite space available, and can't do it all," said Pelgrim.

"You won't listen to me; that's the problem." Fee's voice came to them just before she appeared at the table, brown paper sandwich bag in hand. Henry saw something move inside the bag before a tiny metal head poked out. She quickly shoved it down again. He frowned, trying to figure out what he'd seen.

"Now, Fee, we don't need to hash over old arguments for Lucas and Henry," Pelgrim was saying.

Henry felt Lucas stiffen beside him. "I disagree, Pelgrim. That's exactly what we should do," he said. "That's the reason I've brought Henry into the team. You've stalled, and you need some outside help." Lucas held up his hand when Pelgrim opened his mouth to speak. "No arguments."

If he'd been a bird, Pelgrim's feathers would have been all puffed out. In fact, that's what he reminded Henry of, a big puffy bird, somehow intent on protecting his territory from newcomers, at all costs.

Henry cleared his throat. "I'm not here to cause problems, and when my month is up, I'll disappear again. You don't need to worry about me stealing ideas, and I don't own the copyright on the work I'll be doing over the next month. I'm simply another set of hands to get work done, another brain to bounce ideas off, and another set of eyes to see the problems more clearly."

Everyone except Pelgrim and Fee nodded. He'd need to do a little more work on those two.

"Henry's right," added Lucas. "The contract he signed is rock solid. You can be open with him, and make sure you use his abilities."

He hesitated and cleared his throat. "Your team hasn't made any significant moves forward in almost six months. I wasn't going to mention this right now; but as you're not being entirely cooperative, I need to impress on you all the importance of working with Henry.

"Because, if at the end of this month, you haven't made serious inroads into your concept, I'll have to close the project down and let you all go."

CHAPTER 4

ee watched as Pelly tried to argue with Lucas. She could see he'd made up his mind. That was the thing about Lucas. He appeared all teddy-bear cuteness, but he had an internal steel that allowed him to make the tough decisions. That was why he had a multi-million-dollar research company at such a young age. Certainly not through luck.

The consultant had appeared as stunned as the rest of them at the announcement, which was a point on his side.

Henry, the consultant.

She didn't know what had happened when she'd shaken his hand, but it had been...unexpected. Like her brain and her magic were scrambled at the same time. It was possible the reaction they'd had was some kind of new device being used by the Witch Hunters to find their quarry. Had she given herself away? Was that the big change she'd sensed when Henry had walked in the door?

She considered Henry through narrowed eyes. It had felt organic, natural. A zap of electricity that hadn't quite died down even now. She didn't think the Witch Hunters would approve of something like that; it would go against their fundamental beliefs.

She blinked, trying to get moisture into her contacts. They felt gritty, as if she'd gotten dirt under them. She was also still feeling shaky, and didn't know if that would go away while Henry was around. She hoped so. She couldn't operate with this level of ongoing disturbance.

Had he felt it as well? He seemed so calm. And she didn't think he'd fainted.

Why had it just been her?

Questions were running around in her head, and Fee just wanted to stand up, pull at her hair, and scream. Luckily, she'd cured herself of those kinds of emotional outbursts a long time ago. She pictured herself doing it inside her head, and continued to watch the argument in front of her.

"I'm sorry everyone. I know it's hard. But it's my final decision," Lucas said. He stood up. "I'm offering you Henry as a way to improve your chances because I think it's an idea that has merit. But I can't keep shovelling money at you with no actual results.

"I'll leave you with Henry now. I expect you to get him settled in and discuss your plan of action." Lucas nodded at them all, and then strode toward the elevators. Luckily, the doors opened quickly, and his exit wasn't made awkward by standing there for ages. Fee grinned. She knew about the alterations Lucas had put into the elevators, and they included a fingerprint recognition system that cancelled every other person's call request and went straight to wherever Lucas was waiting whenever he pushed the button.

"I don't know what you think is so funny, Fee, but finding out we will have no job in a month doesn't seem worthy of humor." Pelly was in a fine form, his latent drama queen emerging with force.

Fee rolled her eyes. "Don't give up on us yet, Pelly," she

23

said. It said something about his state of mind that he didn't reprimand her for using her nickname for him. "We've still got a month to prove ourselves, and we've got Henry here to help." She considered Henry, sitting across the table from her, looking like he'd rather be anywhere else in the world. "So what's your expertise, Henry?"

He cleared his throat. "I'm an engineer by trade. But I can put my hand to nearly anything and make it work."

"And you do consulting work?" asked Pelly.

Henry paused. "Ah, no, not usually. This is the first time."

Fee frowned. "So do you work for another tech company? Surely, Lucas would know better than that?" She glanced at Pelly.

"No, I don't work for another tech company." He cleared his throat. "I don't usually work in this field at all."

Fee felt a strange foreboding sensation crawling up her spine. She had an idea that she wasn't going to like the end of this conversation. "So where do you usually work, Henry?" she asked.

"I'm not sure that's relevant. How about we all get on with the work, and try to save your jobs?" said Henry evasively.

Pelly had been watching this exchange, but now he broke in. "No, I think this might be extremely relevant. What is your background, Henry? Where did you go to graduate school? What is your experience in this area? We are being forced to rely on you for our very livelihood. I think you owe it to us to give us an answer."

Henry looked at them for a moment, considering. He sighed. "You're not going to like it, Pelgrim."

"If that is the case, then it's doubly important you share this information with us."

"All right. I'm part of the thrills crew for the Jolly Knight Carnival. I don't have any kind of formal degree or diploma from a college. I just know what I know from hard work and experience." He held his arms wide and shrugged. "It's always been enough for me."

Fee's eyes widened. She was less inclined to place value in postgraduate education than the others, but even she was shocked. Lucas had left them in the hands of some guy from the circus who had no formal education or research experience? How was that possible?

Pelly stood up, his mouth opening and shutting, but no words came out. His jowls flapped up and down, like a demented turkey. If the situation hadn't been so serious, Fee might have laughed.

HENRY SIGHED. It was always this way. As soon as an outsider found out where he was from, they refused to take him seriously, no matter how much he tried to prove himself. His sensible self usually suggested that he didn't tell them, and he often didn't. But he wasn't ashamed of his background, either. So, if ordinary folk insisted on knowing, he told them. Then weathered the consequences.

"You're a carny? Is Lucas aware of this? I'm going to inform him right now!" Pelgrim strode off toward the elevators. He banged the button, but the lift didn't come straight away. He paced in front of the lifts like a caged lion.

"He knows, Dr. Shaw," said Henry raising his voice slightly so the researcher could hear. "He seemed pretty excited about it," he added in a lowered voice, just for the others who were still sitting at the table. He looked around at the remaining researchers. Nolan had been the most interactive so far after Pelgrim, and even he was looking like a deer in the headlights.

The lift dinged, and the doors opened behind them. "I'll

be back with your walking orders, Mr. Kokkol!" said Pelgrim as he stormed through the doors. If he could have slammed the door, Henry was pretty sure he would have.

Eugene broke the silence. "What does the thrills crew do, Mr. Kokkol?"

Henry smiled at him. Eugene was small and shy with dark hair and dark skin. "We keep everything running, all the machinery at the carnival. From the Ferris wheel and the other rides to the trucks, which carry everything between stops and even the computers and ticketing machinery. We don't have the luxury of calling in someone else, so we have to be experts at everything ourselves."

Nolan nodded, his glasses flickering in the light above their heads. "So you've some experience with engineering?"

"Sure, engineering, computing, lighting, almost anything you could think of. I'm the one they come to when they need something fixed."

Fee leaned back. "That's not so bad. Have you ever invented something? From scratch?"

Henry smiled. "That's my favorite pastime, Fee. That's why I'm here. I think like an inventor, and I look at problems in a completely different way."

"It couldn't hurt," said David softly. Henry had to lean in to hear him. "To show him I mean. We *are* stuck." David's eyes darted to the lifts as if to make sure Pelgrim was definitely gone.

Eugene and Nolan nodded, and all three men looked to Fee, who stared at Henry for a long moment, her grey eyes serious. Then she shrugged. "Let's show him Violet."

As one, the other researchers surged to their feet, the excitement suddenly palpable. It was as though a switch had been flicked, and Henry didn't know if it was the disappearance of Pelgrim, or just the delight of a researcher being able to show off their project. It was good finally to see some excitement in their faces.

He stood and walked after them, feeling like he might be able to help them after all.

They took him to a locked side room. Nolan used his thumbprint and a number code to unlock the mechanism at the side, and they all entered the large temperature-controlled room. There was a large, covered object in the middle of the room.

Eugene and Nolan went to either side and pulled the cover off.

Henry just stared. One part of him was horrified. It looked awful, the skin was the wrong color, and was a patchy rubbery texture, which made Henry want to cringe. The wiring was obvious and clunky, and the fingers looked like five fat sausages on each hand.

"I know," said Fee. "We have work to do. But it's coming together."

Henry nodded. Because another part of him could see the possibilities. Visions already were flowing through his mind of the improvements that would make this second skin the most amazing idea that Callaghan Technologies had ever come up with. However, he had to get them on board first.

"It definitely has potential," murmured Henry, walking closer to the suit.

He touched one of the arms. The skin felt like thick rubber, not at all pliable. "Have you talked to a chemist about creating a more... pliable... skin?" he asked.

Fee nodded. "We wanted to, but Pelly doesn't like the idea of involving more people than necessary. Hence his tantrum," she said, nodding toward the lifts. "He thinks we can do it all ourselves."

Henry took a deep breath. He could give them the recipe for the skin he used on Kara's leg. To make it work, they would have to make some improvements to get it thinner. But did he really want to do that? He wasn't sure yet. "It would need to be something that wouldn't be affected by the electronics running through the suit."

Eugene nodded. "We've been trying ourselves, but it's not easy if you're not a specialist. Hence, the Sausage Suit."

Nolan and David both sniggered.

Fee just grinned. "Pelly doesn't like us calling it that. He says it undermines the serious nature of what we're doing."

"What else is going wrong?"

David stepped up to the suit, and pressed a small panel on the side. "Hello, Doctors," said a soothing female voice.

"Hello, Violet," chorused the four researchers in front of him. Henry struggled not to laugh at their childlike delight in the creature they'd created.

"How can I help you today?"

"Can you tell Henry here where you're having problems?" David smiled at Henry.

"Certainly, Doctors. Hello, Henry. My name is Violet, and I am a Second Skin Kinetic Intelligent Neurosystem, capable of organizing and helping in the life of my wearer, as well as diagnosing and/or controlling common diseases. I know the time. I can schedule appointments. I can monitor heart rate, blood pressure, body temperature, metabolism, and stress levels of my wearer."

The voice sounded like she was smiling, and it made Henry smile back.

"But there have been problems. The first is my support structure. As the Doctors have explained, my skin is not optimal and certainly not viable for common consumption yet. Also, the problem of overheating has been difficult to overcome. The wiring system has been problematic, and I am not learning as well as my makers would like."

Henry saw the three researchers look at each other quickly. "What? What else is there?" he asked.

They all started, and looked guiltily at Henry. Fee cleared her throat and spoke. "Well, the bit that Dr. Shaw has been in charge of, creating the nanotechnology, which operates under the skin, hasn't been going according to plan. He's been stalled on some of the technical aspects." She glanced at the others. "It's not entirely his fault; we don't have the right skin for the project."

Henry nodded, suddenly understanding. Dr. Shaw was the one holding them back, but none of them had been able to do anything about it. Even Fee, who didn't seem exactly a wallflower when it came to expressing her opinion. "So you actually know exactly how to move the project forward, but you've all been letting Pelgrim bully you into believing it was something else?" he said softly.

CHAPTER 5

Fee couldn't believe what she was hearing.

He was blaming the fact that Pelly was an overbearing pompous fool on them. What were they supposed to do? Fight him every inch of the way? He didn't understand what Pelly was like. It was an uphill battle to get him to change the brand of tea they had in the kitchenette, let alone talk him into doing anything differently with the actual SSKIN project.

"It's more complicated than that," she said frowning at Henry. "You're simplifying it for your own purposes."

Henry shrugged. "Explain it to me."

"He's in charge. And he doesn't like it when he doesn't get his way," said David in a rush.

Eugene nodded. "He's actually rather intelligent. But once he's decided on a path, he won't listen to anyone else, and it's impossible to tell him when he's going the wrong way."

Henry sighed. "But you all know exactly where the problems are. Why doesn't Pelgrim?"

David blinked owlishly. "Because we don't tell him. We let him believe what he wants to believe."

Fee looked around at the others. Nolan was gazing at the floor, biting one fingernail. Eugene and David were watching Henry with wide eyes. They all looked deflated, like he'd just told them the world was ending or their mother was dying.

But Henry kept talking. "Look, the point here is that it's something you can solve. That's really positive. Imagine if you had no idea where to go, or what to do next?"

If only it were that easy. Fee shook her head morosely. "You don't understand. Pelly won't accept what you're saying. He's going to have a meltdown." It was going to be a nightmare. She desperately wanted Violet to succeed; but from bitter experience, she knew Pelly could be as stubborn as a rock. He'd taken an instant dislike to Henry, and he wouldn't back down from that. Even if Henry could produce some kind of amazing breakthrough, Pelgrim just wasn't going to accept it.

Her usual peaceful work environment was about to be filled with arguments and sulking. And at the end of it, she was going to have to find somewhere else to work because there was no way Pelly was going to admit he was wrong.

"What did you expect when you first saw me?" Henry said, his expression concerned. "Did you think I was going to find some miracle cure, some magic way to make this all work?"

Fee couldn't help it; she flicked her gaze to Henry's face at the mention of the word magic. He was staring back at her, a little bit of knowing on his face. Her heart did a flip-flop. He knew she used magic in her robotics work; she was sure of it. That flash of blue lightning hadn't been natural, and he hadn't so much as mentioned it since. That suggested he knew exactly what had caused it, and why. She wished she knew that much.

Looking away, Fee tried to act as if she didn't understand what that knowing look in his eyes meant.

"We knew it was going to be a disaster from the very beginning," whispered Eugene. "And now we're all going to lose our jobs."

Henry smiled. "It's not going to be like that. I'm going to fix this situation, and you're all going to be free to work on whatever project you want to in the future." Henry patted Eugene on the arm, and Fee felt a sinking sensation when she saw the hopeful expression on Eugene's face.

"Don't go promising anything you don't know if you can keep," she said, frowning at Henry.

He grinned at her. "Don't consign us to the garbage heap just yet, Fee. We have more than enough to work with here. Now that I've met Violet, I know I can work with her, and with all of you. Even Pelgrim."

"You don't know him well enough to say that," warned Fee, feeling like Oscar the Grouch. But she wasn't going to let this guy go all Pollyanna positive when he really didn't know what he was getting himself in for.

Henry shifted to stand directly in front of her. He looked down at her, his brown eyes showing flecks of gold in their depths. Fee swallowed hard.

"I'm not making this up. We are going to make this work, and you are going to keep your jobs. I'll find a way to work with Pelgrim. It's going to happen."

Fee could only look up into his eyes, watching them sparkle with magic.

They were all doomed. But if they were going to be doomed, at least a golden god was around to make it interesting.

HENRY DIDN'T KNOW whether to be annoyed at Fee or intrigued she wasn't falling for his usual ability to make everyone around him feel at ease. All the others were glowing in their newfound positivity and had returned to their desks to work on three separate parts of Violet's problems. Their enthusiasm was contagious; Henry had realized while he was in the room with Violet that he was hooked. They'd given him a problem that needed to be solved, and he'd always been unable to resist a challenge. He would help them as much as he possibly could in the time he had available.

Meanwhile, Fee was sitting at her desk, staring at him with wary eyes.

"Thanks, Frankie, I really appreciate it," said Henry into his mobile phone, trying to ignore the feeling of being watched.

"You better, my boy. You know I hate doing this boring research stuff for you," said Frankie.

Henry could hear the smile in his voice, and knew the younger man wasn't serious. They'd been friends a long time, since, well, before Frankie had become the Chancemaster at the Carnival, and inherited the family powers. He was just keeping up his reputation as a gambler and a wastrel. He led a difficult life, and Henry didn't envy Frankie one bit, despite his abilities.

"Just let me know when you've got information for me. I've got a few things to sort out around here first."

"Are you organizing their lives for them?" Frankie sounded amused.

"I'm helping them keep their jobs," said Henry firmly. Frankie might make fun, but it was serious business now. He wasn't going to let these people lose their jobs.

The elevator doors opened, and Henry looked up. Pelgrim strode back into the research space, the anger still burning over his face.

"I've gotta go, buddy. Storm's coming." Henry pressed the

button on his phone and shoved it in his back pocket. He didn't know precisely how he was going to deal with Dr. Pelgrim Shaw, but he had to begin as he meant to go on.

"What did Lucas say, Pelgrim?" he said, walking over to where Pelgrim was slamming doors and cupboards in their small kitchen space.

"Don't think you've won, carny," snarled Pelgrim.

"This isn't a competition," said Henry quietly. "This is serious. This is about everyone's jobs."

"This means nothing to you! You'll be gone in a month. You don't care whether we survive or not." He banged his coffee cup on the metal countertop for emphasis, spilling some of the milk he'd already put in the cup.

Henry's temperature rose a little. Pelgrim certainly knew the right buttons to push. "I'm going to help you all keep your jobs. I've met Violet, and I've already found several improvements we can work on right away."

Pelgrim's gaze flicked to Henry's, the naked fury in his eyes making Henry want to take a step back. "They showed her to you? Without me?" He turned and looked around at the rest of the team. "How dare you," he yelled, out of control. "That's my project. Mine to show." He turned to Henry. "Or not show."

Henry frowned in the face of the storm that Pelgrim was putting on for them. It was an overreaction to what was happening. It didn't make sense. "What's the real problem here Pelgrim?" he asked.

"The real problem is that Lucas just *fired me*. He said I was being insubordinate and he wouldn't put up with it. Security guards are following me in the elevators, and I have five minutes to pack up my life's work and leave. That's the *problem*."

Henry stepped back at the level of hatred pouring out of Pelgrim. He didn't agree with the decision to fire Pelgrim. He still believed he could work with the man to create something great. "I'll go and talk to Lucas, see if I can change his mind," he said.

"Don't you dare, carny. I'd rather stay fired than owe my salvation to a lowlife like you. The only good news is that Lucas doesn't think the rest of you will be able to complete the project without me, so he's shutting down the whole thing as of now. You're all out along with me." Pelgrim smiled in triumph as the faces on the rest of the research team fell.

"You probably told him to fire us." Fee's voice was high pitched and angry.

"I did no such thing. He knew without being told that I am the pivotal researcher in this project. He knows the rest of you sniveling excuses for scientists could never complete a project like this on your own."

The elevators opened again, and two large men stepped out, wearing identical black shirts and jeans. "Time's up, Dr. Shaw. Did you get your things like Mr. Callaghan instructed?" said one of the men.

Pelgrim jumped. "You will need to wait. I have things I must collect." He raced off to his desk and started rummaging.

One of the big men, walked over to the desk. "Here's a box, Dr. Shaw. You're allowed to fill this up with your personal belongings, but nothing more. And you've got five minutes to do it. We're allowed to drag you kicking and screaming to the reception area if you resist." The guard's voice indicated that he would gladly do that if Pelgrim wished.

But he worked fast and shoved all his personal effects into the box, under the careful eye of the guard. He mumbled the whole time, casting furious glances around the room at the rest of the researchers, and especially Henry.

Henry shivered. The anger in the room was almost a physical presence, as if Pelgrim was pouring all his emotions out into the air around him.

Soon enough, the five minutes were up. Pelgrim stalked to the bank of elevators and pushed the button, ignoring the two big, burly security guards following him. "I won't say goodbye, because I don't wish any of you well. You've been holding me back these last years. If anything, I regret putting so much wasted time into this idea. It's never going to work. You'll thank me for getting you fired as well."

With that, he swept into the metal elevator, and was gone.

Henry let out the breath he'd been holding. "That was intense. You guys might have been right. I don't know if I could have changed his mind."

Fee stormed over to him. "Didn't you hear him? He's ruined it for everyone. We're all out now, and that includes you. You don't get your cushy consultant's fee either."

"Well, now, I do still get the fee, even if Lucas pulls the plug today. It's in my contract. But I don't think Pelgrim was being entirely honest about that. I think Lucas is the kind of person who'd give us all a chance to prove ourselves. And if I'm not mistaken, as soon as your Dr. Shaw is out of the building, Lucas is going to pay us a visit."

"He's not our Dr. Shaw," said Nolan vehemently. "For one, I'm glad he's gone. The room already feels lighter."

"Just make sure that's not because he stole something he shouldn't have," muttered Fee.

Henry grinned. She was being grumpy and pessimistic, but she was also rather funny. He liked it.

CHAPTER 6

$\mathcal{F}$ee couldn't believe her eyes. Henry had been right. Lucas was standing in front of them, as promised, ten minutes later.

"Pelgrim assures me that none of you have the talent to finish the project on your own. Is this true? Do your degrees mean nothing?" he said seriously, his deep brown eyes assessing each of them in turn.

Fee stepped forward. "No, that's not true. Pelly was holding us back. We can make Violet a success. I know we can. You just have to give us a chance." The words came pouring out of her with more passion and conviction than she'd known she possessed. But she *knew* they could do it. She glanced at the others. They were nodding.

"What about you, Nolan? Do you think you can make this work?" Lucas shifted his gaze to the other researchers.

Nolan took a step toward Lucas. "I know we can, sir, especially now we have Henry here to help us."

"David? Eugene?"

Fee realized what Lucas was doing. He wanted all of them

to commit to the project verbally. She motioned with her hand to the other two.

David took a breath and stepped forward. "I believe we will move ahead faster now. Henry has already encouraged us to verbalize that Pelgrim was holding us back."

Lucas glanced in surprise at Henry, who went a little red on his face, but Fee shrugged. They would have had to work on Pelly to change his mind about certain aspects of the research. Now that wasn't going to be an issue that would take up their time anymore.

Lucas glanced around and found Eugene. "Eugene? Are you committed to the team? Can you make this work?"

Eugene grinned, the first relaxed emotion Fee had seen from him. "Of course, we can, Mr. Callaghan. We are all excellent researchers, and we have an amazing project. You won't regret giving us a chance."

Lucas nodded. "That's what I was hoping to hear. I hired all of you because of your excellent resumes and track records. But make no mistake, this doesn't change the one-month deadline. You must show me significant steps forward in this project at the end of four weeks, or I will have to shut you down. Don't forget that." Lucas's puppy dog eyes were hard as steel, and Fee knew he meant every word.

But it didn't matter. They no longer had to deal with Pelly and his stupid ego. "Yes, sir. We understand."

The others nodded and muttered agreement.

Lucas smiled. "Then I'll leave you to it. Keep me informed." He turned and headed back toward the elevators. Henry ran off to follow Lucas, and Fee watched him go. What did he need to speak to Lucas in private about?

"I feel like we should celebrate somehow," David was saying to the others. "Is this the kind of occasion where one would drink bubbles?"

"We should save the bubbles for when we actually get to

keep our jobs," said Fee firmly. "We haven't proved anything yet."

Nolan nodded. "Fee's right. We have a lot to do. First up is deciding how we're going to make up for not having Pelgrim on the team. He might have been an egomaniac, but he was smart, and he did add to the project."

"Almost as much as he took away," agreed David.

Fee smiled. Already the atmosphere was lighter, and it was easier to breathe. She'd been worried that Henry's arrival would mean change for them all; but so far, it had been a transformation that had the potential to make their lives better.

Henry came back into the room and clapped his hands. "I just spoke to Lucas and he's agreed to a field trip for the group. Somewhere that is going to help us get the inspiration we need to get this project humming."

"Where to?" asked Fee. She didn't like the look on Henry's face.

"It's a secret. I'm going to take you all in my car tomorrow to a secret location. So you need to come to work in sensible clothes, good walking shoes. The kind of clothes you might wear on a hike or climbing over rocks."

"And what are we going to do today?"

"Today, we plan our attack," said Henry with a smile. "Today we dream."

HENRY PULLED his car to the curb outside the Callaghan building. He hoped his idea was going to work. Yesterday the mood of the team had gone from excited and hopeful to frustrated and despondent. They hadn't been able to come up with any good alternative ideas, and they obviously missed the influence of Pelgrim. He needed them to break out of their shells and think for themselves. He couldn't just give them all the answers.

The only exception was Fee. She was a bright, shining star in the group. But she didn't have the expertise outside of her passion for robotics to make the project happen on her own. They all needed each other, and the whole team needed to be working at peak capability for them to achieve what they hoped to by the end of the month.

Ahead of him, down the street, he saw Nolan. Yesterday he'd been wearing office gear, but now he was in more casual attire, cargo pants and a Star Wars T-shirt. His bright white sneakers looked like they'd never been worn. He didn't look comfortable. Henry sighed.

He'd come to stand outside the building where Henry had told them to meet him, awkwardly holding a backpack over his shoulder.

Henry pressed the button to lower the window on the far side of his car, and leaned over. "Nolan. Over here." He waved him to the car.

Nolan's eyes glanced over the Charger, obviously impressed. Henry smiled. Even geeks liked cars. He should know.

Nolan opened the front door and climbed in. "Wow, this is amazing. It's a 1970s Dodge, right?" He looked at the dashboard. "Oh, my God, what *is* that?"

"I made a few adjustments to make her more... mine." Henry grinned. He liked showing off his baby. "She's a 1974 Dodge Charger SE. Mint condition."

Nolan smoothed one hand along the dashboard, clearly absorbed in the detail of the additional hardware in the car. Henry glanced at his watch, wondering how long the others were going to be.

"Fee's usually late," said Nolan without looking over. "It's her upbringing. They didn't have clocks." He pushed his glasses up his nose.

Upbringing? "Where did she grow up?"

Nolan glanced at Henry. "In a cult," he whispered.

"Is that what she told you? Are you sure she wasn't having a bit of fun?" Henry could imagine Fee teasing Nolan by telling him something like that.

Nolan shrugged. "Who knows? Maybe. It was at a work function just after she started here; she'd had a couple of wines, and was more chatty than usual. I think she was telling the truth."

Henry nodded and tucked that bit of information away for later.

Eugene and David arrived not long after, both wearing shorts that made them look just as uncomfortable as Nolan. David's long skinny legs were like a lighthouse beacon in the bright, sunny Tampa morning.

Henry raised his eyebrows. It sounded like Fee had them well trained to expect her to be late.

A bright spot appeared in of the corner of his eye, and he saw Fee walking down the street wearing jeans and a T-shirt with Tweety bird on it. Her white-blonde hair was up in a ponytail, and it almost glowed in the sunlight. She wore large dark glasses that hid much of her face, and she strode along the sidewalk with a confidence that belied her previously reserved attitude. Henry felt like he'd been kicked in the gut. She looked amazing.

He couldn't help staring as she spotted the carful of geeks, and came straight over. Nolan got out to let her in, and she climbed in the back with David and Eugene.

"Are you going to tell us where we're going?" she said. Her eyes flashed, and he realized she didn't like the idea of going in a car without knowing where she was headed.

Tough cookies. "I'm going to give you twenty minutes to

guess. The one who figures it out first is exempt from the first competition." He started the engine and took off down the road into the early morning traffic.

"Competition?" All four chorused at once.

"Competition," repeated Henry firmly. "This is an educational field trip, designed to give you the tools you need to make this project work. We're not playing around; this is serious business. Start guessing."

"Museum of Science and Industry," said David quickly. He looked around at the others who were staring at him. "What? I need all the advantage I can get," he said.

Henry shook his head. "No. Guess again."

"University of South Florida," said David.

"Henry B Plant Museum," shouted Nolan at the same time.

"Mariner's Museum," added Eugene.

Henry shook his head. "No, no, and no."

He glanced in the rearview mirror and saw Fee looking at him with narrowed eyes. "Twenty minutes?" she said.

Henry nodded, grinning.

"Oh, oh! I have it. University of Tampa!" said David smugly.

"Nope."

"South University," said Eugene.

Henry shook his head, and turned onto another street.

"Guys, he didn't go to university. He's not taking us somewhere like that," said Fee from the back seat. She sounded exasperated. "Think about it. What do we know about Henry?"

"He got rid of Pelgrim without even trying?" said Nolan.

"He likes cars," said Eugene.

"He didn't go to college," said David.

"Right. And what else?" said Fee.

Henry watched through the rear vision mirror as the

others looked at her blankly. At that moment, he realized she'd already guessed where they were going. Her quick mind had assessed it based on what she already knew about him, and who he was. It was frightening to be so predictable.

"He's from a carnival," continued Fee. "So if he's going to teach us a lesson in working together, or being innovative, do you think he might take us somewhere familiar to him? Where he's sure he can find a few lessons for us?"

The others looked at her a moment, and then a kind of horror appeared on each of their faces. "A carnival?" said Nolan.

Fee nodded. "Perhaps somewhere with loads of mechanical type rides we can look at. And lots of people around to learn from."

Eugene's eyes widened. "We're going on a field trip to the Avalon Heights theme park?" he said in a hushed voice.

Henry smiled around at them all. "That's right. I know a couple of guys there. They're going to let us into the back area on a couple of the rides. Show us around." He waited for their reactions. He figured it was fifty-fifty as to whether they'd be horrified.

He was right.

"I hate theme parks. They're noisy," said David. "And dirty."

"You can never do anything, because too many people are around," said Nolan. He was biting the nail on his thumb, and the expression behind his glasses was anxious.

"Can we ride the rollercoaster?" asked Eugene. His eyes had lit up, and he had a flush on his cheeks.

"They're noisy," agreed Henry, "but that's a good thing; it gives us a chance to do some repairs under pressure. Lots of people are around, so I want you to look at them, really look at them, and decide where and how they might be able to wear your suit. What problems might occur if someone wore a suit into an environment like that? And yes, Eugene, we are going to ride every single damn rollercoaster, until someone comes up with a solution to at least one of Violet's problems."

Fee grinned. "I've never been to a theme park," she said.

Henry stared at Fee through the rearview mirror. "You've never been to one, ever?" he asked, shocked.

"Nope. It's not the kind of thing my parents ever approved of."

"We'll make sure you have a fantastic time today," said Henry. "No holds barred."

"What kind of field trip is this?" asked David in horror.

"One with pressure points. No point in cruising along in life, Dave. You've gotta take it by the horns and make it work for you."

CHAPTER 7

$\mathscr{F}$ee climbed out of the car in the parking lot at Avalon Heights, pulling her backpack over her shoulders. She felt movement inside, and something hard and metal banged against her back. Another of her damn bots had hidden in her bag.

She usually triple-checked before she left home—especially after yesterday when she'd had two stowaways—but she'd been in such a rush this morning that her usual routine had been knocked out of the water. She wondered who it was, but she couldn't check now, in front of the others. As long as it wasn't the Wildling, she'd be okay. She stepped away from the car, and turned around, taking in the theme park entrance in front of them.

She had to hand it to Henry; he really knew how to jolt them out of their normal routine. She tried to imagine Pelly participating in something like this and drew a blank. She shrugged. It didn't matter. He'd drawn his line in the sand, and now the rest of them were being given a chance to see what they could achieve without him. They hadn't done so well the day before. Pelly might have been a pompous ass, but maybe they needed him?

Fee straightened her shoulders. She was not going to let Pelgrim Shaw win.

"Look at all the people. Maybe we should come back another day," said David hopefully.

Henry just laughed. "This is nothing. We're here on a weekday, and it's not even the holidays yet. This is pretty quiet for a place like this, David."

They all followed meekly behind Henry as he led them across the parking lot to the entrance. He paid for them to get in, chatting easily with the woman at the gate and then hauled them off to one side. Fee gazed around curiously, taking in everything from the brightly colored signs to the queues of people waiting for the rides and the various food stalls already selling hot dogs and churros. It seemed like a strange, magical land sitting in the backdrop of another sunny day in Tampa.

She'd never been to a carnival or even a theme park before. It wasn't something her parents had encouraged when she was a kid. They had been more into chanting in the garden to commune with mother earth. And when she got to college, she was too busy working to make ends meet to do the usual fun stuff.

"We're going to wait here." Henry smiled, and where before she'd thought his eyes sparkled, now they shone with an inner energy that was hard to ignore. This was more his kind of place than the research lab. He looked even more like a golden god; and for the first time ever, Fee wished she wasn't a practical researcher who hid in a lab.

She wanted to shine like he did, to feel part of his world. She took a deep breath and tried to take it all in, to make sense of the chaos of this place; the colors, sounds, and smells were pouring over her. She opened up her senses and let it all flow in.

Without warning, she went into overload. Too much was going on, too many people, too many things she could see that needed to be fixed. She wasn't used to it. Instead of feeling a warm shining glow like Henry, all she felt was chaos and disruption running along her senses, pulling her in too many directions.

Just as she thought she might scream, a hand touched her upper arm. She flinched when she realized it was Henry, but she didn't pass out like last time he'd touched her.

"Hey there, Fee. It's okay. Just take a deep breath. Ride the wave," Henry said, his voice soft and soothing, the warmth of his body close to hers helping to stabilize her thoughts. Her body tingled with electricity where he touched her bare skin.

She glanced up into his eyes; for a moment, she was caught in their golden depths. She blinked and looked away. No need to go all gooey on him. His hand lingered on her arm for a moment, and then dropped away. She felt the loss of its warmth, but it had done its work. She was calmer now; the wave of panic had subsided.

"Who'd have thought Lucas would approve a trip to a theme park as a field trip," said Nolan from where he was standing nearby, taking everything in.

Henry cleared his throat. "Technically, I didn't tell him where I was taking you. I just asked for some money to take you on a team-building experience. He was happy to do it, though. There's power in taking time out."

Nolan's eyes bugged out. "He doesn't know?"

"He's going to be so annoyed," said Eugene, awe in his voice.

Henry shook his head. "No, I don't think so. I think he's the kind of guy who understands outside-the-box thinking. He hired me, didn't he?"

Fee couldn't fault his logic. Lucas wouldn't care how they got results as long as they did.

"Hey, Henry! Long time no see, man!" A skinny guy with long hair came up to Henry and gave him a big hug, clapping him on the back, and looking genuinely pleased to see him.

"Grimshaw! Great to see you. How's life treating you at the Heights?"

"Aw, man, the usual. Nothing beats the Carnival, but this'll do a good second. What brings you here?" Grimshaw glanced over at Fee and the others, who had clumped themselves together when he arrived. Grimshaw's eyes gleamed silver in the light then he blinked and it was gone.

But Fee had felt the light touch of Grimshaw's magic pass over her. Aside from her own abilities, she'd come across magic very rarely in her life, but she recognized it immediately. She shivered again. Maybe she shouldn't be worrying so much about whether she was going to lose her job, and start paying attention to Henry and the people he knew.

She'd been hiding for so long from people who hated magic, she had no experience with people who actually used it. She didn't even know if they were friend or foe.

"I've brought these guys here for the full experience," Henry was saying. "I want them to get their hands dirty with a bit of mechanical work on the rides."

Grimshaw nodded. "Well, you've come to the right place. The Twister broke down this morning. I could use some help on it. What's their level of experience?" Grimshaw's expression said he didn't think it was going to be up to much. Fee narrowed her eyes at him.

Henry grinned. "They should know enough about mechanical stuff to get by, I think."

Nolan raised his hand. "Actually, I have very little practical experience in mechanical engineering. My field of expertise is as a medical researcher."

Grimshaw grinned. "They all speak like that?" he said.

Henry nodded.

"This is going to be a fun day. Follow me, and we'll go and see if we can scrounge up some coveralls."

CHAPTER 8

*H*enry watched as they pulled the coveralls—which were in varying degrees of cleanliness and repair—on over their clothes. Fee looked like a drowned rat, hidden inside a suit that was way too big for her. Henry hid a smile. The idea was to take them outside of their comfort zone, maybe learn a little bit about each other on the way, and see if that threw any ideas their way.

He wasn't entirely certain it was going to work. But he'd wanted to do something drastic. Sitting around in the lab getting frustrated wasn't going to cut it. Yesterday afternoon had proved that to him, if nothing else.

Grimshaw had grown up in the Carnival. He'd been on the thrills crew working for Henry's dad, Viktor, but had stayed on in Tampa when he met his wife one year as they traveled the circuit. He'd retained a small part of his magic, but had lost his connection to the Carnival years ago. Henry had never been able to imagine giving up the Carnival, or losing his connection to the magic. But he'd always liked Grimshaw, and when the opportunity allowed, he always visited.

"So any of these fellas any use?" asked Grimshaw in an undertone next to him. "Can I let them lose on anything important?"

Henry considered the three men and one woman in front of him. "I know they're smart. And they have the kind of minds that can come up with new solutions to problems. I think you might be surprised by what they can do." He wasn't entirely sure that was true, if he were honest. But he wanted Grimshaw at least to give them a chance to prove themselves.

"Okey dokey." He clapped his hands together, making Eugene and David jump. "We're ready to go, mateys. Follow me." And like the pied piper, he led them out into the sunlight again, whistling a strange tune that Henry tried to place. Ah, yes, it was the music on the carousel at the Jolly Knight Carnival.

The Twister was an older, miniature rollercoaster at the far end of the park. "We've been thinking about taking it off line," said Grimshaw as he walked toward the ride. "But I've got an attachment to the old girl. So as long as I can keep her working safely, I'm gonna keep her going."

"So what is wrong with her at the moment, Mr. Grimshaw?" asked David.

Grimshaw cackled with laughter. "It's just Grimshaw, man. Grim for short, if you're running out of time. And I'm not sure what's wrong this time. That's what you guys are here for, right?"

Henry caught Grimshaw's eyes. The older mechanic knew exactly what was wrong, but he was playing along for Henry's sake. Henry nodded at him in acknowledgement of the favor.

Grimshaw hustled them toward the far end of the park. They received a few strange looks from the punters around them, but the others were too freaked out to notice. They still were fiddling with their new outfits, trying to make it work in the context of what they were used to. It was rather funny to watch them. Henry smiled. This contract was turning out to be rather amusing.

His eye caught Fee trying to roll up the sleeve on her overalls. They were grimy with oil and grease, and he was impressed that she wasn't more grossed out by them. She had almost tipped over the edge earlier—a lot of people had been by the entrance and he'd figured it was probably that. Once he'd calmed her down, she'd slipped back into her usual quiet, capable—somewhat grumpy—mode.

She did glance around at the crowd every so often as they walked, but they were all doing that. He figured they didn't get out much. The lab was a much quieter, and probably safer, environment.

Her white-blonde hair also made her stand out in the crowds. It wasn't just that she was attractive. A kind of sparkle was in the air around her, something that drew the eye and made Henry want to smile and to run his hands through her soft hair. He shook his head quickly. Enough of that kind of thinking. He wasn't going to be around long enough. And she was definitely not his type. He preferred easy-going women with a ready smile and a simple outlook on life. More like him. Not grumpy, pessimistic women who were definitely hiding something.

She brushed at a strand of hair that had escaped her hair tie and something metallic ran up the sleeve of her coveralls into her ponytail. Her hand went to her hair, and she tried to shake the metal creature out. When she glanced anxiously around and saw Henry watching her, she paused, slowly putting her hand back to her side. Henry smothered a grin.

He'd seen the strange, little robotic creatures on her yesterday. At first, he'd thought he was imagining it, but he'd seen them several times now, and had watched her trying to hide them from everyone else. He had no clue why no one else noticed; but perhaps he was used to seeing things like that, and the others weren't. Perhaps they were all just too wrapped up in their own worlds to see what was in front of their faces. Or maybe there was magic involved.

This one in her hair seemed particularly active, and she was struggling to keep walking normally. Luckily the others were up ahead, chatting to Grimshaw and asking questions about the coaster they were about to see. Henry sped up and casually reached out to Fee's hair, nipping the creature between two fingers.

"Hey!" said Fee, stopping and turning to him, trying to grab back the creature in his hands. "What do you think you're doing?"

He lifted it high away from her and looked at it closely. Between his fingers, a little metal robot fought and struggled to be set free. It had five arms, and at least two legs that he could make out, a tiny head and red glowing lights for eyes. Wires fought for position with metal bearings and nuts. It looked a little loopy.

Henry glanced away from the creature. Fee was grabbing at it next to him, her shorter arms not quite managing to reach his.

"What is it?" he asked, part of him awed. She'd made a tiny creature out of metal bits and pieces. Was it alive? It seemed like it was.

"Nothing. Just give it back to me." Fee continued to grab at the creature, her face a mask of determination.

Henry gave in, dropping his hand until she could grab his elbow and pull his arm down. Electricity zipped along his senses where Fee touched him, and he lowered his arm even further, holding his hand open so the creature stood in his palm. It leaped off and ran straight back up into her mess of hair.

"You know, he's not that well hidden in there, when your hair is up," he said. "Someone will see him."

Fee frowned at him, but she put one hand up to her ponytail. "I don't usually wear my hair up." She grabbed the creature and put it into the front pocket of her overalls. "Stay there," she whispered to it.

"You talk to them? Do they understand you? Are they AI?"

"I don't suppose you're going to let me pretend you didn't see them are you?" she said, grumpily.

Henry shook his head. "This could be the kind of thing that creates a break through on Violet. You're hiding your best work from everyone else on the team."

Fee shook her head. "I'm hiding my worst work, not my best." With a huff of breath, she pulled the creature back out of her pocket and held him in her flat palm. "This is Bing. He was supposed to be able to plait my hair. Instead, he just likes hiding in it, and, if I'm not careful, making knotted nests in it while I sleep. He's not at all useful to the SSKIN project." The tiny creature shuffled side to side for a moment, before running back up her arm and into her hair.

This was her worst? This amazing creature was an example of where she'd gone wrong? "What about the ones that have gone right?"

Fee blinked. "I stopped making them. At least the little ones like this. My apartment was getting too crowded with uncontrollable creatures that didn't do what they were supposed to do."

"You've got more of these roaming around in your place? I'd love to see them sometime." He imagined hundreds of small creatures wandering on the surfaces at her place. It was just crazy enough to enthrall him.

Fee looked up at him, a blush creeping over her cheeks. "I don't think that's going to happen," she said. "I don't generally have visitors at my apartment."

Henry frowned, his visions of crazy robotic minions falling away. "Why not? Don't you have friends over? People you hang out with?" She was so secretive it was almost a phobia.

Fee glowered back at him. "I don't like people at my place, all right? I don't have to justify myself to you."

Henry held up his hands. "I'm sorry. I didn't mean to offend you. It's just completely foreign to me. At the Carnival, we all live in each other's spaces. I can't imagine having a place completely to myself." The more he thought about having a space all his own, the more he liked the idea.

"Come on, you two! We don't have all day," shouted Grimshaw from up ahead. He stood at the side door to a large, brightly colored thrill ride. The Twister.

"This isn't the last of this conversation," said Henry. "But for now, we better catch up to the others."

"There's nothing more to say," grumbled Fee, but she jogged behind him toward the door.

CHAPTER 9

Fee felt Bing wriggling around in her pocket and frowned, looking over at Henry again. What was she going to do? No one else had ever noticed her creatures. Or at least talked to her about it when they did.

Would he try to make her use them for the project? They were all so silly. Whatever purpose she set out to make them for was always subverted by some other nonsensical ability. She generally just left them to do their thing. And being honest, they were good company for her. When she was at home at night in her apartment, she chatted to the creatures, told them about her day, what they were working on, and what new ridiculous statements Pelly had come up with.

She shook her head to clear it. In front of her, Grimshaw was explaining the circuitry of the Twister to the others. Nolan was looking a bit lost, but Eugene and David looked like they'd died and gone to heaven. Gone was the fear and horror of being at a theme park with lots of people. Now they had a problem to solve and they were eager to prove themselves to Henry.

She knew that, because they kept involving him in the

conversation; and every time he praised or even just talked to one of them, they practically glowed. There was some serious hero worship going on, and Henry hadn't actually done anything. Fee got the feeling they thought he'd gotten rid of Pelly for them, but it had been Pelly himself who'd done that. Henry had just gone along for the ride.

Part of her was annoyed with them. They should know better than to imbue some stranger—and that's all Henry was to them, they'd only known him a day—with abilities he didn't possess. Henry wasn't here to save them. He would be gone in a month, and they'd be back to looking out for themselves.

But another part of her was impressed with the way he'd managed to bring Nolan, David, and Eugene out of their shells. They were participating, offering opinions, and laughing together in a way that they'd never done in the lab. If they could find a way to work and talk together, perhaps this might be okay.

"Fee! Fee, come over here," called Nolan excitedly. "Look at what they've got."

She took a step closer and followed where Nolan was pointing. Down below, in the base of the control circuitry was a robot with multiple legs—similar to her robots—but several times larger, in better shape and moving more sedately. She gave a start of surprise and looked up at Grimshaw.

"You can thank Henry for that little innovation. It cleans up down there, makes sure the parts are working, as they should. Also, sets off an alarm when something is wrong, and we can send someone down to manually check on it. Sometimes, I think it just sets off alarms when it wants someone to come and visit." Grimshaw laughed and clapped Henry on the back.

Fee felt cold. Henry had created it? And it worked exactly the way it was supposed to?

∽

FOR THE FIRST TIME EVER, Henry felt embarrassed by one of his inventions. The little cleaning robot at the base of the Thriller's machinery was nothing like the amazing creatures Fee had created. It had no soul, no personality, and no mission other than to do what it was told. No spark.

He glanced over at Fee, saw her horrified expression, and thought he knew why. She couldn't believe how pathetic his robots were compared to hers.

"It's nothing much. Just something I threw together," he said quickly, not wanting to let her know that it had been a major project for him to put something like that together. She must think he was such an idiot.

"Nothing much?" she repeated.

"Oh, I disagree, Henry," said Nolan. "That little creature there is rather amazing. You're just what our team needs to get this project moving. One of Violet's problems is her inability to learn. This little fella here is learning all the time, if what Grimshaw is saying is true."

Henry glanced back at Nolan with a frown. "But Fee—"

Fee cleared her throat and jumped in. "I don't usually make creatures like that. Not that good anyway. The AI side of things is more complicated. I'm a more basic robotics person," she said quickly.

"But—" Henry started to interrupt, but saw the look in her eyes. Ah. She was hiding her critters from the others. Of course. "Sure. Okay. Let's get onto the real problem here, Grimshaw. I'm sure it's nothing to do with Betsy down there."

"Betsy?" Fee blurted.

Henry felt himself going red, but tried to ignore it. "Come on, let's go. I think these guys are ready for the real problem."

Grimshaw sighed and led them deeper into the bowels of The Twister's machinery.

"We noticed the issue yesterday. We took the ride offline straight away." Grimshaw gestured with his arm toward the huge machine. "Most of our rides are computerized, and they have a much smaller command central. But this baby is old. She's also one of our favorites, which is why we keep her running. Not to mention she's popular with the park guests."

Henry stood back as the others crowded around the large command central of The Twister. Buttons were everywhere; and the wires, pipes, pistons, and stampers were all standing still. It was the quietest he'd ever seen the big machine. There was an old computer screen at one end. The Twister was actually run by an operating system. But it was so old they had to make special parts when she broke down.

Eugene had gone straight to the crux of the problem. He was standing beside a cracked valve, and put one hand out to touch it softly.

Grimshaw nodded. "That's right, buddy, it's cracked. So we have to replace it today. But that's not the main problem. What I want you fellas to determine today is what caused the crack. We only replaced that a couple months ago. It shouldn't have cracked so fast."

David moved forward to stare at the problem next to Eugene. "Usually it's caused by stress," he said.

Grimshaw nodded. "That's right. But we've checked every section of the machinery behind and forward of that valve, and we can't see anything causing the kind of stress it would take to cause a crack like that. It makes no sense."

As a group, they focused their attention on the valve, and Grimshaw winked at Henry. He knew Grimshaw would know exactly what the problem was. He was practically a magician when it came to mechanical objects. But when he'd phoned him the day before to ask about heading over, Grimshaw had promised to provide something entertaining for his group.

Henry stood back and tried to watch them all, but his eyes kept being drawn to Fee. She stood back, letting the others charge in and try to solve the problem. Her expression was focused, and she was clearly taking the task very seriously.

Something moved under her hair at the nape of her neck, and he watched as a tiny metal arm poked out and waved at him. He grinned, and waved back at the tiny robot. He'd never met anyone who had strange metal creatures running about her person before. It was a rather attractive quality.

She was like no one else he'd ever met. He wanted to know more about her. Standing here soaking up her features, memorizing the exact shade of blonde of her hair, it wasn't enough. He was drawn to her in a way he'd never experienced before in his life and he didn't understand it. She was gorgeous, sure. But he knew lots of beautiful women, and they'd never bothered him like this. Was it because she was better at making robots than he was? Or the aloof way she carried herself, like she didn't give a hoot what people thought of her, or how the rest of the world acted? Maybe he just hated that she was hiding something and he didn't know what it was, He'd always liked a challenge, a mystery to solve. That's why he invented things.

He felt like he understood the other researchers. He could see what drove each of them, and he knew how he was going to make this project work for them. At the end of a month, they were going to have made huge strides on Violet's problems, and he would have left them with the skills to keep going. It wasn't arrogance; it was just that his skill, his ability had always been to solve problems, and this was just another problem for him to solve. It was a more subtle part of what he did, he knew. When Jack had sent him here, it wasn't because the new Ringmaster had thought he'd solve the interpersonal problems of the researchers involved. He'd expected Henry to use his powerful inventing skill to tip them over the edge into the next level.

But doing this, making them work better together, setting them on the road to success in the future well past the time when he would have left, it was part of what he did.

Only he couldn't figure out how Fee fit in. She seemed to be living in a place outside the reality that the rest of them were living in. She was as big a mystery to him now as she had been yesterday when he'd met her.

There was also the strange electricity that flared between them whenever they touched. It was confusing, and he didn't like it. It put him on edge, made him forget what he was doing and planning. He didn't need the distraction.

CHAPTER 10

$\mathcal{F}$ee kept her eyes firmly attached to the machine part Eugene was handling. She tried to concentrate on what they were doing, to understand the intricacies of what went where.

But all she could think about was the fact that Henry was staring at her, as he had been for almost the whole time they'd been working on the problem. She glanced at her watch. It was almost an hour now.

She frowned. That was too long. He shouldn't be watching her with such studied attention. She turned, and looked at him, catching his eye. Walking over to him, she whispered, "We need to talk." She wasn't going to let him intimidate her like this. He needed to know that he couldn't stare at her all day long. She wouldn't have it.

Henry silently followed her into a room to one side that seemed to be an office. Grimshaw was long gone; he'd said he had other things to do and would be back to check on their progress later. It was a huge amount of trust on his part, and she didn't know if he was relying on Henry to keep his machine safe, or if he just wasn't bothered by what they might do to the Twister in his absence.

She shut the door, and turned. "Why are you staring at me?" she asked, coming right to the point.

Henry opened his mouth, and then closed it. He stared at her some more. "I...didn't..." he said. It was the most uncomfortable she'd seen the golden god look.

"Seriously, you need to stop it. It's not cool." She put her hands on her hips, and glared at him.

Henry swallowed and seemed to pull himself together. "I'm sorry. I'm just trying to figure you out. The others, they're easy. Not too complicated geniuses, who need a bit of recognition to help their confidence and spark their creativity."

Fee nodded. She understood that.

"But I can't make sense of you. You're not shy. You don't want recognition. You invent these amazing little creatures, and keep them like pets on your person. Why do you hide them? I don't understand. And what are you doing in that lab? I'm not sure how invested you are in that project. You don't seem to care about it one minute, and then you're defending it passionately the next. It doesn't make sense to me."

Fee felt suddenly lightheaded. No one had ever questioned her motives, or what she was doing in her job. She'd thought he was being a bit creepy, watching her like that, but now she understood that he was trying to delve deeper into her head.

"You don't need to know any of that stuff. You're a consultant. It shouldn't matter to you what my motivations are. Stop it. That's crossing a line I haven't given you permission to cross."

Henry continued as if he didn't hear her. "And what about when we shook hands? What was that? You *passed out*, for crying out loud. And I felt like I'd been hit by a freight train. It's like there's an electric current running between our bodies every time we connect. I don't know about you, but I've never experienced anything like it before." He paused and then added softly, "Will it happen every time we touch?" His eyes seemed to bore into hers.

Fee imagined his hands touching her bare body and shivered. That wasn't what he meant. Her over-active imagination had taken an innocent question and turned it sexual, just because she'd thought he was attractive from the first moment she saw him. She glanced up and locked eyes with him, and suddenly she was burning. The heat in his eyes shocked her, and she took a step back.

Henry took a step toward her, then another, destroying the gap between them. He put out one hand and touched her gently on the arm. A zing of electricity raced along her skin, and Fee shivered. He stepped closer again, put his other hand around her waist, and pulled her in closer, until their bodies touched.

It was as if a million sparks of electricity were pinging back and forth between their bodies. Every sense was ignited, and Fee didn't know what to do with it all. It didn't seem real, like it was a walking dream she'd stumbled into. She smelled his body, oil and sweat mixed with a sweet toffee scent, like candy apples. He seemed to glow, and when she lifted her hands to his shoulders, thinking to push him away, her hands were caught in the texture of his shirt, and the feel of hard muscles underneath. His neck was right in front of her, and without thinking, she leaned forward and placed a soft kiss right where the vein pulsed. He jerked as if she'd stung him. Given the zing of sexual energy she'd felt through her lips, perhaps she had.

One of his hands came up and grasped the side of her face, angling her toward him. He lowered his lips to hers, and they kissed, softly at first. The blue electricity raced across her lips then down through her body, making her moan against him. It felt better than anything she'd ever experienced before; her body was alive with pleasure. He tightened his arms, drew her closer, and the kiss deepened, became more urgent. His tongue found hers, and Fee wrapped her arms around his neck, pushing her fingers through his hair, and dragging him closer still. She couldn't think about anything except wanting more of him along her body, and gathering more of the exhilarating energy they were creating.

"Henry? Fee? Are you two okay in there? We think we've found a solution!" Eugene's excited voice penetrated the shell of sexual heat that had surrounded them. They both jumped back, gasping for breath. Henry shook his head and looked down at her with a dazed expression.

He cleared his throat. "We'll..." He cleared his throat. "We'll be out in a minute, Eugene. We're just discussing...something."

Fee raised her eyebrows at him and he smiled. A devastating smile hit Fee full force, like the sun being turned on and pointed directly at her. Fee took a step back. It was too much. He was too much. She felt like she had been short-circuited. She'd come in here to tell him off and had ended up trying to jump him.

She'd been right all along, he was a golden god, and she was a mere mortal. She couldn't handle this much sensation; it wasn't meant for her. She shook her head. "I can't," she said, and then opened the door and ran.

CHAPTER 11

*H*enry watched her go with mixed emotions.

He'd never experienced anything like that before in his life, and it scared the hell out of him. He felt completely out of control and confused, and that was not something he liked.

Ever.

He looked at the shocked faces of Eugene, Nolan, and David, as they stood in the doorway and knew this whole thing could easily blow up in his face. It was a delicate process, and what was happening between him and Fee had the power to overturn all the good he was doing with these three.

He walked forward. "I have to chase after her, make sure she's okay. But I'll be back in a moment," he said calmly. It didn't match the turmoil he felt inside; the colors and light were making his insides dissolve into chaos.

"What happened? Is she okay?" said Eugene.

"I've never seen her upset like that," said David. "Not even when Pelgrim was at his worst."

Henry felt like he was being repeatedly punched in the

chest with every passing moment. "It'll be fine; don't worry about it."

He took off without checking to make sure they weren't blaming him for the problem. It would cause problems if they did, but he couldn't think about it right now. He had to find Fee.

He'd thought it was going to be difficult, but the energy they'd created between them still lingered in the air and he sensed her immediately. She was in line nearby to get a funnel cake, one of his favorite carnival foods. It struck another chord of fear inside him. What was happening? Why was it so fierce and uncontrollable? They needed to stop this right away.

He came up behind her and hovered for a moment, unsure what to say.

She beat him to it. "We can't ever do that again," she said without turning around. Around them, the fun and laughter of the theme park continued.

Henry, who'd just been thinking exactly the same thing, frowned. "Why not?" he said. His blood boiled at the thought of never kissing her again.

"Because we don't work together," she said.

"I think we just proved we work very well together," said Henry. Had it been one-sided? Had the connection he'd felt, the electricity that had flowed between them been more powerful for him?

She shook her head and still avoided his eyes, looking straight ahead at the back of the person in front of her in line. "What just happened was a weird chemical reaction, something completely out of our control. It's not normal to have electricity flowing between us like that; we're being pulled together by compulsion rather than real desire. We don't know each other. I'm not even sure I particularly like you. It makes no sense that we would have a reaction like that." She turned to him fully. "In fact, I think you're using your magic on me. You have it inside you. I can tell." She turned away again.

Henry sucked in a breath. "I have never, and will never, use any kind of magic or trickery to get a woman to like me," he said angrily. "I don't know who you think I am, but that's just plain insulting."

"But that's my point exactly. I don't know you. And we won't be doing that again."

"Well, good. Because I don't want to do it again either," said Henry angrily. "I don't like you particularly much either." With that childish—and totally untrue—parting shot, he turned and stormed back to the shed where the others were working. He didn't need her, and if she was going to go around accusing him of things like that, he wasn't going to bother with her at all. He yanked open the door and discovered the other three standing looking at him, worried expressions on their faces.

"Is she okay?" asked Eugene.

Henry pulled up short, and blinked. He never acted like that. He was a calm, methodical guy. Laid back and easy going. That kind of over-the-top reaction was the kind of stupid emotional reaction that he avoided. He never let anyone get to him, and he certainly never lied to them about something like that. He nodded slowly. "She's fine. Just getting a funnel cake, then she'll be back." He hoped. Maybe she was right. Maybe there *was* magic working over them, making them do things they wouldn't normally do.

Henry took a breath. Then another. He needed to calm down, get a bit of space between himself and Fee. Then he would go out again and find her, apologize for his outburst, explain that they needed to keep things professional, and then leave it at that.

It was a good plan, and he felt calmer as soon as he came up with it.

"So how are you guys getting on? What have you figured out?"

The three men leaped at the chance to explain what was happening, and soon he had the three of them crowded around him, talking over each other, and trying to get his attention. Even Nolan, who wasn't an engineer, was into the project, and seemed to be adding the kind of information the other two had overlooked. They were a great team and they'd found the problem that Grimshaw had wanted them to. A broken connection earlier in the system was causing a buildup of pressure that had resulted in the cracked valve.

It was a pity Fee wasn't here, because this was the perfect time for her to be bonding with the rest of them as well. Henry felt a pang of guilt. It was his fault she wasn't here. If he'd managed to keep things professional, as he knew he should have, then it would be fine now. He glanced at his watch. She should have been back by now. He smiled and nodded at the others, but in his head he was wondering how long before he would be allowed to go back out again and look for Fee. What if she decided never to come back? What if she was even now taking a taxi home, all ready to quit her job?

What if he never saw her again?

Henry's eyes flicked to the door. He would just go and make sure she was all right. Maybe she was being harassed by some theme park customer, and needed saving. "Guys, I'm going to check on Fee again; she should have been back by now," he said.

They all nodded in agreement, and he breathed a sigh of relief. They seemed to be worried about her as well. "I'll be back soon, and we can finish this off. But you're doing great. Grimshaw will be pleased."

Their grins lit up the room, and he smiled back, glad he'd bought them here today.

Mostly.

He blinked as he went from the darkened maintenance shed to the outside light. It was a bright and sunny day, and he should have felt happy. His project was going surprisingly well. They'd been working together for most of the morning, and had successfully found—and were discussing excellent solutions to—the problem on The Twister.

The last whispers of energy led him to where Fee was sitting, morosely staring at a large funnel cake, she was holding in one hand. She looked like a little kid wearing her parent's clothes in the giant overalls she'd been given, and her hair was falling out of its ponytail. He saw a glint of metal in the loose hairs at the base of her neck and realized the hair was actually being systematically pulled down. The little metal creature was working studiously to create a nest for itself. He almost smiled. She certainly was a unique individual.

"Hey, Fee," he said softly.

"Hey," she said. She didn't look up, and he had the feeling she'd known he was there the whole time.

"I'm sorry. I'm not normally like that. I didn't mean the things I said."

Her eyes flicked up to his face. "You didn't mean that you don't trick women into liking you?" she said in a whisper.

Henry blinked. What? He thought back to their conversation. "No! I mean I do like you. I want us to be friends. I agree with you that we shouldn't be anything else, and that what happened back there in the office was a mistake. I'd like us to both forget that it ever happened, and try to get back on track. We have a job to do, and the others are relying on us to make sure that we don't all lose our jobs."

"Well, technically I believe you can't lose your job," she said, her eyes flashing.

"Okay, okay." Henry held up his hands. "We need to make sure you guys don't lose your jobs. I'm sorry; I hope you can forgive me and come back to work with the others. They need you on the team."

She looked at the funnel cake and then back at Henry. "What am I supposed to do with this thing?" she said.

"Give it to me, and I'll take care of it." He held out his hand. When she handed it to him, there was a little zing of electricity as their fingers touched. They locked gazes.

"Let's try not to touch each other," said Henry.

Fee just nodded and looked away. "I better get back to the others," she said and walked off.

Henry looked down at the funnel cake in his hand. He took a bite and munched on the crunchy sweetness as he tried to figure out how he was going to survive a whole month.

CHAPTER 12

ee looked down at the thrill ride internal mechanisms, and watched as Eugene used a spanner to tighten the bolts around the new part they'd just installed.

Grimshaw had returned not long before, and asked what they'd discovered about the cracked valve. With a grin, he'd pulled the exact component they needed out of his pocket as soon as they'd finished their explanation. He'd told them to install it and disappeared again before they could ask him anything more.

Eugene talked her through what he was doing, needing another person to confirm he was right. She nodded. She could see what he was talking about, and agreed with how he was fixing it.

But she couldn't help feeling she was just playacting. Like they'd been given a pretend problem to play with, and Henry was sitting back and waiting for them to finish so he could pat them on the head and tell them what good children they'd been.

She didn't like that at all.

She also didn't like the fact that since he'd returned to the maintenance shed, Henry hadn't looked at her even once. Not even to say hello. Or to make sure she was all right. He was completely ignoring her.

Which should have been good. It should have been perfect. She couldn't handle what they'd experienced in the office. It was too much, too big, too full on.

But Henry ignoring her made her want to throw things at him.

"Okay, guys, Grimshaw will be back any minute. How are we going with the repairs?" Henry said.

"We're almost done," said Eugene, his voice exultant.

Fee smiled. They'd done a great job. She wished she felt more excited about it. For the hundredth time, she glanced over at Henry. He was helping David with the final adjustments to his section of the repairs. The two men were talking and laughing together. Fee frowned, and felt like growling.

Which was completely irrational. She shook her head. It wasn't going to work. She couldn't be around him without feeling a rollercoaster of emotions that made absolutely no sense given the small amount of time she'd actually known him.

"Hey, Fee, are you all right?" said Eugene. "I asked you three times to pass the wrench."

Fee blinked and looked at Eugene, who had oil all over his face, and a sparkle in his eyes. "Sorry, I was miles away." She handed him the tool he wanted and then forced herself to watch as he tightened up the last few bolts.

The door opened behind them with a swoosh of air, and Grimshaw strode in. Behind him was another man who was dressed in the same kind of casual outfit as Grimshaw, but had a great big beard and a shock of curly red hair on his head.

"How are you all doing?" asked Grimshaw in his booming voice.

"We're finished," said Eugene with a grin. "You're just in time."

Grimshaw nodded. "Fantastic. Let me introduce my brother-in-law, Seth. He's the real man in charge around here."

They all nodded at the big redhead, who looked solemnly back. "I hope you lot haven't wrecked my baby," he said in a growling voice. Beside her, Eugene paled.

Fee narrowed her eyes. "It's perfect. I think it might actually be better than before it was broken," she said, elbowing Eugene. He grinned weakly at her.

Seth lost his serious expression and grinned. "That's what I like to hear. Now you lot can go and enjoy a couple of rides while we check through and see what you've done to her. Then we'll give you a bit of feedback on what you could have done better." Grimshaw and Seth glanced at each other, clearly expecting there to be a huge number of things to discuss. "Henry'll show you the way."

They filed out of the room, all of them jumpy.

"How long are they going to take?" asked Eugene in a plaintive voice. "I feel like I'm back in high school waiting for my grades."

Henry smiled. "You did a great job. I think they'll even be surprised." He looked around at the thinning afternoon crowds. "We've been in there for most of the day," he said. "I think it's time we had some fun." Henry grinned and then gestured for them to follow him to the nearest ride.

David started to look a little green around the gills, but Eugene and Nolan crowded in behind Henry when he joined a line. Fee brought up the rear, unwilling to get too close to Henry.

The rollercoaster wasn't the worst one in the park; there were no double loops or hanging upside down. In fact, it had way more kids on it than the other rides. Henry had chosen an easier one, because he knew how David felt about them. Fee clenched her hands, trying not to think how nice that was.

He was still making David do it, when he clearly didn't want to.

They climbed in the seats, with Henry and Eugene in the first two seats, Nolan and David in the second two. Fee climbed into the third set of seats, and had a young teenage girl sitting next to her. She was delicately pretty and the only reason Fee knew she was older than she looked was by the group of teenaged girls she was with. They seemed to be whispering and giggling an awful lot together as they waited by the entrance.

Fee smiled at the girl, who smiled back shyly. When the black padded safety mechanisms came down and locked into place, Fee sat still and took a breath.

The roller coaster took off up the usual steep hill, and Fee tried to steady herself for the coming ride. Instead, her gaze fixed on the back of Henry's head, which she could see through the seats in front of her. What was happening between them? One minute they were going hot and heavy in the office, and next minute they were barely speaking.

She felt like she was a teenager again with a crush on a boy.

Only for her, it hadn't been the usual high school crush, because she'd been homeschooled at the Great Mother plantation. All the kids expected to hurry through their meagre learning, so they could head outside into the great outdoors, where they could work on the farms.

She'd gazed worshipfully at Tall Oak, one of the older boys who had strong arms, and a way with the horses. It had all ended abruptly when he'd run away from the farm with one of the older girls.

But she still vividly remembered the pangs of angst, the terrible emotions of being a teenager. Especially because she had been a teenager who so completely did not fit in at a rural commune where living off the land was paramount.

The first downhill slope of the ride came up, and Fee screamed as her stomach dropped out from under her. The rest of the ride was a blur, filled with screams and yells of surprise. She was glad they hadn't gone on one of the big ones first.

As they climbed shakily off, Fee gave the young girl an encouraging smile. She looked like she was about to cry.

"Are you okay?" Fee asked, momentarily concerned.

"I didn't do it. I was supposed to do my prank, but I was too scared. They'll kill me."

Fee frowned. "What kind of prank? Who will kill you?"

The girl shook her head. "Nothing. Don't worry." She took off at a run.

Fee considered following to make sure the girl was okay, but Eugene grabbed her arm before she could take a step.

"Hey, come on, Fee. We're going to do the Ferris wheel. David says he thinks that one will be easy. I wanna see him hurl."

She grinned. Like Eugene, she didn't think David realized what he was getting himself into.

It might be funny to watch.

She glanced around, wondering about the young girl. She shrugged. The girl would find her friends again. Maybe whatever prank she'd been planning would be forgotten in the fun of the theme park.

Again, they lined up, and this time, Eugene angled himself to sit next to David, grinning back at Fee. Nolan ended up sitting next to a pretty, young woman, and Fee somehow ended up next to Henry.

As she scrunched herself up into one corner of the bench seat, she wondered how she'd managed to get herself into this position. Henry was trying not to look at her, despite being right next to her, and after another moment or two of crushing herself against the side, Fee changed her mind.

Why did she have to be the one to try to avoid him? She moved over. What did she care if she touched his leg with hers?

She placed her hands onto the metal bar in front of them. What did it matter if their hands accidentally touched in the middle? They were both grown adults, and just because he was acting like a child, didn't mean she should as well.

The ride lumbered forward, the little car rocking slightly as it moved upward. The scenery below them levelled out, and Fee could see the surrounding views of Tampa. The river meandered slowly to their left, the lush green vegetation of the wilderness preserve visible on the other side. And directly in front of them was the city, with the water of the bay sparkling in the distance.

"It's lovely," said Henry softly.

She glanced at him. He was staring at her, the heat in his eyes unmistakable. She glanced back out at the scenery before them. "Yes. Lots to see in Tampa," she said. Her voice cracked and she cleared her throat.

"I'm sorry, Fee. I've been acting crazy."

Fee nodded. "I guess we both have."

"Can we call a truce? Agree to take better care of each other?"

Fee nodded, not sure what else to say.

Henry moved his hand over so it covered hers for a moment. Without warning, hot sparks of desire hit her right in the belly. Fee gasped, and next to her, Henry pulled back as if he'd been electrocuted.

"Why is it doing that? What is happening to us?" asked Fee, her voice high pitched and hysterical.

Henry just shook his head. He opened his mouth to say something, but a terrified scream from above had them both scrambling to see what was wrong. Fee's eyes locked on the same girl who'd sat next to her on the last ride, as she dangled out of a Ferris wheel carriage overhead. She was holding on with one hand and screaming hysterically.

Without hesitation, Henry stood, making their little seat swing back and forth. "Hold tight," he said. "This is probably going to make the carriage rock."

Then he climbed through the side and out onto the metal spokes of the Ferris wheel. No one at the base of the wheel had noticed the girl, so the ride was continuing its slow motion movement around.

"Hey, down there. Turn this thing off!" yelled Fee toward the operator in the distance below, as loudly as she could. But there was too much noise from the rest of the theme park, and no one heard her.

She looked up to where Henry was climbing, and her heart jumped into her throat. As they went around the curve of the Ferris wheel the carriages turned, and so did the spokes of the wheel. As they neared the top of the Ferris wheel, the spokes went from lying flat, to being perpendicular to the ground, and Henry had to climb carefully using the bars between the spokes, as well as the spokes.

He made it seem easy, climbing as if he'd been doing it for years, and Fee realized that he probably had. He'd grown up in the Carnival, and hadn't he said he'd worked on the thrill rides? He'd probably done this kind of thing his whole life. The thought settled her stomach down a little, but she still watched his every move with one hand over her mouth.

As more people noticed what had happened to the young girl, they began calling out to the operator below. Eventually one of them must have noticed, and pushed some kind of emergency stop button.

But the emergency stop jerked the Ferris wheel to a sudden halt, making all the carriages swing dangerously back and forth. There were screams from several people around the wheel, and the petrified young girl who had been hanging precariously lost her grip.

By this time, she was high in the air, almost to the top. She screamed as she fell, grabbing at nearby bars, trying to halt her descent.

Fee felt a wrench on her magic, making her physically jerk backwards. It felt like someone was dragging her across hot coals. She gasped for breath as a flash of blue lightning split the air between her and Henry, and then the girl found purchase on a cross bar. Seconds later, Henry was there, holding onto the teenager as she sobbed into his arms.

Fee stared as Henry grasped the girl with one arm and climbed to the nearest carriage using just his other arm and his legs. He was like a spider with his incredible balance and strength. She also noticed a blurring around the edges of what she could see of him up there. He was using magic to help save the girl, and he was hiding it from the other people on the ride. The only reason she could tell was because he was still using her magic to amp up his own.

She couldn't be angry with him; after all, he'd saved the young girl from what would have been a certain death if she'd fallen.

But it frightened her to know that he could just reach out and take what was hers so easily.

CHAPTER 13

*H*enry climbed down out of the carriage, still holding the young girl in his arms. She was quieter now, but had been hysterical for much of the ride down, and he'd sat with her, trying to calm her down. If there had been a way to get her down without continuing the journey on the ride, he would have done it.

Now there were medical people rushing toward him, and he gladly handed the girl over. She protested weakly, but he sent some calming thoughts in her direction and she quietened down. She needed proper help and care, and he didn't know how to give it to her. They would call her family to come and take care of her too.

He looked around for Fee. Drawing the magic from her had been instinctual, something he'd done on the spur of the moment when he needed it most. He knew he would have questions to answer from her, but he just needed to see her, to calm his own mind.

Out of the corner of his eye, he saw Grimshaw striding over. The older man was going to be furious about the repercussions of this day's events on his rides. Henry shrugged. He hadn't told the girl to climb out up there.

He'd asked her why she'd done it, and she'd whispered something about a dare. His own teenage years had included multiple dares from his older brothers. They were all bigger and stronger than he was; ready to knock him around for being too different from the rest of them. He'd probably done much worse than climbing the Ferris wheel—but then he'd been a carny kid.

So yeah, he understood the young girl's motivations. He just wished she'd chosen something a little less dangerous. And he had a terrible feeling she was younger than she was trying to pretend.

He could feel the shakes setting in, the result of doing something far more dangerous than he was used to these days. He'd climbed riggings, wasn't afraid of heights. But climbing a moving wheel was a level of stupid that he didn't like to think about. And if he hadn't been there, that girl would have died. He knew it without a doubt.

Grimshaw clapped him over the shoulder. "What the hell happened up there, man?" His voice was accusatory, as if he thought it was Henry's fault.

Henry raised his eyebrows at Grimshaw, but didn't get a chance to respond.

"He just saved that girl's life; that's what he did," said Fee, striding up to the two men like a little ball of fury. "If Henry hadn't been there to risk his life, that girl would be splattered all over the ground and you'd have an even bigger mess to clean up." She pointed her finger at Grimshaw as if daring him to disagree.

He frowned down at Fee for a moment, and then his shoulders sagged and he looked back at Henry. "I know, man; I'm sorry. Of course, you saved the day. It's just going to be a bitch around here for a while. Some kid almost falling from the Ferris wheel? We're going to have to close her for a while, figure out how to stop that from ever happening again."

Henry nodded. He knew exactly what Grimshaw was talking about. "Sorry, Grimshaw," was all he could think of to say. His brain was fogging over a little. He swayed a little where he stood.

"Hey, man, are you okay?" said Grimshaw, grabbing Henry's arm and holding him steady.

"I think... I think I may be having a reaction to using so much magic, so far away from home," said Henry groggily.

"We need to get him out of here," said Fee's voice behind him.

He felt her hands holding him on his other side. The usual hum of electricity felt like an old friend rather than a disturbance. He resisted the urge to snuggle in close to her as she helped him walk down the path.

He only made it a few steps before his vision went blurry, and then he felt nothing at all.

CHAPTER 14

ee tried to keep him standing, but it was only because Grimshaw was on the other side of her that she managed to keep him upright. He was damn heavy. "Can you help me get him back to the car?" she asked Grimshaw, who nodded.

"I'll just pick him up. It'll be easier that way."

Fee looked around for the others, and gestured to David, Nolan, and Eugene when she saw them hovering to one side. "We have to get Henry to a doctor," she said as they hurried over.

Grimshaw shook his head. "He won't thank you for it, Fee," he said in an undertone. "This is just magic burnout. He'll want to head home and rest it off."

Fee tried not to notice that Grimshaw was talking openly to her about magic. It meant he knew she'd understand what he was talking about. All she could concentrate on for the time being was getting Henry somewhere safe.

"Are you sure?" she said.

"Positive. Just take him home and let him sleep it off."

Fee didn't know where home *was* for Henry in Tampa.

But she would deal with that once they were all in the car. She smiled slightly. That would be the one high point of this day. Getting to drive Henry's car. She had a feeling people weren't given this privilege very often.

She and the others trailed along after Grimshaw as he carried Henry out of the theme park and toward their car. He let Henry down slowly, and Fee grabbed his other side again. "Let's put him in the back seat, so someone can hold him up, make sure he's okay for the ride home," said Fee.

But it wasn't as easy as it should have been to get Henry into the car. He seemed to be all heavy arms and legs, and none of them worked as they should to get him into the back seat.

"We'll have to just put him in the front," said Fee in exasperation.

Grimshaw wiped sweat off his face and nodded. "He's sure fighting getting in the back."

Fee frowned. Henry was completely out of it. He wasn't able to fight anything.

In the end, they got him settled into the front passenger seat. Fee slipped into the leather seat next to a sagging Henry, and hoped he'd be okay. She grabbed a sweater from her bag, and shoved it under his head.

She turned to Grimshaw. "Thanks for your help," she said, holding out her hand.

He grinned and pushed aside the hand, grabbing her into a big hug. She didn't know what else to do, so just hugged him back. He clapped her on the shoulder, and then turned to the others, hugging each of them, and giving them words of encouragement. They brightened under his attention, the same way they had from Henry's. Fee shook her head. It was amazing what a bit of attention and validation could do for a person. Especially from someone they looked up to.

"I better head back. Seth was sorting it out, but he'll want some help. Wish me luck."

"I'm sorry our visit had to end like this," said Fee.

"Come back anytime. I'll get you a free pass," said Grimshaw with a wink. He waved and then headed back to the main entrance at a run, his long legs eating up the distance.

Fee turned to the others, holding the driver's door open as they climbed into the back. She glanced up at the sky and was surprised to see dark clouds lingering overhead. It looked like it was about to rain—just what she needed.

"This isn't as cool from the back seat," said Nolan.

Putting her hand on the smooth exterior of Henry's beautifully restored Dodge Charger, Fee wondered if this was such a great idea. She'd grabbed the keys from his pocket, and she knew she had to get him somewhere comfortable where he could sleep off the magic. But Henry had seemed attached to his car. What if something happened?

Fee took a breath. She'd just have to drive slowly.

Turning the key, the motor hummed to life, sending vibrations through the car. Remembering the alterations Henry had said he'd installed in the car, she wondered if there was anything she should know. Glancing to where he was slumped sideways in the seat next to her, she hoped not.

"Do you even know how to drive a car like this?" asked David nervously.

Fee smiled into the rear vision mirror. "Of course. Why wouldn't I?"

Just the fact that I grew up in an agricultural cult that believed anything motorized was the work of the devil. That was all.

She'd made up for it once she left. She'd learned to not only drive a car, but also how to gut and put one back together again. She'd had a lot of catching up to do, and she'd gotten into it with gusto.

But this car was something else. She could feel the rumble of unidentifiable extra additions underneath the usual motor sounds. She smoothed her hands over the leather on the steering wheel. She had no choice but to drive his car: they needed to get him home.

Pushing her foot slowly on the accelerator, she drove out of the parking lot and turned onto the road, trying to keep her speed down. They made it to the freeway before big drops of rain started splashing onto the windshield.

Fee fumbled around, pulling on levers and pressing buttons.

"It'll be that button on the left," said Nolan.

"No, the lever to the right of there," said Eugene.

Fee pressed both and found the lights and the horn before she found the wipers and set them to keeping the rain off the windshield. She held onto the steering wheel tightly with both hands, trying to keep the car in the correct lane, and at the right speed, with very little visibility. They were halfway home before the rain slowed down and then stopped, and Fee heaved a sigh of relief. She didn't want to crash Henry's car, especially not when he was unconscious inside it.

Now that the rain wasn't pouring down, it didn't take long before she got tired of the slow speed and her foot pressed a little harder on the accelerator. Without even seeming to, the car increased in speed. It was such a smooth ride that Fee had to glance down at the speedometer to make sure they were actually going faster.

She pushed on the accelerator a little more, and felt the power behind the engine's hum. It thrummed through her whole body, making her shiver with delight. Driving this car was an experience she would never forget.

"Maybe we could drive around the block a couple of times when we get back," suggested Eugene. "Give us all a go at the wheel?"

Fee laughed and shook her head. It was bad enough that she was driving Henry's baby. "I think we'd better just get Henry home as soon as we can," was all she said.

They arrived outside the Callaghan Tech building. "This is us, boys," she said as she climbed out to let the others exit the back seat.

"Are you sure you're going to be able to handle him?" asked Nolan once he was out of the vehicle. "We barely got him in there."

Fee nodded. "I'll be fine. It's not far. I'll get my neighbors to help me if I need to."

"If you're sure...?" Nolan was looking at her dubiously, but there was no way she was going to let any of them come to her apartment. She'd realized it was her only option on the way here. She had no idea where Henry was staying, and if it were some kind of magical stupor, she'd have more luck looking after him than the others.

And she *would* have help getting him from her internal garage up to her apartment—she just wasn't going to tell these guys that. "Worst comes to the worst, I'll leave him in the car," she joked.

"Surely that wouldn't be good for him?" said Eugene worriedly as he came to stand beside Fee and Nolan.

"I'm kidding, Eugene. I'll get him safely tucked up in a bed, no worries."

David climbed out last, but he didn't add anything to the conversation. He looked pensive, glancing back at Henry a couple of times before he came to stand next to the others on the sidewalk. It had been a long day for all of them.

"Okay then. We'll see you tomorrow." Nolan gave her an awkward hug, something he'd never done previously. It was weird, but Fee appreciated the effort. She hugged him back, and then gave the other two a quick embrace as well. It was something she'd never have dreamed she'd do three days ago.

They'd enjoyed their day today, despite what had happened to Henry. It was going to change how they worked together from now on.

Fee climbed back into the car, waving one hand out the window as she headed off, and drove the short distance to her apartment block at a more sedate speed. She didn't own a car, but she had a parking spot in the underground garage assigned to her apartment, so it was always there for visitors.

If she were ever to *have* any visitors, that is. Henry's car was first that had sat in her parking space since she'd moved in five years before.

He was still out cold, so Fee went to the small lock up at the front of the park, and pressed the buzzer she'd put inside. "Yes?" asked a robotic voice.

"Max, I'm home. And I need your help. Can you meet me downstairs in the parking lot?"

"Certainly, Wild Feather. At once."

"I've told you not to call me that," said Fee grumpily.

"You tell me lots of things, and I ignore most of them," replied Max calmly.

"Just get your butt down here to help me." Fee tried not to feel like too much of a failure as yet another of her inventions talked back at her.

HENRY WOKE groggy and with a splitting headache, in the arms of a creature he couldn't quite explain. He was being carried up a set of stairs in multiple metal arms that seemed to flow around him like an octopus. He squinted, and realized that was exactly what it was modelled after.

"Wild Feather, he is awake," said a robotic voice.

"I've told you a million times, not in front of other people."

"This is the first time I have actually been in front of another person, and you definitely haven't told me a million times, Wild Feather. I count five times, at most." The creature was reprimanding Fee like it was her mother. Henry shook his head trying to figure out if he was dreaming.

Henry heard Fee's muttered reply from behind the creature, but he couldn't see her. He tried to twist around, but found himself held too tightly in multiple grips.

"Please do not move, sir. It may cause me to lose my balance, and fall down the stairs." The voice was polite and matter of fact, and rather musical, if he were honest.

And obviously another creation of Fee's. Or should he call her Wild Feather? He tried to push down the desire to snigger. He'd assumed Fee was short for Phoebe or Fiona or some other name she didn't like. Wild Feather was a whole other level.

They'd arrived at a landing with a single metal door, and Fee squeezed past her creature to unlock it. She pushed the door wide open and Henry felt like he was floating as he was carried through the door on multiple legs.

"Where shall I put the patient?" asked the voice.

"Put him in my room, Max." She paused. "I'll be in to see you in a second, Henry. Just let Max take care of you."

Henry didn't reply; he was too busy looking around at the strange and wonderful cave he'd just entered. The windows all had blackout curtains, and instead of overhead lights, fairy lights twinkled across the ceiling like stars. A couple of round globes hung down like giant planets, letting off more light. In the main room they'd entered the only furniture was a couch and a dining room table and chairs. The rest of the space was filled with computing equipment, TV screens, and other gadgetry he wanted to get a closer look at.

He shifted in the arms of his transportation.

"Please, sir, I am not as stable as I may at first appear. You

89

will need to remain still for this situation to end successfully."

Henry settled back, trying to remain still, and wondering what problems this amazing eight-legged creature had with balance. Maybe he could fix it.

Max lay him down on the bed, and Henry had his first full glimpse of the creature. He was well and truly designed after an octopus, with eight constantly moving legs keeping him standing upright. His head was a small computer screen with wires and metal behind it keeping him together. His body was a basic metal casing that didn't move with the amazing agility that he could see in the legs. Henry kept staring at the limbs, which seemed to be comprised of thousands of tiny joints, giving the octo-creature the ability to move in all directions as if he really was an octopus in the sea.

"Can I get you anything, sir? I believe Wild Feather will be in momentarily."

Henry shook his head, and then wondered if Max could understand visual cues.

"Very well, I will leave you."

Yes, he did. Henry was enthralled. He'd never done much work with robotics before coming to Callaghan Technology, and he didn't know how a creature like this might work. It seemed magical; and given what he knew about Fee, it probably was.

More was going on here than met the eye. And he was going to find an explanation for all of it.

CHAPTER 15

$\mathcal{F}$ ee fluttered around in her kitchen, preparing a hot coffee, and then an iced tea, for Henry. She couldn't decide which would be best for him in his current state. She didn't actually want to talk to him face to face. She'd been working on instinct when she brought him back to her cave; and now he was here, she wished she'd never done it. It felt uncomfortable and awkward.

She felt a chittering vibration in her hair, and put one hand up to Bing, pulling him out of the nest he'd been hiding in.

"I'm going to have to wash my hair again tonight, using double the conditioner to get that knot out," she scolded. He stood on her palm, and chittered back at her, unconcerned. She put him down on the bench, and he skittered off along the surface, skidding at the far edge, and disappearing over the edge. She grinned. He was a bit of a daredevil.

She sighed, thinking about her interaction with Bing. An outsider would think she was crazy, talking to her creations like that. She had to watch herself in front of Henry.

It was because no one else ever came to her private sanctuary. She wasn't used to being on best behaviour here. She'd lived in the same apartment for the last five years and never had visitors. Not even a door-to-door salesman.

Now Henry was in her room, in her bed, and she was hiding in the small kitchen space, trying not to freak out.

Max emerged from the bedroom, and looked in her direction. He had sensors all over his body continually providing him with information, so he didn't technically need to look at her to see or sense her. Fee figured he did it out of politeness, which was one of his overriding command features.

"He is waiting for you. I do believe he is very weak, and should return to a sleeping state as soon as possible. Do you wish me to carry the liquid sustenance you have provided?"

Fee shook her head. "I'll take it."

"There is another problem I have not ascertained?"

"No."

"Then why are you still in the kitchen?"

Fee sighed, and picked up the tray. "No reason," she said.

She tiptoed into her room, feeling like it didn't belong to her any more. Henry's presence on the bed took over the room, making it seem small and cramped.

"I made you something hot...and cold. I wasn't sure what you might feel like."

Henry smiled weakly. "A cold drink would be good. Do you have anything for a splitting headache?"

Fee nodded and went to the en suite, where she grabbed a couple of pills from her cabinet. She saw a glimpse of her face in the mirror. She was pale with dark smudges under her eyes. Rubbing her face, she tried to bring a little color back into her cheeks. Sighing, she went back out into her bedroom.

"These should help. And I think you need to sleep. You can stay here and get some rest."

Henry nodded and took the pills, taking them in one swallow. "I don't want to put you out."

Fee shook her head. "It's fine. I have work to do anyway. Just rest."

He seemed like he wanted to ask more questions, but Fee shook her head. "I'm not going to answer anything else until you've slept." She snapped a finger and all the lights in the room went out, including the fairy lights on the ceiling. "Rest. You'll feel better for it."

She walked back out into the main room, closing the door to her bedroom softly behind her. She looked around her apartment for a moment, and then huffed down onto the comfy couch. What had she been thinking bringing him here? It was insane. No one was allowed here. It was the one place she could be comfortable.

She harrumphed, and then switched on her laptop, restlessly flicking through a few of her usual online forums on robotics and computing. Nothing exciting going on there except a few arguments over the best way to solve a particular software issue. Putting the computer away, she turned on her television, and flicked through a few channels, trying to find something good to watch. Over 100 stations, and there was nothing on.

She glanced at her bedroom door, wondering if he was asleep yet. Maybe she should check on him? Make sure he was all right?

"Would you like some dinner?" asked Max.

Fee jumped. "Don't sneak up on me like that," she said sulkily.

"I think you will find I made the same amount of noise as usual." He paused. "Dinner?"

Fee nodded. "Sure. Maybe in a half hour? Nothing fancy, just some eggs or something." She glanced at her room. "I'm going to check on the patient."

"My sensors say he is sleeping."

"Even better," she replied.

She opened the door carefully, trying not to make any noise, and then poked her head around the edge. "Fairies," she whispered. The fairy lights overhead came on. Now she could see a big lump in her bed. She crept into the room, stopping at the closest edge of the bed and stared down at Henry. The glow from the fairy lights radiated over his face; Fee felt like a moth drawn to a flame, unable to stop the attraction that might very well be the death of her.

He looked peaceful in sleep. Not more relaxed, because the man could hardly get more relaxed than he was when he was awake. Just more peaceful, like his brain had stopped thinking quite so hard.

She sat down in the armchair near her bed, which was covered in clothes she'd either tried on or decided not to wear sometime that week. Staring at his face, she tried to understand what was happening between them.

Asleep, he looked less like the golden god he'd seemed at the beginning, and more like a rather alluring man. She put her head to one side, trying to understand the attraction she felt for him, and the raging sexual response she'd felt when he'd kissed her. It made no sense to her analytical brain. She'd never been one to leap into relationships, and she'd certainly never kissed anyone the way she'd kissed Henry.

It had to be something to do with the blue electricity that sparked between them every time they touched. Some kind of magic was compelling her to feel this fascination. She leaned back in the armchair and watched him in the dim light, trying to figure him out.

She woke, hours later, with a blanket over her, and a cold plate of eggs sitting next to her on the floor. Her eyes were scratchy from her contacts and she had a painful crick in her neck. Her legs were stiff from the weird position. She stretched out and tried to shake herself awake.

The bedside clock said it was four in the morning. Fee's stomach rumbled and she considered the cold eggs for a moment. But no, that wasn't going to happen.

She stood up, and tiptoed out of the room, closing the door and heading to the kitchen. Pulling out bread and meat, plus cheese and tomatoes, she puttered around the kitchen, making herself a couple of sandwiches and a coffee. In one corner of the room, Max was silent and recharging. He turned himself off at 11 p.m. every night by going to his charge station, and setting the alarm for 6 a.m. She had a solar panel attached to the roof of the building, and he ran off the sun. It was a handy system.

She wasn't sleepy anymore, so headed back to the bedroom to watch her patient some more. Something drew her back in there, an unexpected need to be close to him now that she had him here. She told herself it was because she still hadn't figured him out. She wanted to take advantage of his lack of awareness while she could.

Picking up her first sandwich, she had just bitten into the juicy goodness when he spoke.

"Any more of those for me? I'm starving," he whispered.

Fee jumped for the second time that night. Looking over at him, he was in exactly the same position, but his eyes were open, watching her intently. She shivered.

Without a word, she picked up the plate and handed it to him, keeping hold of the half a sandwich in her hand. He probably needed the energy more than she did.

He sat up, leaning his back against the wall behind him and she realized he'd taken off his shirt to sleep. He was delightfully tanned, with a broad muscled chest—not a desk-based researcher, that was for sure. She realized she was staring and blushed, glad for the dim lighting in the room.

"This might just be the best sandwich I have ever eaten," he said with a groan. "I was starving."

Fee smiled. "I think that might be a bit of an exaggeration."

"Magic always does that to me." He watched her carefully. "You'd know about that, wouldn't you?"

Fee looked away, trying to decide what to say. She didn't need him knowing any more about her and what she could do.

"I've felt it—your magic, I mean," he said. "And I've seen it. Those little creatures you design, they're full of your energy."

Without thinking, Fee flicked her eyes to Henry, and she was caught in the deep golden depths.

"Don't try to deny it," he said softly. "I used some of your power to help save that girl on the Ferris wheel. We both know it."

"I...wasn't." She paused and licked her lips. "I've just...never met anyone who talks about it before."

Henry's eyes gleamed with amusement. "There are many people using magic out there in the world. Although I've never met anyone who does it quite like you."

Fee narrowed her eyes. Was that an insult? Was he saying that she wasn't as good as the people he knew? "What do you mean?"

"I've never seen anyone who could give souls to metal creations. It's amazing." Henry's voice was awed.

Fee swallowed. "It's nothing, not even a talent. Even Max, he talks back to me, and never does what I ask him to."

"That's because you've taught him to think. I've never seen any other robot do that. At least not yet."

"He's not AI. He just seems like it because he backchats." Fee was shaking her head. Henry had it wrong.

"He's as close as anything I've seen or heard of. And giving him eight arms like an octopus, that's a stroke of genius. Although I can't figure out how you make his legs so fluid, so exactly like a real octopus in water." His voice was excited, and Fee had to remind herself not to be drawn into his enthusiasm. It was hard, because she found him infectious, in the same way that Nolan, David, and Eugene were now hero-worshipping Henry. She wanted to curl up at his feet and listen to him talk.

She shook her head. "Do you do that on purpose?" she asked, annoyed.

Henry blinked owlishly in the dim light. "Do what?"

"Trick people around you into being all fired up."

He pulled back a little. "I like people to be excited about what they're doing. That's all. It's not a trick." He sounded hurt and Fee cursed her antisocial skills.

"I'm sorry; I didn't mean it like that. Too much alone time. It just feels like you're a freaking planet and I'm a tiny little moon orbiting you. I try to get away, but nothing I do will let me go. All I want is to be closer to you."

Henry grinned. "That's an interesting analogy." His eyes gleamed and he leaned forward again. "So you want to be closer to me?"

Fee rolled her eyes. "Not if you talk to me like that." She stood up, and went over to retrieve his empty plate from where he'd placed it on the bed next to him. "I'm going to do some work. May as well, I don't think I'll get back to sleep now." She reached out, but instead of grasping the plate, she found her arm encircled by his hand.

"What are you doing?" she said, tugging at her arm.

"Stay here with me. Let's talk some more." He patted the bed beside him with his other hand.

Fee swallowed hard, looking into his eyes. He looked like a golden lion, eyes gleaming, his expression focused on one thing: her.

This was what it felt like to be the prey.

Fee shivered. "I don't..."

"Please? I don't think I can get back to sleep either." His voice was soft, hypnotic, and Fee found herself sitting down on the edge of the bed.

"What do you want to talk about?" she said.

Henry shrugged. "Anything." He paused. "You. How you came to be here, living in this amazing apartment, working for Callaghan Technology." He didn't let go of her arm, but slid his hand down toward hers, and clasped it tight. She tugged at it experimentally, but he didn't let go.

"I went to college at MIT, graduated early with my PhD in robotics, and was headhunted by Lucas at an alumni event. I've been here about five years. That's the whole story."

"You're hardly old enough to have done all that."

"It didn't take me as long as some people to finish my PhD," she said. "Or my Master's."

"How long did it take?"

"I was done with my PhD in a year and a half," she whispered. Most men were intimidated by what that meant. At least all the guys she met at MIT.

Henry just looked impressed.

"That's pretty amazing," he said. "*You're* amazing," he whispered. The next second he was pulling her toward him, and she let him. Their lips touched, and the electric current she was coming to recognize burned through her veins, making her moan with the heat of it.

HENRY COULDN'T BELIEVE he was doing it again. He'd decided to stay away from her, had assured himself he didn't need the hassle of getting involved, and that whatever was going on between them, the electricity made it worse not better.

And yet.

Here they were, kissing like their lives depended on it. Desperately, he deepened the kiss, trying to get closer to her. To somehow be a part of her. To understand this thing between them that was so uncontrollable and crazy.

He put one hand around her, and pulled her to him, lying back down on the bed. She moaned but otherwise didn't reject him. Pushing her T-shirt up her back, he savored the sizzling feel of her skin under his palm. It was soft and silky smooth with just a bite of the electricity he'd become accustomed to when he touched her.

His lips continued to devour hers, the heat making him groan. He pulled away and kissed his way along her neck and across her collarbone. Fee leaned back to give him room, and he felt her lacy bra under his hands. He moved his hand around to cover her breast, molding it to his hand, and she moaned. He played with her nipple experimentally through the thin material, and Fee pushed her breast closer, wanting more.

Just then, an alarm sounded next door.

Fee jerked back, looking around her as if she'd forgotten where she was. Henry could only watch as she moved away from him with a panicked expression, pushing herself back off the bed, and pulling her T-shirt back down.

She stood for a moment staring at him with wide eyes, then turned and fled through the door.

CHAPTER 16

Fee opened her eyes and looked around.

She was lying on the couch in her living room where she'd fled, convinced she was never going to sleep again. She must have dozed off after all. Morning light was peeking in through the sides of her blackout curtains and she wondered what the time was.

Was Henry awake? How was she going to face him again after what had happened?

Her contacts were painful and scratchy, and she rubbed at her eyes, wishing she dared take them out. She would have to wait until she could have a shower. She didn't want to remove them in front of Henry.

The door opened and the man himself poked his head through. He looked ruffled and gorgeous, especially when he grinned. "Rise and shine, sleepy head," he said as if nothing had happened. "We've got a big day today." His hair was wet from a recent shower, although he was wearing the same clothes as yesterday.

Fee frowned, and grabbed her phone from the coffee table. It was nine o'clock; usually she'd be at the office by now. She sat up abruptly. "Oh, no! We're late. The others will wonder..." she trailed off and looked at Henry, a blush spreading over her face.

"They already knew you were going to take me home to your place, right?" said Henry soothingly. "They're not going to think anything of you being a little late." He didn't seem bothered by the memories of what had almost happened between them. Perhaps it wasn't a big deal to him. Fee tried to muster the same casual attitude.

"Have you had a shower? I need to get clean before I can face the office."

Henry nodded and came further into the living room. He gestured to her bedroom. "It's all yours."

She stood and walked past, trying to keep as far away as possible. A faint hum of electricity made the hairs on her arm stand up as she walked by him, but she managed to ignore it. Once she was in her room, she shut the door and leaned against it, closing her eyes and letting out her breath in a big exhalation of air. What the hell was happening to her?

She took a deep breath and straightened up, shaking out her shoulders. She could do this. There was no way a guy was going to mess with her so totally that she had a melt-down in her own bedroom. She strode over to the en suite, turned the shower to stinking hot. She took out her contacts, and placed them in solution before getting out of her clothes and climbing into the shower. After a breathless few minutes getting herself clean and then drying off, she returned to her bedroom, a soft towel wrapped around her body.

There was a fair bit of thumping and walking around from next door. She could hear Henry's voice, and the low thrum of Max answering. She almost went out to see what was happening. But common sense prevailed. She had to finish getting ready for work.

She grabbed a plain black shirt and trousers from her

drawers, and dragged them on. She put her contacts back in and used the special eye drops that helped with the pain from having them in too long. A few minutes on her makeup and hair, and she was ready to face whatever was happening in the other room.

She quietly opened the door. Henry was sitting with Max, playing cards. It looked innocent enough. But Max could be tricky, and she was discovering that Henry could too.

"What are you two doing?" she said.

Henry glanced back at her. "I'm teaching Max to play cards," he said blandly.

Fee narrowed her eyes. "What kind of cards?"

"Poker."

"Do you think that's an appropriate game for an impressionable robot to be learning?" she asked sternly, forgetting her embarrassment.

Henry looked up, a surprised expression on his face. "Of course. He learns not only the mechanics of how to play, but also about cheating, bluffing, and tells. It's the perfect game to help Max with his interactions with humans."

"It seemed an appropriate use of my time, since I have already prepared your breakfast," said Max.

Fee raised her eyebrows but said nothing more. Heading to the kitchen, she poured herself a cup of coffee from the fresh brew waiting for her, and then leaned back against the counter, taking a sip and watching Henry under lowered lashes. He wasn't paying any attention to her at all. She didn't know whether to be offended or relieved; but if he could be blasé about last night, so could she.

Her usual oatmeal was waiting on the stovetop, and she brought a bowl back to the couch, sitting next to Max, watching silently as they continued their game.

"Shouldn't you be a little more concerned about getting

to work?" she said before placing a spoonful of oatmeal into her mouth.

"I'm going to have to go to the hotel to get some new clothes anyway," said Henry with a grin. "I figured I was going to be late. You, on the other hand, are going to be late with absolutely no excuse to hold it together."

Fee narrowed her eyes. "I have five years of credibility to see me through being late one morning. And they knew I was looking after you. I'll just say you were a difficult patient."

For a moment, Henry's eyes flared at her across the coffee table. The heat in his gaze was unmistakable. "You tell them anything you like," he said. "You and I will know what really happened."

"What really happened?" she asked softly, still caught up in his tawny gaze.

"You ran away from me, just when things were getting interesting." He glanced down at his cards, frowning. "Maybe it was for the best; I don't know." He placed a card on the table, his agile fingers making Fee blush even harder as she watched them.

Abruptly, she put her half-eaten bowl of oatmeal down on the table, and stood. Smoothing down her shirt, she cleared her throat. "I'm going to work, and you need to get your clothes." She looked down at Henry expectantly.

He sighed and reluctantly got to his feet. "I suppose I can't stay here forever. As much as it's fun playing with Max." His jeans hung off his hips and she caught a glimpse of his tanned stomach under his shirt. For a second, visions of his naked chest under her flashed through her head. It felt like an addiction, the way she was feeling about Henry right now. She didn't trust it, which was a large part of the reason she'd run out on him. She wasn't going to let some bewildering magic she didn't understand force her into bed with a man she barely knew. It might be sizzling hot between them, but it wasn't real.

At least, she didn't think it was.

Henry had been watching her face carefully, and now he moved to stand next to her, closer than strictly necessary. "We should go," he said, suddenly seeming nervous.

"I guess," replied Fee, even though moments before she'd been pushing for it. The hairs on her arms raised up, and goosebumps raced along her skin. She met Henry's gaze and saw her own sudden craving reflected in his face.

Henry took another step toward her, putting one hand up to cup her cheek, and lowered his head. His kiss started softly, as if he was asking a question, but soon deepened into something more thrilling when Fee put her arms around him, crushing her body to his. Electricity sizzled through her, and she felt like she was tumbling over a waterfall with nothing more than a barrel to keep her safe. Their usual electricity sizzled and adrenaline rushed through her veins. She couldn't get enough of him, his touch, his body, his smell.

She was well and truly under his spell.

The stray thought was enough to snap her out of it, and send panic through her body. She made a noise, trying to step back out of the embrace. Henry didn't let her go immediately, his dazed expression saying he was just as caught up in the moment as she had been.

"I need to get to work," she said, backing away from him, holding her hands out in front of her as some form of protection.

Henry rubbed his hand across his face, and nodded. "You're right. That was...not a good idea."

He followed her silently out the door, and watched as she locked the door.

"I'll give you a ride back to Callaghan, and then go grab my stuff," he said as they walked toward the elevator.

She nodded. "Sure." The tension was thick in the air around them. Fee didn't know how to break it, or fix it. But if it continued like this, the others were going to know soon enough that something was going on between them.

She needed to tone it down, to pull back from this craziness, or something bad was going to happen.

She could feel it.

CHAPTER 17

*H*enry stood in the reception area at Callaghan Technologies trying to calm his racing pulse.

He was showered and clean, and had put on new clothes. He was ready for the day. He just hoped this burning desire to see Fee again didn't ruin his ability to come up with some new ideas for Violet.

He smiled at Wanda as he walked past on the way to elevators, noticing again her glasses slipping down her nose.

She didn't give him as much of a glare as she had done on his first day, but she didn't exactly look approving either. Perhaps if he fixed her glasses she'd be nicer to him. He shook his head. He needed to be focused on the research team, not on fixing glasses for grumpy receptionists.

The only problem was that instead of focusing on the research, his mind went straight to Fee. It was a massive distraction they didn't need, either of them. How was he going to get anything done when his libido kept getting in the way?

Just the thought of last night was sending his imagination

into a spiral, and hardening up his body in places that he didn't need. He literally had to make himself think of ice-cold water, baseball, and other unsexy things to get himself to calm down.

What was happening? He felt like his body had been invaded by some hormonal teenager, complete with a horrendous sex-obsession. With an effort, he pushed down his body's urges and focused on the task. Today they needed to buckle down and work on Violet's main problems, see if they could take anything they'd learned from the previous day and bring it into her design.

The doors opened and his heart leaped into his throat before he firmly swallowed it down again. He was going to be all business. If he was going to save their jobs and the project, he couldn't afford to be anything else.

He glanced toward Fee's desk first; he couldn't help himself. But he made sure his expression was blank, and he didn't give away what he was feeling. She looked up at him, her expressive grey eyes like liquid pools. He looked away, unable to handle the instant connection created just by gazing into her eyes.

"Hey, Henry! How are you?" Nolan came up to him, a concerned expression on his face. David and Eugene followed closely behind. "Fee said you'd slept the night through?"

Henry grinned. He hadn't slept the *entire* night. "I feel great now. It was just a reaction to what happened on the Ferris wheel. Too much exertion all in one go. I'm a researcher, not a climber."

Nolan gave him a pat on the shoulder and a relieved smile. "We were worried you might not be able to finish the contract. That something might be wrong with you."

"Oh, no, it'd take more than that to keep me down," he said with a smile.

"It seemed almost magical, what you did," said David, watching Henry closely.

Henry let out a bark of laughter. "It was terrifying, that's for sure. Thanks for being so concerned about me, but I'm fine now. Let's get to it. We're at the conference table first and then we'll go hang out with Violet for a while." He turned to where Fee was still hiding behind her desk. "Fee, come on, we need you as well."

Once he had them all gathered around the table, he pulled out a large whiteboard on an easel and some whiteboard pens. "So first, Eugene, I want you to list Violet's best points down on one side of this board. What's great about her? What is working well?" He handed a blue pen to Eugene when he came to his side.

Eugene glanced around at the others, and then shrugged and went to work.

"Tell us what you're writing, as you write it," encouraged Henry.

"Well, she has a lovely voice," he said quietly.

Nolan sniggered. "That's because you made it the same as that singer," he said. "What's her name? Taylor something?"

"What else?" said Henry, giving Nolan a quelling look.

"She actually works rather well when it comes to taking body temperature, blood pressure, and her other diagnostic features."

Henry nodded encouragingly.

"Her organizational capabilities are rather clever. She hooks into Google and can ask it anything the wearer wants to know."

"Okay, great, those are three big aspects of the project, well done." He looked around at the others. "Now, David, can you please write down where she isn't doing so well?"

David stood awkwardly, and went to the front of the room. Despite the fact it was just the five of them, he blushed. "Her skin is all wrong," he said quickly. "Too thick and bulky. Too rubbery. She also overheats easily and we lose all her best features. And her wiring system isn't working, probably something to do with the overheating, although we haven't been able to figure that out yet." He wrote all three problems down in an illegible script.

"Fantastic, David. Anything else?" Henry looked around at the others.

Nolan shrugged. "Pelgrim's work on the nanorobotics is all wrapped up in this as well. There will be issues with figuring that out now that he's gone."

Henry nodded. "Perfect. That gives us some specifics to work with." He stood up and started pacing around the table. "Does Violet currently do anything that the current crop of wearable products doesn't? That their watch couldn't tell them?"

They looked at each other again and deflated. "Probably not," said Eugene.

Henry stopped. "Then that's where we start. What can we add into Violet's schematics that no one else will have? And how do we make her useful to a particular niche of people?"

To one side, Henry saw Fee nod her head. "We were going to make her skin impervious to outside forces, maybe bullet proof," she said. "That would be different."

Nolan paused and glanced at Fee. "And we had that idea to have her monitor vitamin levels and then be able to help the user absorb them through the skin."

"What about making the skin give the person information they didn't even know they needed?" said Eugene. "Like the ability to learn their habits and make educated guesses about what they might want? Make her more like a friend who knows you rather than a machine."

Henry paused at that concept, a part of him creeped out. But it was all fodder for the mill, and he wasn't going to stop them at this point. "Keep going," he encouraged. "All ideas are good ideas at this point."

"She could fly," said Eugene.

"She could do diagnostics while you're asleep," said Nolan.

"She could make you invisible," added Fee, grinning.

"The skin could be strong enough to help people with amputated limbs walk," said David.

"Her skin could provide fingers and hands for people who don't have them," added Nolan thoughtfully.

Henry looked around at the group. Their excitement was palpable: eyes were sparkling, they were all shouting over each other, and good-naturedly trying to be heard. It was as if they were a different team.

He held up his hands. "Okay, okay. Now let's go back and look at these ideas and see how we might incorporate them into what we're doing." Henry stood up and walked to the front again. He stood looking at the two lists, trying to see where things matched up and where they didn't. "The connecting point for all of this is the skin. I think once we get the skin right, everything else will fall into place. The overheating and the technology problems."

The others nodded. There was an air of expectancy in the room.

Henry tapped the whiteboard again. "When we were at the theme park yesterday, did you see anyone who might be interested in purchasing something like Violet? Anyone who would think that being covered entirely in a second skin would be a good idea?"

The researchers glanced at each other, and almost as one, frowned. No one spoke up.

"Who are you aiming this product at? Who would buy it?"

"We don't... that is, we thought it would be useful in the medical field," said Nolan. "People who were sick."

"So again, the kind of ordinary people we saw yesterday. What would make them wear the suits?" he asked. Henry looked around, willing them to get what he was trying to say.

"Being honest, I don't think anything would make them want to wear a full skin suit, unless they had to," said Nolan. "Unless the suit could save them from dying."

Fee cringed. "So we have people with no other option as a potential audience for Violet? That's awful."

"So what might make those people from the theme park use it if they weren't sick?"

Nolan was tapping his finger on the table. "What if it's just a section of the suit? Couldn't it be parts of a whole? An arm for a person who needs a new one, a leg or two for someone who has none? A chest for someone who needs protection or heart monitoring? And then maybe the whole suit for someone who really needs it?"

Fee looked up at him, her eyes wide. "All made with the same uber-tough skin that has the ability to be a computer, a bullet proof vest and medical diagnostic all in one."

"Not one whole Violet, but parts of the whole," whispered Eugene. "Different body parts for different people, but with the same processor working through each product, able to do the same things, but with adjustments on particular units, like the hand for an amputee."

The team looked around at each other, their eyes wide with the possibilities.

Henry nodded. They were getting the idea. "So we go down this list and find the specific talents that we wish Violet to possess; the non-negotiables we *have* to configure into her system, based on this new idea of smaller parts of the whole. That will then lead us to the next step." He reached down into his bag and pulled out a sample of the skin he'd created for Kara that he'd had Frankie courier down to him. "I may have something that will help once it comes to figuring out the skin."

He passed it around to the others. It was thin, lifelike and could be changed to conduct electricity if they wanted it to.

They each touched the soft fake skin, passing it around the table.

"It looks like you've cut it off a person," said Eugene with a shiver.

"It's warm," exclaimed Nolan as he touched it.

Henry nodded. He'd worked hard on that aspect of the fake skin.

Fee took it last, and Henry watched her reaction closely. She softly touched the skin with her hand. She looked up at him, awe in her eyes. "You designed this?" she said.

Henry shrugged. "We needed it for a friend at the Carnival. It was part of an artificial leg. I wanted it to look real."

"It's amazing. Like nothing else I've ever seen."

Something inside Henry clicked into place. "If you want it, I'm going to let you use it for Violet. It's still my product, and it will probably need some work to ensure it's right for this environment, but I think it will help."

CHAPTER 18

"*I* think it's time to call it a day," said Henry.

Fee let out a relieved breath. They'd been working hard all day, getting the formula for Henry's fake skin sorted, and deciding how they could make it better, and work in with their other ideas for what Violet would be able to provide. It was the most progress they'd made in a long time on the project. It felt good.

"How about we all go to that bar just down the road? Have a bit of a celebration?" Henry's suggestion was met with silence. They weren't used to having a social life, to people inviting them to do things.

"Sure," she said tentatively. "Sounds good." They *should* get out more. Yesterday's field trip proved that, if nothing else.

"I don't know," said Nolan.

"I should really get home," added Eugene.

"I don't like crowds," said David, scowling.

Henry sighed. "Remember the theme park yesterday? It was fun. We had a good time. I think you should all trust me.

Come on, guys, I won't take no for an answer." He stood up and gestured at the others to do the same.

They looked at each other and nodded. If it were for the team and the project, they would do it. They would do anything.

It was as if Henry was asking them to go stand in front of a firing line, instead of having a beer and fries with some friends. "Come on, it'll be fun." She glanced at Henry. She hoped.

Henry managed to gather them all together and get them out into the early evening Tampa warmth. Fee ended up walking beside Henry and they walked in silence, occasionally hurrying up the others who were inclined to dawdle.

They pushed open the doors to the bar, which turned out to be a rather stylish wine bar. It transpired that Nolan and Eugene were both wine buffs, telling the others what to order from the menu. Henry obediently ordered the merlot Nolan suggested, and Fee quietly let Eugene pick a Pinot Gris he insisted was the best she would find anywhere. David sniffed and ordered a beer. "Just to annoy them," he said to Fee.

"Pity there isn't a jukebox," said Henry, his eyes laughing.

Fee laughed outright at Nolan and Eugene's expressions. "He's only saying that to wind you up."

Their drinks were delivered by a bored waitress, and for a moment, they all stood looking at their drinks.

Henry broke the moment by lifting his glass high in the middle of their table. "To the best research team I've ever worked with," he said.

They all lifted their glasses. "To the best research team in the *world*," added Nolan.

The others nodded and smiled, and Fee grinned. It was great to feel part of the team, to know that they all wanted to be there, and that for the first time in months, they were heading in the right direction. She leaned over to Henry and whispered, "We're the only research team you've ever worked with, right?"

He laughed, a deep throaty sound that made Fee shiver. "Maybe. I'll never tell," he said with a smile. His golden eyes twinkled, and Fee physically had to resist the pull of attraction she felt toward him.

"So what other research have you done, then?" she asked, loud enough that the whole group could hear.

Henry leaned back in his seat, the very picture of a relaxed cowboy. He took a breath. "Well, I've done whatever was needed. I know a bit about engines, cars, motors, and such. I can fix a carnival ride at a thousand paces."

"But what else? What other things like the skin have you worked on?" Fee pushed, unsure why it was so important to her to know.

"I invent what's needed. You tell me you need something, and I find a way to make it happen. I'm a fixer, a creator. It's just me."

It was vague, and Fee wanted to know more. "What's the most fun project you've ever worked on? Something you're really proud of?"

Henry frowned at Fee for a moment. "I enjoy everything I do. It's the problem solving that I love, more than the specifics of what I'm doing. It doesn't matter what I'm fixing, as long as I make it work. You should know about that, with your robotic creations."

Fee froze. She'd forgotten to tell him not to say anything about that. She shook her head at him, glaring at him to make him realize she wanted him to stop, but he ignored her.

"Have you guys seen Fee's inventions? I'm surprised she's not using more of them on the Violet project," he said.

Nolan, Eugene, and David all looked at her with questioning eyes.

She shot a panicked glance at Henry, and then looked back at the others. "It's nothing really. Henry's exaggerating. None of them work properly."

"None of them work properly? I was playing poker with the biggest, baddest cheat of a robot this morning, and I don't know anyone else around here who could say they'd made a robot that backchats *and* cheats."

Fee's face was now flushed with heat, and she kicked Henry under the table to get him to shut up. She didn't like anyone knowing about the robots. The Witch Hunters knew about her little creatures and she didn't need anyone making the connection. The fact that he was so casually telling the team, who she'd managed to keep clueless for five years, was making her angry and panicky at the same time.

"Fee? Have you been holding out on us?" said Nolan jokingly.

She shook her head violently. "They're just a bunch of silly robots, which do silly things. Nothing we could use."

"I beg to differ," said Henry.

Fee looked at him, feeling like she was about to cry. Why did he have to go and spoil everything by being a big mouth? This was exactly why she didn't let people into her life. They thought they had a right to tell her secrets, to let people know things she didn't want them to know. For the first time all day, she was able to harden her heart toward Henry. She wasn't going to let him any closer. They'd kissed a couple of times, and it had been nice, but it wasn't going to happen again.

"I think the way you've designed Max's legs could be something extremely useful to the Violet project. And that little robot that swims must have special electronics that allow it to stay under water so long. You should bring them in and show them to the others."

"You're wrong," said Fee softly. "They're prototypes that

aren't ready to be seen. I resent you mentioning them in front of everyone." She gave him a hard look.

"You're holding out on the team," said Henry, his face equally grim. "We can't get this done without everyone pulling their weight, and currently you're not telling the others everything."

Fee felt like she'd been punched in the stomach. He was accusing her of being a cheat, of letting the others down? Who did he think he was?

She stood up, and lifted her drink. She took one last sip of the deliciously fruity wine, and then deliberately threw the rest of the liquid in his face. "Go to hell," she said, and walked away.

CHAPTER 19

*H*enry wiped the wine from his face and admitted he deserved it. He shouldn't have brought up her creatures in front of the others without talking to her about it first. He'd known she was hiding them. But some perverse part of him was doing it deliberately. This inexplicable connection between them was too much; it was all happening too fast and his sense of self-preservation was attempting to back up a bit. He'd been trying to take their growing attraction down a notch by pissing her off.

Added to that, he didn't like talking about his research. It made him uncomfortable, and he was good at deflecting. Unfortunately, he'd been spot on about her creatures being a taboo conversation. He'd gotten the reaction he expected, and exactly what he'd deserved.

Maybe it's for the best, said a voice deep inside. You don't need a complication like Fee, a woman who makes you feel like you're in a lightning storm when you kiss. Imagine what it would actually be like to make love to her. It was too much, too complicated.

There was a little bit of relief as he watched her storm out the door.

Next minute that relief turned to anxiety when he saw whom she bumped into at the door.

Dr. Pelgrim Shaw.

Henry stood up and strode over. He felt rather than saw Eugene, David, and Nolan follow him. He felt like a mother hen, fluffing up her feathers to make an intruder go away.

".... I see you're still holding out some pathetic hope of doing something without me," Pelgrim was saying to Fee, looking down his nose at her.

"At least, I've got a job," she replied just as Henry arrived behind her.

Score one point for the woman with the crazy robots.

"Not for long," said Pelgrim with a snide smile on his face. "Lucas admitted to me he was going to allow you to work out your month and then let you go. He doesn't expect you to make any serious inroads in that time, especially not without a lead researcher."

"You'd be surprised what can be achieved in a month," said Henry mildly, before Fee could say anything more. "Some of my best work has been achieved in less time than that."

Nolan stepped forward. "We're actually out celebrating because we've made some rather startling break throughs. It's been a particularly successful day."

Pelgrim glanced over Fee's shoulder at Nolan. "What would you know? You're just a medical researcher. You couldn't possibly comprehend the complicated nature of this kind of technology. You were brought on board to help us with the basics. Like a junior researcher, only with less pay."

Nolan stepped forward, as if to hit Pelgrim, and Henry held him back. "He's not worth it, Nolan, and he's not correct. You're important to the team. We need everyone's

119

expertise to make this work." Henry glanced over at Pelgrim. "Just because he's too stupid to see that is his fault, not ours."

Pelgrim's face darkened and he turned his glare onto Henry. "And you, a bum and a carny, unable to get a degree anywhere, so you tout yourself as a consultant? A conman, that's all you are, and as soon as Lucas sees reason, I'll prove to him how useless you are. I know you all played hooky yesterday, and went to a theme park instead of working."

Henry just raised his eyebrows at Pelgrim. He'd been on the receiving end of similar slights—in fact, many worse—in the course of his years. People tended to think badly of the Carnival folk, and when things went wrong, the Carnival was to blame.

But Fee wasn't used to it. Before he could stop her, she took a step forward, pulled one arm back, and slammed her fist into Pelgrim's face. He staggered back, holding one hand to his nose as Fee jumped around shaking her hand. "Ow, that hurt," she said, tears in her eyes.

Blood appeared on Pelgrim face, his hand soon covered in blood from his nose. "I'm bleeding," he said in outrage, a strange nasal lisp in his voice. "You punched me."

Henry pushed Fee behind him as Pelgrim thrust himself to his full height and stepped forward.

"You should go," Henry said. "At the very least, to the bathroom, to staunch the flow of that blood."

Pelgrim pulled back his other arm, and tried to hit Henry, but he was slow and awkward. Henry felt like he was fighting a sloth. He easily blocked the incoming punch, and then twisted Pelgrim's arm painfully up his back.

"Let me go, you bum! I'll call the police. This is assault."

"I have witnesses who will corroborate the fact that you punched me first," said Henry. "And you'd probably be laughed out of the police station for saying that Fee attacked you. She's two feet shorter than you and more than 100 pounds lighter."

"Let me go." Pelgrim's voice was tarnished with anger, but it couldn't be helped. There was no way Henry would have let Fee fight her old boss by herself. He let go of Pelgrim's arm, and the other man stepped immediately back out of reach.

"This isn't the last you'll see of me," he said and stormed out the door of the bar.

"Did anyone else feel like they'd seen that exit line in a Marvel comic book?" said Eugene.

The others sniggered.

"You okay?" said Henry to Fee.

She nodded, holding her hand and staring off after Pelgrim.

"I think I better drive you home," he said.

Fee glanced up at him, startled. "No way. Just because you protected me from Pelly, doesn't mean I forgive you or want to be around you. You're still an ass." She stormed out the door.

Henry glanced back at the others.

"Go," said Nolan, shooing him out the door. "We want her to be safe. And Pelgrim isn't one to give up on a fight."

Henry chased down the road after Fee. Instead of heading to her apartment, she was walking back in the direction of Callaghan Technology.

"Hey, Fee. Wait up. I'm sorry," Henry called out.

She ignored him and kept walking. Henry jogged a few steps and caught up with her, slowing to walk beside her.

"I'm sorry. I made a mistake. I know I should have talked to you before bringing up your creatures."

"Too late," muttered Fee, her blonde hair swishing angrily over her shoulders as she strode down the footpath.

"I think you should let me walk with you, just for now.

Pelgrim's not exactly a nice guy. You don't have to forgive me, just let me keep you safe until you get home."

Fee stopped and glared at him. "The problem with that plan is that you'll think you've done something to help me, and you'll expect me to forgive you. Which I don't. So you can take your "keep Fee safe" idea and shove it where the sun don't shine. Go back to your drinking buddies and have some more wine. Because I don't need you." She stormed off, and Henry let her. But he wasn't going to let her roam about on her own with Pelgrim still angry with her.

Especially if it was because of what he'd said or done. He followed at a distance, making sure she made it to the building and got in with her swipe card.

He let himself in as well, and waited by the reception area for her to come back, settling himself into Wanda's seat. He noticed Wanda's glasses sitting on the desk, and picked them up, turning them over and over. He looked at the items on the desk, pulling open drawers until he found what he needed—small thin staples and a metal paper clip or two—and settled in to make the changes Wanda needed, while he waited for Fee to come back down.

He was concentrating on his task, and didn't notice how much time had passed until he looked up at the big clock on the wall. Half an hour and she still hadn't returned. He placed Wanda's newly corrected glasses back where he'd found them and walked to the elevators.

When the elevator opened on the research lab floor, he pushed himself to standing, and strode quietly into the dark-ened space.

"What on earth are you doing?" asked Fee from her corner.

Henry took a breath. He felt heat going up his neck and face, and was glad for the semi-darkness of the lab. "I was worried about you," he said.

"I thought I told you I don't need your help. Especially if the first thing you do is break my trust and tell my secrets."

Henry walked slowly to where she was sitting at her desk. "I'm sorry, Fee. That was dumb, and I totally get why you're annoyed at me. You have every right." He stopped in front of her desk. "But I did mean it when I said you should be using your creatures here at the lab. I think some of Violet's problems could be fixed by using the technology you've invented for Max and the others."

Fee went very still. She didn't say anything at first, as if she was still processing what he had said. "I keep them secret for a very good reason," she whispered. Then she shook her head. "None of them ever turn out right, anyway. They're my failures."

Henry shook his head. "If they're your failures, why do you keep them around?" he asked softly.

When she didn't answer, he replied for her. "It's because they're tiny individuals, with enough heart and soul to capture yours. Which means they're more alive than any other robotic creation I've ever heard of or seen. You've used your magic to create something spectacular."

Fee shook her head, but didn't say anything. Just at that moment, a little metal spider creature came scuttling out from under a pile of papers on her desk. It took a running leap into the bowl of water at one side, creating a little splash of water over Fee's arm.

Henry grinned as Fee wiped the water off with her hand. "See? You somehow created a waterproof skin for that one, didn't you? He spends all that time under water and doesn't have a single spot of rust or corrosion to show for it, and his electronics are perfect. That's amazing."

"He's crazy," Fee blurted. "He doesn't do what he was supposed to do; he just swims around in a bowl of water all day long."

"It doesn't matter. You learn what you need to from him, and move on."

"If I did that, I'd have so many tiny robots running around that my apartment would be overrun with them. I can't bring myself to destroy them once they come into being."

"You don't have to destroy them. And you can be judicious about making them as well. Decide on the features you want to replicate, what has worked particularly well in each of your creatures, and focus on that aspect." Henry felt his enthusiasm rising to the fore, and tried to dampen it down. She'd said she didn't like how he'd tried to convince people the night before. But it was hard.

"What are you doing?" Fee asked in a strange voice.

Henry blinked. "I... uh... I was trying not to be too enthusiastic?"

"You look like you need to go to the bathroom," she giggled.

Henry took a breath. At least, she'd relaxed, and wasn't as angry with him anymore.

"Do you really think my creatures would be helpful for Violet?" she said.

"Definitely. I'll show you, come on." Henry grabbed her hand and dragged her over to the locked room that held Violet. "Open her up," he said.

Fee fumbled with the security fingerprint and number pad but finally got the door open, and they both went in. Henry looked up at Violet, still amazed by the sheer audacity of what they were trying to achieve with her, despite her sausage fingers. The door swung shut behind them, locking back into place. The room was dimly lit by lights all around the base of the room, and Violet stood in the middle. The sophisticated computer operating system was let down by the bulky skin they had encased her in, and it made Henry even more determined to use his recipe to create a skin that was more appropriate. But first things first.

"She could use the kind of technology you used on Max's legs to make her arms and legs flow better. Do you really want Violet to have fat sausage fingers?" he said with a laugh in his voice.

Fee went to stand closer to Violet, and reached out a hand to touch the patchy skin they'd been using. "It is pretty awful, isn't it? It's so strange to realize we have other options now and that we don't have to listen to Pelly's dictates on what we can and can't do."

Henry nodded. "We'll be able to prove to Lucas that it's actually going to be easier to finish this project without Pelgrim."

"I hope so."

"I know we will. I can already see so many possibilities for Violet, including using your ideas. You need to have a little faith—"

Just then, as one, the lights went out across the whole lab and they were plunged into darkness.

"Fee?" said Henry. "What just happened?"

CHAPTER 20

he sudden full darkness took a moment to adjust to, although not as long as it might have if they'd had full lighting. She squinted over at Henry and his vague shape came into focus. He was still waiting for her answer to his question.

"I don't know," she said. "This hasn't ever happened to me before."

"Have you been here at night?"

Fee nodded and then remembered he couldn't see her. "Sure. I've worked here at all hours of the day and night. This isn't normal."

She put her hand out in front of her and made her way slowly to the door, and pulled on the handle. It was locked solid. She pressed a button on a keypad. Nothing. No sound. "I think we might be stuck in here," she said.

Henry appeared behind her, and bumped his body into hers. Electricity shivered across her skin, making her entire body tingle. She moved away, telling herself sternly that she was still annoyed at him.

"Maybe we can circumvent the locking system," was all he

said. A small pinpointed light came on. Henry had a flash-light on his key chain. *Of course.*

She watched as he fiddled with the keypad and used a tiny screwdriver—also on his key chain—to pull off the front casing of the door lock. Even as she watched him do it, she knew it was no use. Lucas was a security fiend, and made sure everything they used was double and triple protected in any kind of emergency. But she was curious to see him at work, trying to fix something, so she kept quiet. Maybe he would prove her wrong.

She knew the kind of state she went into while she was building robots, a kind of magical trance, and she wanted to know if he did it the same way. No one else she'd ever known had had magic like she did. Or at least had ever admitted to it. She'd always wondered if her mother had magic too—because where else would her magic have come from but her parents?—but her mother had never spoken of it. It would have meant her life if she did.

Henry's magic was soft and gentle, and it came on slowly, easily. It wasn't overpowering; it was calm and collected, a little bit like Henry. She held herself still, and watched with complete attention as he attempted to get them out.

Eventually he shook his head and heaved out a breath. "Nope. It's too tightly locked down. He's got password on password on password in here."

"I think Lucas has a bit of his own magic," said Fee. She shook her head when Henry glanced up at her sharply. "Nothing major, just a strong sense of intuition for the right technology at the right time. And also about security. I have a feeling we might have to wait this out."

"What? Here?" Henry looked around. "In the dark?"

"Are you afraid of the dark, Henry?" said Fee softly.

He paused. "Not likely. It just seems a little convenient. You've managed to get me alone with you locked in a small space. It seems like you might want to have your wicked way with me," he said teasingly.

"Give me a break," said Fee. "I'm still pissed at you. You broke the trust between us; you knew they were a secret." She took a step away from him. "I don't forgive that easily."

Henry sighed. "I know, and I'm sorry. I really am." He paused. "Do you want to play truth or dare? I'll tell you the truth of why I really did it."

Fee's eyes went to his face, trying to read his expression. It was too dark, despite the light from his tiny flashlight. "I haven't played that in a long time. If ever."

"Is that a yes or a no?"

Fee glanced around them, at the bulky shape of Violet in the middle. "I guess there's nothing better to do."

"Damn right there's not," agreed Henry. He led Fee over to the side wall, and they both sat down leaning against the cold wall. Fee shivered. It was much colder in this room than outside in the usual Tampa heat. Damn climate control.

Henry immediately pulled off his sweater and handed it to her. "Here you go. I'm used to the cold weather," he said. "It's not going to run out of air in here, is it?" he asked.

Fee shook her head. "I don't think so. It's just colder than anywhere else."

Henry shifted slightly, and his shoulder brushed hers. A tingling sensation spread out from her shoulder.

"So," said Fee, clearing her throat. "You choose truth?"

Henry nodded. "I do."

"So I ask you a question I want answered?"

He shrugged. "I want you to ask me why I did it. But you could pick something else to ask me about."

Fee considered it a moment. "No, you're right. I want to know why you told them about my creatures when you knew they were a secret."

Henry sighed and looked at her. "Because I'm scared of

how I feel when I'm around you," he whispered. "I've never felt anything like it, this constant desire to be close to you, to learn more about you, to talk to you...to touch you. It's becoming almost painful when we're apart. So I was trying to push you away by saying something I knew you would hate."

Fee took in a shocked breath. Of all the explanations she had been expecting, that was not one of them. She didn't know what to say. "Uh..."

"I know; it's way too honest for where we're at." Henry shrugged. "You see? This is what I mean. We're moving too fast, and I can't stop it. I can't stop myself saying these things to you."

"Okay," said Fee, her whole body trembling. "Let me think about that for a while." What did she have to say? She didn't know what she thought, although she understood where Henry was coming from. It felt like they were hog tied to a freight train barreling at full speed toward some unknown, and possibly deadly, destination.

"Sure. In the meantime, I get to do a truth or dare with you," said Henry.

Fee sighed. "Truth."

"Where did you grow up?"

"Arkansas." That was nice and vague.

"You know what I mean. Not the state, what kind of place was it? Why did you leave?"

Fee took a breath, trying to sort out her tumbling emotions over Henry's declaration from her dislike of talking about her past. She was too confused to hold back. "It was a commune, although looking back it was more like a cult," she said. "It was all natural, mother earth type stuff. No technology of any kind."

"That must have been hard on you, given your fascination with robots."

Fee nodded. "Yeah, it wasn't easy. But I found a friend when I was about twelve years old. A woman who lived on the edge of our farm, in an old house. I found out later that she actually owned the land belonging to the commune, and they just rented off her."

"What did she do?"

"She took me under her wing, taught me about the outside world. She had a computer, so I learned how to use one, looked things up on it. Learned about the outside world. It was amazing. She helped me pass my high school equivalency test, and she helped me get into MIT on a scholarship. I'd be back there looking after the cows or harvesting the crops, still feeling like there was something missing, if it wasn't for her."

Or maybe I'd just be dead.

"Wow, that's amazing. Is she still there? Do you still see her?"

Fee shook her head softly. "No, she died when I was in my fourth year of college." She paused. "She left me everything. I still own the property that my parents and the cult live on. She wanted me to carry on the tradition she'd started."

"You let them keep farming there?" Henry's voice was surprised.

Fee shrugged, trying to decide how much to tell him. "There was no point disrupting them." *Keep your enemies close, as the saying went.* "They believe technology is the devil, and avoid it at all costs." That was enough information. He didn't need to know the whole grisly truth. She glanced at him, just a shadowy figure in the darkness of the room. "Your turn. Truth or dare?"

"I'll take a truth, I think."

Fee considered a moment. "Tell me about the Carnival where you grew up."

"That's not a very difficult truth," said Henry.

"I wasn't trying to trick you. I just want to know about it."

"My father is the Thrillmaster, the man in charge of the thrill rides. I have five brothers. We're all mechanically minded, but no one else invents things like I do."

"Tell me about the magic."

Henry smiled. "Ah, yes, the magic. It's how everything runs at the Carnival. It's like an amplifier, it takes our natural talents and makes them stronger, better. When everything is in balance, we live and breathe through the magic. It runs our lives, and it protects us from harm. Mostly, anyway."

"What does that mean?"

"We've had a few problems recently. The magic isn't as strong as it once was, and someone was trying to harm us. But it's getting better again, we're healing."

"Why would someone want to harm the Carnival?" Fee asked, but she knew all about people who hated magic. It seemed plausible they'd target the Carnival, just as they did people like herself.

"Magic can work either way. It can take you from the ground and raise you up, make you something far greater than you ever were before. Or it can dig you down deep into the earth, where darkness reigns."

Fee shivered. "So there are bad guys with magic who are after you?"

"Something like that," said Henry, laughter in his voice. "My turn. What's your real name?"

Fee thought back to her apartment. She knew Max had used her full name at least twice. "You already know it."

"Then explain it to me. What does Wild Feather mean?"

She exhaled sharply. "It's just the stupid name my mother burdened me with when I was born. It's the kind of name we all had at the farm. Her name is Summer Dawn. She had a dream, saw an eagle flying, and decided to name me Wild Feather. I guess it could have been worse."

"How so?"

"She could have named me Bald Eagle."

"Baldy for short?"

Fee giggled. "Or Eggy?"

Henry paused a moment. "My full name isn't Henry," he said.

Fee waited. When he didn't say anything more she asked, "What's your full name then?"

"Henrification."

"What does that even mean?"

Henry shook his head. "Nothing. It's a carnival tradition to name the kids strange long names. We all pretty much shorten them. And some of us even get names that actually make sense. But not me. My mother just liked the name Henry, and named me this longer version of it for the sake of it."

"Sometimes traditions can be crazy."

"Yep."

"That didn't count as your turn though. I didn't ask you to tell me that."

"What do you want to know, then?" said Henry with a smile in his voice.

"Have you ever seen this blue electricity before? Do you know what's happening between us?" Fee held her breath, waiting for his answer.

Henry was silent for a moment. "I wish I had an answer to that, but I don't."

"Then I get another question. That was a terrible answer."

Henry let out a bark of laughter. "I don't think that's in the rules. But okay, ask away."

"Have you ever been in love?" she asked softly, her heart beating rapidly inside her chest.

Henry stiffened beside her, and Fee regretted the words

as soon as they were out of her mouth. It gave away too much of her own thoughts.

"No," he said softly.

She let out her breath slowly, mostly relieved he didn't try to make unreasonable claims. Mostly.

"What about you? Have you ever been in love?" he asked.

Fee blinked. "I've had lovers, but no, none of them were more than a fun way to spend time while I wasn't studying."

"No one since you've been in Tampa?"

"No. I...like to keep to myself. It's better that way."

"What does *that* mean? Why is it better?"

Fee hesitated, torn. She wanted to tell him about the Witch Hunters, who they were and why they were after her. But he'd just shown her that very evening he couldn't be trusted to keep her secrets. "I'm grumpy and I hate it when people want me to be chirpy in the morning," she said instead. "At least I can be as mean as I like to Max and his feelings won't be hurt."

"I can't imagine you being mean to Max."

"Happens all the time. But he loves it. Says it's good for his robot shell to get tears on it." She grinned, enjoying the banter.

"Okay, your turn. Do you have another question for me?" said Henry.

"What's your biggest failing?"

"Aside from telling your secrets?" he said softly.

She scowled at him. "I'd almost forgotten about that, and now you've reminded me again." Maybe he'd done it on purpose.

Henry let out a breath. "I'm the youngest of six brothers, and they're all bigger and stronger than I am. I was the weird little brother none of them really understood. They bullied me, made fun of me, dared me to do crazy things, and generally made my life difficult while I was growing up. But it means I'm a determined bastard. I refused to let them win, and it's taught me that I can achieve whatever I want through sheer unadulterated stubbornness. People say it's a failing."

"It's either your greatest fault, or your biggest asset. I can't decide which." Fee hesitated. "Do you get along with your brothers now?"

"We get on fantastically well. They're a good bunch of guys." Henry shifted his position against the wall. "What about you? Do you have any siblings?"

"No. Just me." She would have liked to have brothers or sisters, even if they did tease her mercilessly. "It must have been nice to have a big family."

"I was just thinking that it must have been nice to have a small family," said Henry. "I guess we always want what we can't have, huh?"

"I guess."

"Next question?"

Fee shook her head. "No more questions." She leaned on Henry's shoulder. The electric current tingled, strangely comforting. "I don't forgive you. But I'm tired."

Henry moved his shoulder, so Fee's head was on a slightly more padded area. "Go to sleep. I'll try to stay awake in case the lights come back on."

She was so tired; she couldn't bring herself to answer. It was late. She felt like she'd been on an emotional roller coaster. She needed some rest. She closed her eyes, and drifted off, thinking of a young boy called Henry running around amongst the Carnival tents.

CHAPTER 21

*H*enry sat very still, watching the morning light creep into the room through the bottom of the door.

He was stiff and tired, but he'd not been able to sleep. Fee was snuggled in against his body, and he had one arm around her, keeping her against him. It was hard to tell if the power had come back on. The lights in this room had never returned, but perhaps that had more to do with a timer than the power cut.

He'd had time to think, during the small hours of the morning, but he hadn't come to any conclusions, other than he wasn't going to hurt Fee again like he had the day before. It had been a stupid self-defence mechanism, and he was annoyed that it had been his knee jerk reaction.

She'd not replied to his almost-declaration, and that made his palms sweat uncomfortably. Although the fact that she was now snuggling up to him gave him one answer.

Noises outside made him aware that others were now coming into the lab, and he gently patted Fee's side to wake her up. No need to get discovered in even more of a compromising position than they were already in. She woke slowly, disorientated at first.

"I'm going to try and get their attention," said Henry, when she'd pulled back and was sitting up under her own steam. She nodded.

He stood and went to the door, rattling the handle. Still locked. "Hello? We're in here! Let us out!" He banged on the door a couple of times for good measure.

He heard voices and then the sound of the lock being deactivated on the other side. The door opened and Nolan stood frowning at him.

"What on earth are you doing in here?" he said.

"The power went off last night, locked us in." Henry wondered how it looked to Nolan. Did he think they'd been doing something dodgy? Stealing secrets? Making love? He gave Nolan a tired smile. "It's been a rough night."

Nolan glanced over Henry's shoulder at Fee. "This has never happened before," he said. His tone suggested that something was going on. But he didn't know what.

Henry turned to Fee. She was standing up, gathering herself. She walked over and brushed past him to walk out the door, blinking in the full light of the lab.

Nolan looked back and forth between Henry and Fee as if they were crazy. Eugene walked over, his face a question.

"The power went out while we were in there checking out Violet. I don't even know when it came back on."

"How could the power have gone off? It has a generator back up. You'd have to cut two lots of power," said Eugene.

Something pinged at the back of Henry's mind. "It's not simple to cut the power? It's never happened before?"

Eugene shook his head. "It makes no sense that it would have been entirely out."

"Then we need to let Lucas know something happened last night. Because it definitely went out on us."

"I'll call him," said Nolan. "He'll want to come down and have a look."

Henry sat down at the meeting table. He had gone from being embarrassed at being found in there, to being worried about what the hell was going on.

~

LUCAS ALMOST JUMPED out of the elevator, concern on his face. "The power went out completely?" he said to Fee, the first person he saw.

"Yes," said Fee, nodding. "No one else has reported it?"

"No. And I don't understand how it went off like that. It shouldn't be able to happen. We have sensitive materials that could be ruined if they lost power."

Fee nodded. "What do you want us to do? Can we help?"

Lucas shook his head. "I'm going to check into the systems." He glanced over to where Henry was snoring gently with his head on the boardroom table. "In the meantime, I think you need to take Henry home and let him sleep," he said.

Fee followed his gaze, and nodded. "I'll take him home, then get changed and come back in."

Lucas nodded absently, but Fee could see his mind was already working on the problem.

Going back to her desk, she grabbed her purse. She could feel something rummaging around in there, and poked her finger in to confirm that it was her little kleptomaniac, rather than something less palatable. A glint of metal and a pair of crab-like claws settled her fears.

She was about to leave, but stopped a moment to consider the little metal spider swimming around in his little pool of water. She wanted to have a closer look at all of them, to see if Henry was right. Maybe they'd be more useful than she'd thought. She scooped him up and put him in her purse as well. He started chittering angrily at her.

"Keep quiet if you know what's good for you," she whispered.

She went over to Henry, and shook him awake. He groggily let her lead him to the elevators and down to his car. He even let her sneak him into the passenger's seat, and she had climbed into the driver's seat, before protesting.

"You're half asleep," she said firmly, and put the car in gear.

He'd fallen asleep again by the time she was two blocks out, so she decided to take him back to her place again and had the car in the underground garage before she thought any better of it. She managed to get Henry to wake up enough to get him up the stairs and into her apartment before he crashed again on her bed. She stood looking at him sleeping for a moment, before sighing and going back out into the kitchen.

"Well, Max, he's back," she said.

"Yes he is, Wild Feather."

She stretched herself out, as she waited for the kettle to boil for a coffee. Her two little critters climbed out of her bag, slowly making their way along the countertop before disappearing over the edge. They'd come back later once they'd finished searching the area for their own particular obsessions.

On her third yawn, she decided that they wouldn't need her at the lab for a while, and she went back into the bedroom. Her eyes were painful from the contacts, and she realized that putting in some eye drops wasn't going to cut it. She was going to have to take them out. She'd just make sure she woke up before Henry and put them back in before he saw anything unusual. It was such a relief to have them out she stood blinking into the mirror for a few minutes, letting the drops soothe her scratchy eye balls, then she changed into a T-shirt and pajama bottoms to wear to bed.

That was when she realized that she had a problem.

She stood next to the bed considering her options. In the end, she decided she'd been lying next to Henry all night; it wouldn't matter if she slept next to him on the bed. She climbed slowly onto the mattress, lying down next to him on top of the sheets, and closed her eyes.

She opened them a few minutes later when his arm snaked around her stomach and pulled her close against his warm chest. She stiffened, ready to push away from him as soon as he tried anything more, but Henry didn't move. She slowly relaxed back against his warm body, allowing him to spoon her to him, the low hum of electricity making her senses swim. Her eyes drifted shut, and she was almost asleep when his hand moved up, cupping one breast, his fingers flicking softly over her nipple as it hardened under her T-shirt.

Instead of moving away, like she knew she should, she arched her body into his hand. His mouth came down on her neck, nuzzling into her skin, sending little sparks of sensation along her body. She shifted restlessly under his lips, wanting—no, needing—more.

Moving so she faced him, Fee reached up with one hand to grasp him behind the head, pulling his lips to hers. The moment they touched, the electricity that had been humming in the background flared up, igniting multiple blue-stained lightning bursts over their bodies. The air sizzled and desire burned through Fee, so strong she thought she might implode with the sensations exploding through her body.

"Why is that happening? What is happening to us?" she asked.

Henry shook his head. "I don't know. Maybe we can

figure it out." He paused, and lowered himself to her mouth again. "Later."

She sighed against his lips. "Later," she promised before kissing him again.

THE SOUND of a phone ringing shrilly in the background woke her from a deep sleep. Henry was breathing gently next to her and Fee glanced at her watch. They'd only been asleep for an hour. In the background, she heard Max answer the phone. He came into the bedroom.

"It is your workmate Nolan. He says it is an emergency."

Fee sat up, climbed off the bed, grabbing her T-shirt and pants on the way to the telephone.

"Hello?"

"Fee. You have to get down here," said Nolan, his usually calm voice cracking. "It's carnage. The lab exploded. It's Eugene. He's hurt."

"Okay, calm down. What happened? How badly is Eugene hurt?"

"I don't know. The ambulance took him away. He was pretty badly burned. He was trying to save Violet."

"Save Violet?"

"Everything's gone, Fee. All our research. Violet. Everything's all gone."

CHAPTER 22

*F*ee stood next to Henry, looking up at the Callaghan Technology building. A piece was blown out of the side about half way up. Their floor. Plumes of black smoke were still emerging from the affected area, and parts of the floors below and above it were crumbling, sending occasional lumps of concrete down. Lucas was pacing outside the entrance to the building. It was his life's work inside. No wonder he was frantic. She would be too.

The emergency services barrier was keeping everyone else well back. A faint hum on the edge of her senses made Fee shiver.

"Were you guys actually in there when it happened?" she whispered to Nolan, standing on her other side. How had they made it out alive?

He shook his head. "Eugene and I had gone with Lucas to the generator floor, and we were helping him check through the security system. That's the only thing that saved us." He paused to take in a ragged breath. "Eugene only got so badly hurt because he rushed back upstairs, and tried to get into the lab. He rushed at the flames."

Fee winced. The medics said he had first and second degree burns over most of his body, and that it would be a while before he was fully recovered.

"And David?" asked Henry.

"He came running as soon as he saw the explosion. We were supposed to be meeting him for coffee in the café across the road, but got sidetracked by the security breach." Nolan wiped his hand across his face. "David and Lucas pulled Eugene out and carried him down the stairs. They were burned as well, just not as bad. David was really upset. He went in the ambulance with Eugene."

"Do they know who did it?" Another ripple of unease rolled over her body.

Nolan shook his head. "The arson investigators are searching now."

As they watched, two men went up to Lucas and pulled him aside. One was an older man dressed in the dark blue of a fire official, and the other was a younger man in a suit.

"That's him. The fire marshal," said Nolan. "I don't know the other man."

"We need to hear what they're saying," said Henry. He grabbed Fee's hand, and they rushed over.

"...We believe it was a bomb, Mr. Callaghan. Set by someone who knew the system very well. Possibly a disgruntled employee. Do you have anyone who fits that description who we could talk to?" the man in the suit was saying. He was mid-thirties, with sharp eyes and trendy shoes.

Fee's mind went to one person. "Pelgrim," she blurted before she could stop herself.

Everyone turned to look at her.

"And who is Pelgrim?" asked the man in the suit, pulling out a pen and notebook.

"Your disgruntled employee. Lucas fired him a couple of days ago," said Fee.

"And you are…?" he asked, taking in Fee's hastily donned jeans and T-shirt. He wrote something in his notebook.

"They're employees from the research lab," said Lucas to him. He turned to Henry, Fee, and Nolan. "This is Agent Franklin of the FBI and Fire Marshal Driskell. They're leading the investigation into the explosion."

Fire Marshal Driskell cleared his throat. "It's mainly up to the FBI now we've determined it was a bomb. We'll just be helping out if needed."

Agent Franklin narrowed his eyes at Fee. "What makes you think this…" He looked down at his notes. "This… Pelgrim would have planted the bomb?"

"Surely, he wouldn't have…?" said Nolan, rubbing his neck where it was erupting in a red heat rash.

"Did you see his face last night?" said Fee. "He was livid. I'd never seen him like that."

Beside her, Henry nodded. "He'd be a suspect, that's certain."

Lucas pushed one hand through his hair, making it all stand on end. "We're all suspects, if it comes to that," he said grimly, looking over at the fire investigator.

The man shrugged and nodded. "In situations like this, it's usually someone who knows the building well, and has a very personal reason for doing it. Agent Franklin and I will talk to all of you separately."

"What do we do in the meantime?" asked Nolan, uncertainty in his voice. They all looked at Lucas.

He sighed. "I don't know. Give me time to think about it. For the moment, go home, take a break for the rest of the day, and I'll give you a call when I know more."

Fee's heart dropped. This was it. He was going to close them down.

"We can recreate Violet," she said. "We were going to redo her skin anyway. This isn't the end."

Lucas nodded absently. "Fee, I have to think about it. I'm not going to make any rash decisions, don't worry."

Fee felt as if the ground had dropped out from under her, and she was tumbling down a giant hole. A tingle of magic stirred against her skin.

"Come on, I'll take you home," Henry said, putting his arm over her shoulders and gently pulling her away. "Nolan, do you need a ride?"

Nolan shook his head. "I have my car." His whole body was slumped.

"Will you be okay?" Fee asked him. "You can come back to my place with us," she added, feeling strangely protective.

Nolan shook his head. "I'll go to the hospital and check in on Eugene and David."

Fee nodded. "Can you call and let me know how they're doing?"

"Of course." Nolan gave them a small wave and turned in the other direction. His shoulders were hunched and he walked as if the world's weight was on his shoulders.

Fee knew how he felt. It wasn't just about losing their jobs. They had been attacked, and it felt personal. It was pure luck no one had died.

Her heart lurched. It was pure luck it hadn't gone off last night while they were trapped inside. She glanced at Henry. His face was grim.

"We could have been in there," she whispered.

"But we weren't," he returned immediately, indicating the thought had already occurred to him.

The taste of bile rose in her throat. They could easily have decided to stay in the lab until the security breach had been figured out. Their lucky escape from whoever had set this bomb was full of what ifs, and if onlys. Her stomach churned with each new thought.

If only she'd associated the power cut to a bomb.

If only she'd insisted they all leave the lab.

What if they'd stayed?

What if Lucas hadn't led the others out of the lab and down to the generator level?

What if this was all her fault?

Fee leaned over and threw up in the gutter. Henry was there immediately, holding her hair and rubbing her back. Like the proverbial lightbulb turning on inside her head, she realized what her magical senses had been trying to tell her since she arrived at the scene. It was like a punch to the gut. This really was her fault.

"It's going to be okay," he said. "We'll catch whoever did this."

"How? How are we going to do that?" said Fee, as she wiped her face with her sleeve. She felt dizzy, and leaned into Henry, seeking comfort in his warmth.

"It's not up to us," said Henry gently. "It's up to the FBI agent back there. He'll do his job, and find the person responsible."

Fee shook her head. "We have to do something," she said feebly. "They won't find anyone."

"What makes you so sure?" She could almost hear Henry's frown in his voice.

"Because there's magic involved here. The kind that I haven't felt in a long time. Witch Hunter magic." Fee felt like there should have been a drum accompaniment to her announcement, or a theatrical music emphasis. As it was, all she got from Henry was silence. She glanced up at him, but he truly just looked blank.

"What's that?" he asked.

"You're from a Carnival full of magic users, and you've never heard of the Witch Hunters?" she said incredulously. She could feel the hysteria rising up through her body, begging to break free.

"Let's get you home, and you can tell me more." Henry glanced around. "I don't think this is the right place to be telling me your secrets. Wait here."

Henry raced over to Lucas, and spoke in low tones to him, gesturing over to Fee. Lucas looked in her direction, and nodded. His face was covered in black smudges, and his eyes looked like dark pools in his usually relaxed face.

Tears welled in Fee's eyes. This was all her fault.

Henry ran back over. "Come on, let's go," he said, as he wrapped an arm around her shoulders and guided her back to his car. The ride to her apartment was a blur and as soon as she let herself into the apartment, she headed for her room. "I'm going to take a shower and get clean," she said.

"I'll make coffee," said Henry.

As she stood in the shower under the hot spray, she tried to organize her thoughts. The only other time she'd experienced the wrath of the Witch Hunters had been when she'd left the commune. She'd told her parents she was leaving, and they'd tried to convince her to stay. She'd admitted she was different, that she needed to go out into the world and find her place. She'd shown them her first-ever creation, a little robotic creature called Junebug. Her father had leaped back, horrified to see a metal creature move around like it was real.

"Get thee gone!" he'd yelled. "'Tis the devil's work! Martha, she has the devil inside her."

"No, no, Dad. It's a simple robotic structure. Here, I can show you," she'd tried to explain it to her father, but he'd stormed out of the house.

Her mother had shook her head sadly. "We'd hoped it skipped past you, Wild Feather. It's why we're here, why we live like this. Your father can sense when others are using the devil's magic. He knows how you created that thing. You must leave now. It's his responsibility to do something about it, and I know he doesn't want to. Go."

Her mother had gently shoved Fee toward the door. Fee had protested, sure her father would understand if she gave him enough time.

She'd been wrong.

CHAPTER 23

*H*enry stood waiting in the kitchen, a mug of coffee steaming in his hands, mulling over what Fee had told him so far. Witch Hunters? It didn't sound good. Worse than that, it sounded ominous. He hoped he hadn't dumped the Carnival in a whole new mess of problems.

They already had sufficient on their plate at the moment.

His mobile phone beeped and Henry jumped. He glanced at the screen. It was his father.

"Hey, Dad," he said.

"Hey, Henry." Viktor paused.

Henry's intuition kicked up a gear. "What's happened?" he said.

"Missy's in trouble. They're sending a small group to try to rescue her and a few others...including Zeph Jolly," his father said.

"Zeph? What's he doing there?" Rilla's brother hadn't been at the Carnival since they were kids.

"Rilla's mother was missing. She's one of the people they're trying to rescue."

"And the reason you didn't call me earlier was...?" said Henry, annoyed. He was the best person to go on a rescue mission like that.

"You're busy. We can sometimes manage to handle things without you, you know." Viktor's voice was heavy with sarcasm.

Henry took a breath. "So you haven't heard how it's all gone? Are they okay? Where did they go?"

"They went to this place called The Experiment in L.A. Another carnival, but they use curse magic. Turns out it's where Tilly is from."

"I'm coming home," he said immediately.

"No, Henry, you have to stay and finish that contract. It's part of the last payment, and Rilla says we're close enough that we won't make it if you don't stay. We can handle things back here. I just wanted to let you know what was happening, keep you informed. And hear your voice." The last was said gruffly.

"That might not be an option any more, Dad. There's been some drama at my end as well."

"What's happened?" asked Viktor sharply. "I *knew* I needed to call."

"The research lab was bombed this morning. All the research that I'm supposed to be working on was destroyed."

"Were you hurt?"

"I'm fine. One of the researchers has some serious burns, but everyone else is okay."

"What are they going to do?"

"I don't know. It's only just happened. I'm not sure if they'll keep the project going or not."

"Let me know as soon as you know."

Henry smiled. "It's good to hear from you Dad." He paused, thinking. "Hey, Dad, have you ever heard of a group called the Witch Hunters?" If anyone was going to know about them, it was his father.

"The name rings a vague bell. But I'd have to look them up. Doesn't sound good."

"I don't think it is. But can you check them out for me? It's probably going to be important."

"Of course. You take care of yourself down there, son."

"I will. Call me when you know more about Missy and the others."

"Will do."

"Talk soon, Dad."

Henry pushed the button and stared off into space. He hated that he was here so far away from his family and unable to help. He was usually part of missions like this one; his ability to think on the spot and create gadgets usually was useful. He itched to get back home and help.

Just at that moment, Fee emerged from her bedroom. She looked clean and fresh in denim shorts and a T-shirt, but her face was paler than usual, and she looked tense. It reminded him he was needed here too.

"Feeling better?" he said. There was something different about her. She looked more vibrant, despite her obvious distress over the bombing.

She nodded, but he could see she wasn't. He went over and gave her a hug, wrapping her inside his arms. The usual electricity buzzed between them, but now it was somehow comforting. She snuggled into his chest and sighed.

Henry let the feeling of rightness flow over him for a moment, before pulling away and looking down into her face. "Now tell me about these Witch Hunters."

Fee stiffened, but she nodded. "It's hard for me to talk about it," she said. "I've been hiding from it for so long."

"It sounds like it's important. We need to figure out who did this to Lucas," said Henry.

"It's an attack on all of us," snapped Fee, her eyes flashing.

Henry inhaled a surprised breath. "Your eyes. You have green eyes." His first thought was Garth's eyes and how they changed color when a Gift started.

Fee blinked and then tried to hide her face. She groaned into his chest. "I went down to the building without my contacts. They all saw me," she mumbled into his shirt.

"You wear grey contacts to hide your real eye color?"

Fee nodded against his chest.

"So tell me, who are the Witch Hunters?" he said softly.

"They're a secret organization working to destroy any magic they find." She paused and lifted her head, staring up at him with wide green eyes the color of the sea on a stormy day. "My father is one of them. So is my mother."

It took a moment to comprehend what she was saying because he was so entranced by the emerald green of her eyes. Then Henry blinked as it filtered into his brain. No wonder she didn't like talking about her past. "Wow. That *is* big."

Fee nodded. "They operate totally under the radar. Most people don't even know they exist; they're quite deadly."

"What makes you think it was them?"

"There was a faint hum, something on the edge of my senses back there. I recognized it as the same magic my father used on me when I left. He was trying to kill me."

"I'm so sorry, Fee."

She shrugged one shoulder.

"How do they find the magic users?" he asked.

"That's the irony. They have their own magic to see the magic in others. When I showed my parents my first creation, my father knew instantly what I was. I only just escaped with my life."

Henry tightened his arms around her again. Her own

father? He didn't know what to say, other than to offer comfort with his arms, his warmth.

Fee sighed. "I was never that close to him, he was full of fire and brimstone as I was growing up. I guess he was expecting my magic to emerge at any moment. I think it must be in my family somewhere."

"So when was the last time you saw your parents?"

"When I was seventeen. I'd been secretly planning to leave. I'd gotten a scholarship to MIT, and Geraldine, the neighbor who taught me all those years, helped me escape before my father could do more than gather his resources."

"What about your mother?"

A look of pain passed over Fee's face, and she closed her eyes. "My mother told me to run when father left to get his tools, but she stood by while he attacked me. She didn't try to stop him."

"I'm sorry, Fee. That must have been awful."

Fee shrugged into his shoulder. "I don't often dwell on it. She made her choice. I made mine."

"What choice did you have? When your father was trying to kill you?"

Fee sighed. "I could have stopped them. I've had opportunities since I left. When Geraldine died, she left me all the land they have their farm on. I could have kicked them off."

"But you didn't? Why?" Henry could feel the tension in her body.

"It's easier to fight a battle when you know where the players are. If I kicked them off, how would I know where they were?"

Henry nodded. "Makes sense, I guess."

"It wasn't an easy decision to make. I wanted to kick them off the land so badly, to make them pay for what they did to me, and what they do to other people. But I didn't. Instead, I installed someone in Geraldine's place, to keep an eye out for kids like me. To make sure they don't try to hurt anyone else."

"So you have a gatekeeper down there?"

"Yes."

"Can we call them? Ask them what's happening? Maybe this attack has something to do with your parents?"

Fee nodded. "They're not the only Witch Hunters in the U.S. It's possible that it's not them. But it's a good idea, I'll phone her now."

CHAPTER 24

*F*ee's hand shook as she replaced the receiver.

Alberta had used the code words they'd devised to let each other know if there was something wrong. As soon as she'd said something about baking peanut butter cookies for Fee, it had been obvious the woman was scared.

She'd told Alberta not to worry, she was sure the cookies would be delicious, and hung up.

"Someone was there, or they were listening in." Fee's mind was whirring with the possibilities. "We have to get her away from there."

Henry shook his head. "We have enough on our plate here, Fee. If this really is the work of Witch Hunters, I'm not sure we can..."

"I have to! I put her in that position. She's my responsibility." Alberta was a lovely older woman with sharp eyes and a bad hip. She wasn't up to protecting herself from crazy zealots. That hadn't been her job, she'd just been supposed to keep an eye out and let Fee know if anything suspicious

154

happened, all while living rent free in a nice house, with a bit of an extra pension.

"Then I'll go with you."

"You don't have to." Fee's stomach lurched at the idea of going on her own, but she didn't want Henry to go with her out of a sense of duty.

"I want to. You'll need backup. And with the lab destroyed, it's not like I've got much to do around here." Henry frowned. "Although I do think we should find out more about who might have done this before we go anywhere."

Fee nodded. "First I'm going to call Nolan and see how Eugene and David are." She reached out her hand to pick up her phone, and it rang. "Hello?" she said.

"Fee, this is David."

"David! How are you? How's Eugene?"

David paused, and Fee heard him take a shaky breath through the phone line. He was obviously upset. "I'm fine. Eugene is in a serious condition. He has burns to most of his body. The damn fool ran back up into the lab."

"I heard. I'm so sorry."

David cleared his throat. "Lucas just rang and told us the FBI has found evidence the bomb was definitely set to go off while there were people in the lab. They're targeting us. It was only because you were at home and the others trooped down to the generator rooms that we avoided casualties. The FBI agent thinks we're all still in danger, so Lucas wants to put us all in protective custody, paid for by the company, until this blows over. Even Eugene."

Fee scrunched up her face, trying to understand. "Protective custody? What does that mean?" Her intuition was pinging big time. She glanced over at Henry, who was frowning.

"Lucas has found somewhere we can all go. It's a friend's

holiday home, with a security team suggested by the police. He wants us to wait out the investigation safe and sound." David sounded scared and breathless at the same time.

"For how long?"

"As long as it takes. Although Lucas said the FBI agent seemed confident he was going to find who did this pretty fast."

"Where would we be going?" She had no intention of going into some kind of indefinite lockdown with the team, not when Alberta needed her help. But that didn't mean she wasn't curious.

"I don't know. They said it had to be secret for our own protection."

A shiver went down Fee's spine. "What about Henry?" She frowned over at Henry, who was watching her attentively.

There was a pause. "Lucas said he spoke to Henry, and he's decided to go back to the Carnival."

Fee's stomach dropped out, and she opened her mouth to refute what David was saying. But she closed it again, and tried to keep calm. David was lying to her. But why? Was he part of this? She needed time to think.

"Do you think it's safe, David?" she asked instead, trying to stall for time.

David hesitated. "Lucas wouldn't harm us. He's a good guy."

Fee tapped one finger on the tabletop next to her. David hadn't exactly answered her question. She said the only thing she could think of. "Okay, I'll go with you. But I have to pack up my things. I can't go immediately."

"I knew you'd do it, Fee," said David, sounding relieved. "You just need to pack enough for a couple of weeks. A van will pick you up in an hour."

"Okay. An hour. I guess that's enough time."

"You'll need to be fast." David's voice was calm, more confident now.

"Okay, I'll see you soon," said Fee, hanging up the phone. Her breathing was fast, and she tried to make herself calm down.

"It's David," she said. "I think he's part of it somehow. He just lied to me about you going back to the Carnival." She frowned, realizing she hadn't made sure it wasn't true. "You didn't talk to Lucas and tell him you were going back to the Carnival, did you?"

Henry shook his head. "No. But tell me exactly what David said. We have to make sure it's really him."

"He said Lucas had spoken to you, and you were going home to the Carnival."

"So Lucas could have been the one lying?"

Fee stopped and thought about it for a moment. "I guess so. But David sounded weird on the phone, like he was worried I'd say no to going."

"You *are* saying no to it. He was right to be worried." Henry grinned at her.

She rolled her eyes. "They'll be here in an hour. We have to pack everything and get out of here in half an hour."

"They could already have someone watching the building," warned Henry.

Fee stared at him. "Then we need a distraction when we do leave, so we can actually escape."

"I like the way you think," grinned Henry. "Quick, grab everything you need, so we can get out of here. What about Max?"

Fee looked at her favorite invention and hesitated. He'd be useful to have here, to turn lights on, and make it seem like she was home. But there was a high likelihood someone would search the apartment when she didn't jump nicely into their kidnapping van. "We take him with us. They *all* come with us."

She ran to her bedroom and grabbed a large bag, stuffing as many of her clothes in as she possibly could. She got her toiletries from the bathroom, and even grabbed her tool kit. "Come on you lot. Out you come." She gave a low whistle, and several small metal robots crawled out from hiding places around her room.

Most of them she convinced to climb into a small wooden container that she dumped her costume jewellery out of. But Bing insisted on climbing into the nape of her neck and snuggling himself into her hair. It was strangely comforting, so she let him hide there, and carried all her stuff back out into the main room.

"Why does this feel like I'm saying goodbye to my apartment?" she said to Henry, who was searching through her electronic equipment.

"Maybe it's your intuition," said Henry looking up from his task with raised eyebrows.

"Or maybe I'm just being melodramatic," she said staunchly. It would be fine. But just in case, she went back to her room and grabbed her little cardboard box of mementoes from under the bed.

As she stuffed it into her bag, she again stopped to watch Henry as he rummaged around the room. "What are you actually doing?" she said.

"I'm trying to create a distraction," he said.

"And what exactly is the distraction going to be?"

Henry glanced at her over his shoulder. "I thought perhaps you could have some kind of a breakdown, and refuse to come out to the van. If I can get the parts together to make a fake you to sit by the open window, you can record something that will start when they trip your detection software downstairs."

Fee raised her eyebrows at him.

"Don't try to tell me you don't have anything like that. I can see the set up for it here. Plus Max told me about it."

"Are you sure it will work?"

"Sure it will. I've set up systems like this loads of times at the carnival. It'll keep them distracted, and give us more time to get out of here."

"There's a back entrance to the parking garage," said Fee. She'd made sure about back entrances and other options when she first moved in.

"Even better. We can escape out the back while they're trying to reason with you out the front. Quick, come give me a few hysterical cries," he said with a grin.

Between them, they configured a basic sequence that would respond to knocks at the door, and to anyone who called out to her from below. Fee kept glancing at the clock on her wall, willing time to slow down so they could get it done in enough time.

As they worked together, Fee was impressed again by Henry's skill with making things. He seemed to know instinctively what to do and how to do it and his hands moved at high speed creating whatever they needed. She felt the hum of magic surrounding them. It was good to have someone else who had a similar power to her own.

"Okay, it's done," said Henry. "Let's get the hell out of here."

Fee nodded. It was basic, but exactly what they needed. It would recognize a van and begin the sequence as well. And it was going to take photos of the van and anyone who got out, and forward them to Fee's phone.

They grabbed her bags and headed out the door. "Come on, Max, you're coming too," Fee called to the robot where it stood to attention by the door.

"Certainly, Wild Feather." Max moved toward the door with his multiple-legged gait and closed it behind him.

They had to make room for Max and the bags in the back of Henry's car and wasted precious minutes squeezing his tentacles into unnatural positions.

Henry started the car, and instead of peeling off out of the building like Fee was expecting, he drove at the correct speed out of the back exit and down the road.

"Come on, get going," she encouraged, looking over her shoulder out the back window.

"We don't want to call attention to ourselves. This car is already pretty noticeable, we don't want to make it worse," said Henry, as he peered around them along the road.

"What are you looking for?"

"Spies. Scouts. Lookouts. Anyone who looks suspicious, who might report us back to their bosses."

Fee nodded. That made sense. "So where to now?"

Henry hesitated. "I need to go back to my hotel room. There's something I need."

"Okay then. Let's go."

"There's a chance they might be watching my hotel room," said Henry slowly.

Fee turned to face Henry as he focused his attention on driving along the city street. "Why would they be watching you? I'm the one they're after."

Henry took a breath. "Didn't you say they had ways to detect if someone was using magic? I used my magic in a pretty public place the other day, saving that young girl on the Ferris wheel. If they've been watching you, they might have seen it."

"Then why are we risking it? Surely we can buy you new clothes or whatever?"

"I have a journal and a diary with names and contact details in it. If this really is the Witch Hunters, I can't let that get into their hands. It would give them an entirely new set of magic-users to take aim at."

"How would they know where you are? David would have no way to find out."

Henry shook his head. "I'm not convinced it's David. What if it's Lucas? He knows exactly where I am. Or Pelgrim? He could have followed me home at any time these last few days." He tapped his finger on the steering wheel.

"I'll go in, try to see if I can ask someone from the hotel to get my bags for me."

"What if they're waiting in the room? They'd never let a hotel worker leave with your bags."

"Do you have a better plan?" Henry glanced at her curiously.

"We could use my little critters," suggested Fee. "Stay hidden, send them in to get bits and pieces. They might not be able to get everything, but they could safely get a phone and address book."

Henry glanced at Fee a moment, surprise on his face. "Can they do that? Follow direction?"

Fee winced. "They're a bit like a pack. They'll go where I ask them, as long as Bing goes with them."

"The one from your hair?"

"The one from my hair."

CHAPTER 25

*H*enry crouched behind the hedge at the back of the hotel, scanning the area, for anyone who might be watching for him. He couldn't see anything suspicious, but that didn't mean a thing. It wasn't as if he was an expert at this kind of subterfuge.

They were planning to get as close as they could to the hotel, and then send the critters up to his room. He was going to burn the damned address book when he got it back. It had just never occurred to him how dangerous it was until now.

Behind him, Fee crouched with her arms curled against her, holding four small robots, including the spider-like swimmer, the kleptomaniac with hundreds of arms and legs, a cute little one that looked like a ladybug that Fee said was her first-ever creation, and a strange wild-looking one with tiny scissors instead of one arm, and long wires curling across its tiny faceplate as if it was the drummer in a Bob Marley tribute band. Bing was up in her hair, one hand outstretched like he thought he was an expedition leader.

Henry shook his head. He just didn't understand how Fee could call them her failures. They were the most incredible things he'd ever seen. "Are they ready?" he asked.

"As they'll ever be. I think we need to get them close to your room before we unleash them." Fee looked at him and his breath caught. He kept forgetting about her new eye color, and then being surprised by it all over again.

"We'll need to be on the lookout the whole time." He didn't know if he was being paranoid or not, but Fee's description of the Witch Hunters had raised a chill up his spine. He didn't intend to get caught by one of them, not for anything. Aside from anything else, he wasn't sure there was anyone at the Carnival who could rescue them. They were all preoccupied with getting Missy and the others out of the trouble she'd gotten herself into.

"I'll do my best, but I'll need to keep an eye on the critters as well," said Fee nervously.

Henry took a breath and tried to decide if he really needed to go into the room. The answer was still yes.

Annoyingly he was on the third floor of the small hotel; it had seemed advantageous when he first arrived. But he had an external balcony, and Fee assured him the robots would be able to climb up the outside and the little thieving one would be able to pick the lock with ease. He shook his head. This day was going from bad to just plain crazy.

Half bent over, they raced around the side of the pool, trying to keep under cover, and watch out for suspicious behaviour at the same time. It was harder than it seemed, because everyone looked suspicious when you were worried. All they could do was to keep going, and hope for the best. Henry ducked past another tree, and came to a stop outside the window of the room directly below his. "This is it. They'll have to climb up from here. Third floor."

Fee nodded and lifted her hand up, letting each of the five metal robots off onto the concrete. They climbed up the side of the wall as if it was flat, speeding up to the top floor. They jumped over the balcony edge and disappeared from sight.

"They know it's the bag on the bed, right? The one with the address book in it."

"It's fine. If they get the wrong one, we can send them back up again. They're happy to run about."

"Yeah, but I don't know if we have time for that. Whoever it is, they're serious; they're willing to blow up a building to get to you." Henry felt like he was being overly paranoid, especially given the look that Fee shot him, but warning signals were blaring inside his head. It didn't feel safe, and he needed them to be leave as soon as possible.

They waited in silence for a few minutes, with Henry darting glances to the surrounding areas. Fee was watching for the critters to come back, and didn't seem as concerned by an ambush downstairs.

A crash sounded upstairs in the room, and Henry jerked up to standing position.

"What was that?" whispered Fee. "Was that in your room?"

Henry shook his head. "I don't know."

As they spoke, three small metal objects came hurtling out of the room and over the edge of the ledge, only just hanging on as they ran, clinging to the edges of his black bag. Henry gave a sigh of relief. They'd got it.

"Where are June Bug and the Wildling?" asked Fee anxiously as they scuttled down the side of the building and dropped the bag into her hands.

The one with eight legs pointed six of them back up to the room, and chattered in a language only it could understand. Bing raced up her arm and into Fee's hair, quivering. The thieving one bounced up and down in agitation.

"Did someone try to catch you?" asked Fee.

Affirmative chattering came from all three.

At that moment, two more creatures came flying out the window, but this time they were flying as if they'd been thrown. A large man appeared at the balcony and looked around. Henry pulled Fee quickly backwards under the balcony, holding a hand over her mouth when she went to speak, and hoping they hadn't been seen.

"They're around here somewhere. I can smell them. And those dirty little robots are everywhere. Like vermin, they are."

"Good thing you squashed two of them then, isn't it," said another voice.

Henry held Fee tight as she struggled at the mention of her critters being hurt. They had to wait until the two men went inside.

"Do we hunt him down?"

"Nah. Boss said to search here, and catch him if we saw him. Did you see him?"

"No."

"Then we don't have to bother chasing anyone."

"I don't want to be the one to tell them we lost the circus dude. They were real particular about wanting to ask him some questions."

"But we didn't lose him; we ain't seen him. As long as he gets the woman, he'll be happy. She's the one he's after."

They went back inside, their voices dimming. Henry loosened his grip on Fee, and she darted to where the two tiny critters had landed on the concrete, their bodies broken and motionless. She crouched down and picked them up carefully, tears rolling down her face. He recognized Junebug and the strange Wildling from the midst of the broken pieces. The other three critters ran over and hid in the pockets of Fee's jacket.

Henry came up beside her, the bag in his hands. He put one hand on her shoulder. "Fee, we have to go," he said softly. "We were lucky they only sent two of them here."

Fee nodded, and let him lead her away, clutching the broken critters to her chest.

CHAPTER 26

*T*he car sped away from the hotel, and Fee had no idea where they were going. But she didn't care. Holding the two small creatures in her hands, silent tears traced their way down her cheeks.

They were both crushed beyond recognition. Junebug was the first robot she'd ever made, and the Wildling had been an adorable but crazy part of their small clan. They'd been with her for a long time now, and to lose two of them at once was a blow that went straight to Fee's heart.

"You must think I'm stupid, crying over a couple of metal robots," she said to Henry.

He shook his head. "No, of course not. They were special." He paused to go around a corner. "Can you repair them?"

Fee shook her head. "I don't think so. They've been so damaged. He must have stomped on them. They're completely crushed."

"I'm sorry." He genuinely did sound sorry.

"Thanks," she whispered. Thoughts started to clamour for attention in her brain. "Where are we going?" she asked.

They'd been so focused on getting out of there she'd forgotten to make sure he was on the same page as her.

"Out of town. To rescue your friend, Alberta. We'll collect her, and take her with us. I just need you to tell me where the farm is."

"About an hour north of Little Rock, Arkansas."

Henry nodded. "So we could get there in less than a day."

Glancing over at Henry, Fee frowned. "Only if we drive all night."

"Do you want to get there as soon as possible?" asked Henry, his eyes on the road.

Fee sighed. "I guess so. But we should share the driving."

"Sure. I'll take first shift."

Fee looked back at the road ahead of them. "Where are we going after that?"

"The Carnival. I can protect us there."

"But what do we do about the Witch Hunters?"

"We'll cross that bridge when we come to it. First we have to make sure Alberta is safe."

Fee felt something relax on the inside. He really *was* going to help her save Alberta. "But what about Lucas and the others?"

"They'll have to take care of themselves. You heard those guys back there. You're the main target. The bomb was for you."

Fee shivered. Surely, it couldn't all be for her? She led a quiet life, going between her little cubicle at Callaghan and home. What harm was she doing? "I'm sorry you're tangled up in this," she whispered.

Henry shook his head. "It's not your fault. But we do need a bit more information. I'm going to call a friend."

He pressed a button on the dash and said, "Frankie."

The sound of a phone dialling, and then ringing filled the

car. Fee raised her eyebrows. "How many modifications have you actually done?" she asked.

Henry shrugged. "A few."

"Hello?" a male voice answered the phone groggily.

"Tell me you weren't asleep, Frankie. It's the middle of the day," Henry said in a joking tone.

"Henry?" The voice still sounded half-asleep. "What do you want?"

"I need some help. I've run into some trouble."

"What kind of trouble?"

"Someone trying to blow us up kind of trouble."

Frankie snorted. "That's not difficult to believe. What did you do?"

Fee giggled and glanced at Henry. His face showed amusement at his friend's ribbing.

"And who've you got with you there? That didn't sound like one of your laughs."

Fee put a hand over her mouth. Was she supposed to keep quiet?

Henry sighed. "She's one of the researchers at Callaghan Technology, where I was working. She uses magic like we do. We think she's being targeted by an organization called the Witch Hunters."

"And you want me to find out more information about them?"

"Yeah, the Witch Hunters, plus a few people who might have helped blow up the Callaghan Technology building."

Frankie whistled through his teeth. "Geez, Henry, what have you gotten yourself into?"

"I don't know, but I hope Jack took payment of my fees before the contract started. 'Cause I don't think I'm getting paid for this one if he didn't."

Frankie barked out a laugh. "Give me these names, and I'll get onto it straight away."

Henry glanced at Fee as he spoke. "Three names. Dr. Pelgrim Shaw, Dr. Lucas Callaghan, and Dr. David... Fee, what's David's last name?"

"David Gardner," she supplied quietly. It was a sad list, because she couldn't say without a doubt that anyone on it was innocent. She hoped Lucas wasn't part of it, but what did she really know about him? There was his ability to create commercially accepted designs, which she had always attributed to a little bit of the magic that hung around him. But maybe she'd sensed Witch Hunter magic?

"I asked Dad to check the Witch Hunters out too, so check in with him, see if he found anything," said Henry.

"What do you know about them already?"

As Henry told Frankie everything he knew, Fee shook her head slightly, trying to clear it. She was used to having the Witch Hunter axe hanging over her head, and thought she'd done enough to ensure she would have enough warning of an attack. But she'd obviously become too complacent. She'd overlooked a major attack. Now she just didn't know who might be responsible.

What if Eugene had been killed? It would have been her fault. She shivered, the reaction going through her whole body.

"I'll check them all out, and get back to you, Henry. You take care of yourself down there."

"Thanks, Frankie. I will."

The phone clicked off, and Henry glanced at Fee before putting his foot down on the accelerator. They were on the freeway now, heading north. It would take more than a few hours to reach their destination. Fee wriggled around in the bench seat, trying to get comfortable.

"There might be a blanket or something in the back," said Henry. "Something to lean on."

Fee turned around, and almost knocked her nose on one

of Max's tentacles. "You see anything back there, Max?" she asked.

Max's legs moved around, and a blanket appeared, smoothly sailing over his tentacles like a boat over water. "Is this what you wanted, Wild Feather?"

Fee sighed. At least some things never changed. "Yeah, thanks, Max-a-million." He didn't care about her using his full name, but it made her feel better nonetheless.

Fee rolled the blanket and hung it over the seat, creating a pillow for her head. It had been a long 24 hours, and she was exhausted. "Is it okay if I grab some sleep?" she asked Henry.

"Of course. I've got Max here to keep me company."

Fee nodded and closed her eyes. Images flashed across her eyelids like an action movie: Pelgrim yelling at them, being stuck in the lab, the burned out hole in the side of the Callaghan Technologies building. It had her heart racing and her blood pumping so fast that she opened her eyes again.

"Just take some deep breaths," said Henry, glancing quickly over at her. "And try not to think about it."

"Easy for you to say. You're not the one trying to sleep," grumbled Fee.

She closed her eyes again and took some deep breaths. She was asleep in minutes.

CHAPTER 27

*H*enry glanced over at Fee.

She was sound asleep, her blanket pillow keeping her head up, her hands still clasped around the broken critters in her lap. They'd been driving for six hours, and she'd done a good job of catching up on her sleep.

"So, Max, what else can you tell me about the Witch Hunters?" The robot had been keeping him entertained: they'd played eye-spy, which was difficult with a very literal robot who had a dodgy sense of humour, and talked about robotics and artificial intelligence. When he talked about Fee while she was asleep, Max used her nickname, not the full name he always used when talking with her face to face. It was kind of spooky.

"I only know what I have been told or overheard in my time," he replied.

"Which is...?"

"They are devout, and firmly believe in their right to kill those with magic, whatever the cost. They believe magic is a scourge they have been tasked with destroying."

Henry shook his head. He didn't know how they'd

managed to stay under the radar at the Carnival all these years, but he was glad they had. These people sounded horrific.

Maybe blessing magic didn't count? Henry tightened his grip on the steering wheel. And maybe it did. "What else?"

"They are generally rural based, although not all of them eschew technology the way Fee's parents do."

"And her parents?"

"After her first run in with her father, Fee escaped, but knew she would have to keep an eye on him to keep herself safe. She has a few simple spy cameras set up at the farm, with help from Alberta, and of course Alberta herself to keep an eye on things."

"Where do the feeds for those cameras go?"

"Her phone. But I saw her checking earlier, after her conversation with Alberta. They were no longer in operation."

"That doesn't bode well for Alberta, does it?" Henry had a terrible feeling she would already be dead.

"No. It does not."

Henry continued to brood for a while, wondering if they were making a huge mistake by traveling to get Alberta. What were they going to do after that?

The phone went off, sending vibrations along the steering wheel.

"Hello?" he said.

"Hi, Henry. This is Lucas."

Henry slowed his speed, and sat up slightly. "Lucas."

"Where are you? I've been trying to get in touch with you and Fee. The FBI agent wants to talk with you."

Henry couldn't tell if that was sinister or not. "We ran into some trouble. Have you heard anything new about the bomb?"

Lucas sighed. "They think they've narrowed the suspects

down. It appears it wasn't a very sophisticated bomb; they scored more points for ingenuity than finesse."

"So not a professional, but someone who was smart enough to figure it out for himself?"

"Or herself," said Lucas softly.

Henry glanced over at Fee. Her eyes were open. They widened slightly at the implication.

"You think Fee had something to do with this?" asked Henry.

There was a pause at the other end, and then Lucas sighed. "I don't want to think that any of my staff were involved. But that's what FBI Agent Franklin is telling me. Fee is the only person who has disappeared."

"She's not the one who did it. We're hiding out because she's the *target* of the bomb," said Henry. No way was he going to let Lucas go on believing that Fee was guilty.

"Is that what she told you?" asked Lucas softly.

Henry took a breath. "What makes you think she did it?" he asked.

"At the advice of the FBI, I've offered everyone in the lab protection at a friend's beach house. Fee is the only one who hasn't come in and taken advantage of that."

"You've got everyone else all together in one house?" asked Henry. He was suddenly worried for Nolan and Eugene, the only two he was fairly certain had nothing to do with the bomb.

"Yes. They're all here. Except Fee." Lucas's voice was accusatory.

"Is that for their protection, or so it's easier to find them when they decide who did it?" Henry asked tersely.

"Of course, it's for their protection. Agent Franklin is actually leaning toward Pelgrim as the main suspect. It's just that actions speak louder than words."

Henry couldn't decide if Lucas was sincere. He'd never sensed anything other than integrity and honesty from him, but he was also in a position to make all of this happen. He'd known where Henry was staying, and would have known exactly how to get past the security to plant a bomb.

"Okay, we'll come in," said Henry. Beside him on the seat, Fee shook her head violently. He put a finger to his lips, trying to let her know he was just playing for time.

"That's great," said Lucas, his voice sounding relieved.

"We'll be a few hours. We have a couple of things to do first, and we were headed out of town."

"Really?" Lucas sounded worried. "You know that just makes her seem guiltier, right? Are you sure she's as innocent as you think?"

Henry paused. Was Lucas trying to convince Henry or himself? Was someone there talking in his ear, telling him this stuff about Fee, or was he the one in charge? It was impossible to know. "Of course, she's innocent, Lucas. If you knew Fee better, you'd know it too."

"How well do you actually know Fee, Henry? You've only known her a couple of days. Perhaps if *you* knew her better, you'd know she was capable of this." Lucas paused. "Let me know when you get closer, and I can tell you where to come."

"Sure." Henry pressed the button to end the call before Fee could burst out with anything that would let Lucas know she'd heard the whole conversation.

"We're not going back," said Fee, turning in her seat, her eyes sparking green fire.

"Of course we're not going back. We have no idea who is working with the Witch Hunters, and Lucas is a prime suspect. I just wanted to give us more time."

"Oh." Fee sat back against the seat again. "That's all right then."

"What did you think about Lucas's voice? Did he sound suspicious to you?" asked Henry.

Fee shook her head. "I don't think so. But he thinks I did it, doesn't he?"

"I think he doesn't know what to think. Either that or he's the one who bombed the damn building. Maybe it's not just about you? Maybe he's trying to get the insurance money?"

Fee shook her head. "I definitely felt the Witch Hunter energy there. I don't think this is a simple case of insurance fraud. And don't forget the men at your hotel room."

"So you think Lucas is part of it?"

"I was sure it was Pelly at first. Then David blatantly lied to me. But you're right; it could also have been Lucas using David to put his message across." Fee put her hands to her scalp and pulled at the hair. "I don't know what to think anymore. I wouldn't have said anyone was suspicious until we got bombed. Except maybe Pelly after he was fired. But the energy at the Callaghan Technologies building was real."

"Then we have to figure out who might have done it, and find a way to stop them."

"Have you thought about the fact that they could all be innocent and this is an outside job?" Fee didn't like having to think of them all as possible suspects.

Henry sighed. "Yes, I have. It seems more logical that it's an inside job, though. The FBI's investigations backed up that idea too."

Fee thought about that for a moment. "I guess it would make it easier to get past all the security. Less likely to be noticed. But they destroyed Violet. All our hard work down the drain." Fee felt sick at the thought.

"Which makes it seem more likely it was Lucas. He didn't think that the project was going anywhere. He was pressuring you all, brought me in to save it, but could have been planning to simply close it down and fire you all. This gives him the opportunity to claim insurance, get some of his money back."

"So you think Lucas is guilty?"

Henry shook his head. "I don't know yet. But he's looking like a good suspect. Especially given that phone call we just had."

CHAPTER 28

*F*ee woke to the vibration of the car under her body and the morning light from an early sunrise. She blinked open her eyes, and turned to see Henry concentrating on the road ahead of them.

"Morning, sleepy head," he said with a grin.

"How are you still awake?" she croaked out, trying to get her bearings.

"I'm used to all night drives. We do it every time we change towns for the summer season. I usually drive one of the trucks, so this is like child's play in comparison."

Fee nodded and swallowed over her dry throat.

"There's water by your feet, and we're coming up to a diner where we can get some coffee and something to eat. According to the road signs anyway." Henry seemed far too chirpy for this hour of the morning.

Fee leaned down and grabbed the water bottle, taking a grateful swig. The cool water soothed her throat, and she felt almost human again, when she screwed on the lid and leaned back in the seat. "Where are we?" she asked, looking around at the fields.

"Not far from your farm. After you finished your turn driving, I figured I'd let you keep sleeping and just drive the rest of the night. I wanted to get us there as soon as I could."

"I can't believe we're almost there."

"We need to figure out exactly what we're going to do," said Henry slowly. "Once we get to Alberta's house, I mean. Can we trust her enough to take her to the Carnival with us?"

Fee immediately shook her head. "No. I need to take Alberta back to Little Rock where I can protect her."

"How are you going to protect her exactly? They've already proved they can hide right in front of you and you won't notice. We need to go somewhere I know we will be safe. And that's the Carnival Compound."

Fee winced, but held her ground. "I have an apartment in Little Rock. I keep it stocked up with supplies, just in case. We can go there."

Henry shook his head. "It's too close to where your family is based. By the sounds of things, they've figured out what you've been doing, and they've learned enough that they found you."

"I think it was just a fluke. Some kind of error I made. I'm positive my apartment is still safe."

"How?"

"I have a security system in place. Nothing has been disturbed."

"They could still know about it somehow."

"Maybe." Fee hesitated. "But I don't think we should lead them to the Carnival either."

Henry was silent for a moment. "There's a chance they've left Alberta alive because of her lack of magic. Is that right?" He looked at Fee, his brows raised.

She nodded, her hands going clammy as she realized how much danger she'd put the older woman in. She'd been so arrogant in thinking they'd never realize, and now Alberta might be the one to pay for it. "I hope so." Fee paused to consider. "Although they didn't seem too worried about hurting people when they bombed Callaghan Technology."

Henry watched the straight road ahead for a moment. "I've been thinking about that. It was actually quite targeted. A small bomb that only damaged your lab. No one else besides Eugene was hurt."

Fee nodded slowly. "So the person cared enough to try to limit the damage to other people?"

"I think so. It gives me some hope for Alberta."

"But not for me?" Fee said softly.

"Or me," said Henry with a crooked grin. He became serious. "These Witch Hunters, they scare me. The Carnival is built on magic. If they ever decided to focus on us, it would be a disaster. We have to make sure we don't lead them to the rest of my family and friends. I can't be responsible for that."

"Then we should go to my apartment, not the Carnival. That's the only way to ensure we don't do that."

Henry sighed. "I'm just not sure I can protect you on my own," he said.

"I don't need you to protect me. We'll figure something out together. We're not completely helpless, you know." Fee frowned at him; he grinned back and their gazes caught. Her stomach did a little somersault. He didn't have to be here, but he'd wanted to help her. She shivered, despite the heat in the car.

She was becoming more attached to Henry the longer they spent together, but all her self-preservation warning systems were telling her to back off. Any kind of relationship between them seemed destined to end badly. They lived completely different lives on completely different sides of the country. Not to mention the psychotic killers who were out for her blood, and the entire Carnival of people he had to protect from the same killers. He wasn't going to choose her over them. A lump formed in her throat and she looked away, trying to think of something—anything—else.

The phone rang as she was trying to get herself back under control.

"Hey, Frankie," said Henry. He cleared his throat.

"Henry. I've been looking into those Witch Hunters. You need to get your butt as far away from them as possible. They're out to get anyone with magic, and that includes all of us at the Carnival. I talked to Indigo and she says they're worse than curse magic users. Your Da agrees."

Fee could see from Henry's face that using curses was bad.

"What did Indie know about them? Anything useful?"

"The Carnival had a run in with them a century or so ago. They killed about 50 Carnival folk before they could be stopped."

Fee's breath went out of her lungs in a rush. She'd known she was in danger. She'd been dealing with that since she was seventeen years old. But to learn there were others who were in danger, and had been harmed by the Witch Hunters in the past? Her decision to leave her parents alone suddenly seemed naive.

"How did they get rid of them?"

"They killed them all. Every single damn one who knew about the existence of the Carnival. It was the only way." Frankie's voice was grim.

"So if they find out about us again..."

"We'd have to do the same thing, or they'd keep coming after us, again and again."

Henry let out a long breath. "Okay. Thanks Frankie. Anything on the other names?"

"Well, they're a mixed bunch. Pelgrim Shaw is under investigation for your explosion; he's their main suspect."

Fee's eyes widened. "How did he find out...?" she said.

She could almost hear Frankie's grin from the other end of the line. "I have my ways, Fee. Don't you worry about that."

"What about the others?"

"Lucas doesn't seem to have a background, which is never a good sign. He appeared from nowhere at a college out west, and then did his post graduate at MIT based on the quality of the research he'd been doing. He started and then built up Callaghan Technology into a multi-million dollar company. He's squeaky clean, but it's too squeaky clean. He's hiding something."

Fee's eyes widened at this description of Lucas. Was Henry right? Did her boss have something to do with all this? She'd not really believed it until this moment.

"What about David?" she asked.

"David's interesting, although less suspicious. He grew up in an extreme sect of the Mormon Church living an even more austere lifestyle than was usual for those folk. Up to the age of seventeen, he was fully devoted to his family and his religion, was engaged to a suitable girl, and was all set to live his life the same way as everyone else. Then he turns eighteen, and up and leaves all that behind, deciding to go to college instead."

Fee blinked. "That's not such an unusual story," she said defensively. It was exactly what she had done after all.

Henry glanced over at Fee. "What happened to him when he went into the outside world?"

"Not much. He did his work, got a post-graduate degree in computing. He was quiet, kept to himself, and didn't do anything out of the ordinary."

Fee sighed. "So does that mean he might be involved?"

"I don't know. He comes up pretty clean, aside from his

decision to completely break from the rest of his family like that."

"Did you find out anything about Pelgrim?" Fee was curious to see how his life would be boiled down by Frankie.

"He's far more standard. Rich parents, top marks at school, smart guy all the way. Kind of arrogant based on some of his correspondence. Nothing that points to his involvement in the bombing, except that he was extremely angry with Lucas for what he believes was unfair dismissal."

"That's a pretty big arrow, Frankie," said Henry caustically.

"Sure. It makes him an obvious choice. And I guess the obvious answer is often the right one. But I don't know; he doesn't seem like the type to put himself to all the effort involved in that bomb. I'm not sure he'd have the balls to actually do it."

"Based on what?" asked Fee.

"The internet is a powerful tool in the right hands," said Frankie in a deep voice.

Fee giggled. She liked Frankie, whoever he was.

"Then who did it?" asked Henry.

"My money is on one of the other two. But I don't know which one. If you wanted me to guess, I'd lay odds on Lucas; he's got the balls and the money."

Henry glanced over at Fee and she shrugged. She didn't have any insights. "Okay, thanks Frankie."

"All good, my friend."

"Have the others come back from L.A.?"

"Not yet. Last I heard, Tilly was in, and the others were waiting for the big performance to nab them."

"Is Missy okay?"

"Don't worry, Henry. She'll be fine. I'll let you know more as soon as I know anything."

Fee felt the stirrings of jealousy in her stomach. Who was

Missy? And why did Henry care so much about her? She watched Henry's expression as he talked to Frankie. Was he in love with her? She crossed her arms over her chest and tried not to care about it.

"Thanks, Frankie. Talk soon."

"Take care of yourself. Yell if you need anything."

Once the call was disconnected, Henry glanced at Fee. "Who do you think? Lucas or David?"

"I don't know," she said, shaking her head. "At least we ruled out one of our suspects. But if Pelly is still the main suspect of the investigators in Tampa, they won't be looking at anyone else." She paused. "Should we try to tell them what we think?"

Henry snorted. "What, that we think Lucas or David might be guilty based on hunches? They'd never believe us."

Fee sighed. "I guess you're right. Then what do we do now?"

"What we've been planning to do. Get Alberta and go to your apartment. Then we can plan from there. But first, I'm starving."

CHAPTER 29

*H*enry pulled into the diner, parking the car near the exit. He stretched his arms and yawned. He was looking forward to coffee, and hopefully a decent break. He needed to be fresh when they approached Alberta's house.

He glanced over at Fee. She was awake, but in her own little world, looking out the window.

"You coming in with me?" he said.

She glanced around at him, her eyes blank for a second. Then she smiled. "Oh, sure. Sorry, I was miles away."

"Bringing back memories for you?" They weren't far from her parent's farm. About half an hour if he had his distances right.

She nodded. "I haven't been back since I was seventeen," she whispered.

"What about when your friend died?"

"I was too afraid. I didn't want to be recognized, so I made the lawyer sort it all out. He even spread around the rumor that Alberta was Geraldine's cousin, so it seemed like she'd inherited the house."

"Do you trust the lawyer? Could he have told your parents where you were?"

Fee lifted her shoulders in a delicate shrug. "I thought I could trust him. He didn't have anything to do with them, and he knew it was vital to keep them ignorant about the situation. I always assumed the client confidentiality thing would keep him quiet, but I guess he could have said something. It's getting hard to know who to trust."

Henry reached out and pushed a strand of hair away from her face. The usual electricity raced up his arm, but he tried to ignore it. "You can trust me," he said.

Fee gazed up at him, her eyes large on her face. "Thanks. That means...a lot."

Without thinking about it, Henry leaned in and kissed her gently on the lips. A burst of electricity flared between them, sizzling hot. Henry couldn't help himself; he pulled her closer and hungrily kissed her. He felt like a teenager, out of control and not understanding what was happening between them. Instead of resisting him, as he half expected, she wrapped her arms around his neck and drew him nearer.

His hand clenched where it was holding her hair, and he deepened the kiss, his tongue dancing against hers. His hand rose of its own volition and pressed against her breast, massaging the soft mound, playing with the nipple through her clothes. He felt it harden against his fingers and she moaned against his mouth.

Sparks flew and Henry lost the ability to think. All he could do was feel Fee's body against his, their lips and tongues together and the electricity that danced between them every time they touched. It never seemed to calm down.

If anything, the energy they created seemed to multiply around them. Henry felt like they must be glowing, the power was so bright. But he didn't care. All that mattered was the woman next to him, her lips on his.

A knock on the window of the car broke them apart. A policeman stood at Fee's door, frowning at them. They pulled apart guiltily, like kids caught doing something they shouldn't. Fee rolled down the window.

"Hello, officer," she said meekly, her lips red from his stubble.

"This is a respectable town. We don't need outsiders necking in the parking lot."

"Sorry, officer. It won't happen again," Henry leaned over and spoke, not wanting Fee to take the brunt of the officer's ire.

"See that it doesn't." The officer turned and stalked back toward a cruiser on the other side of the parking lot.

Fee turned to Henry, her eyes wide. She gave a half smile. "So I guess that will teach us for necking in the car, right?"

He smiled back, not sure about calling the extreme emotional and physical experience they generated when they touched something as lame as *necking*. "Let's get something to eat," was all he said.

They headed into the small diner, and found a seat at a table near the door.

"Can I get you something?" asked a waitress who looked like she'd rather be anywhere else.

"I'll have a cheeseburger and a coffee," said Henry.

"I'll have the chicken pot pie and a root beer," said Fee.

They both avoided looking at each other a moment or two, until Henry couldn't handle it any more. "What's the best plan for getting Alberta out?" he asked.

"I was hoping we might be able to go up to the front door, tell her to come with us, and then get back in the car and leave," said Fee, with an expression that said she knew how silly that statement was.

"We should scout it out first. Is there a spot where we can leave the car and go in on foot?"

Fee considered a moment. "It's been a long time since I was here, but I think I remember a spot."

"Great, so we—"

Henry's phone rang in his pocket and he stopped talking to grab it. He was expecting Frankie to ring, and didn't want to miss his call. He didn't look at the screen, and said "Hey."

"Henry, this is Lucas. Where are you?" Lucas sounded terse.

"Lucas." He looked over at Fee. Her eyes were glued to his face.

"You were supposed to be back here by now."

"Look something came up. We had to do a detour. But we'll be there soon."

"Pelgrim has a solid alibi. The FBI is looking for other possible suspects, and Fee is firmly number one. They want to speak to her." Lucas paused. "And you."

"Look, Lucas, you need to stall them. Tell them she didn't do it, that she was the target."

"I don't know if that's the truth, Henry. I'm starting to wonder if you're not working with Fee as well, that this is some big plot to destroy me."

Henry was so startled his head jerked back a little. "Of course it's not, Lucas. We're not the ones you should be looking for. Fee is in danger, so I've taken her somewhere she'll be safe, that's all."

"Well, the FBI don't see it like that. They've issued a bulletin that you're a person of interest in the bombing. They'll be looking for you. Both of you."

"What are you talking about? How can they do that?" How the hell had they managed to get on top of the list of suspects? He thought of the police officer who'd just caught them kissing in the car. At least it hadn't reached this far yet.

"You shouldn't have run. It makes you both look suspicious."

Fee started gesturing in front of him, making strange motions.

Henry frowned at her, and tried to concentrate on his phone call. But before he could say anything in reply to Lucas, Fee grabbed his phone and cut off the call.

"Hey, what did you do that for?" Henry said.

"It was taking too long. They could have been tracking us. Lucas has a team working on a project like that."

"Did you hear what he said?"

"Something bad, I'm guessing."

"They have us pegged as the prime suspects for the bombing. They think we did it because we didn't go to the beach house with the others." Henry grinned. "Mostly you. I could probably talk my way out of it. I get the impression that Lucas thinks you're leading me astray."

"What are we going to do?"

Henry sighed. "I guess we'll have to go back down there at some point and get this all sorted out. But first, I think we should eat a good meal. I'm starving."

He could see a burger and a chicken pot pie heading their way, and he wasn't going to miss out.

CHAPTER 30

*F*ee crouched among the trees looking at the house in the distance. It looked the same as it always had. A two story wooden house, built at the turn of the century when more and more of the farms in this area were being carved out of the land. Smoke curled out of the chimney, keeping the cold of the late winter weather at bay.

But something was off. She knew it in her bones, and couldn't explain it. Glancing at Henry, she could see he knew it too. His face was grim, and he was staring at the house as if he could see through the walls to what was happening inside.

"So we probably shouldn't just drive up, then, huh," she whispered.

"No, I think that idea is out."

"We need to get closer."

"Is there anyone else who comes around to the house? A gardener or a housekeeper or something?" asked Henry.

Fee shook her head. "Alberta's still pretty agile. She does all the work herself."

"Is there any other way to get into the house?"

She narrowed her eyes at the house, and tried to think.

"Front door, back door. Bad idea." She glanced toward the old barn and a vague notion of Hetty telling her one time that there was some kind of old tunnel. But did it go to the house? And was it still open? She didn't know. She glanced at Henry.

"Go on, tell me," he said.

"There's an old tunnel in the barn..." she started. "It might not go to the house, and it might not still be open; it's a long while since Geraldine talked about it," she finished in a rush.

Henry narrowed his eyes toward the old structure. "It's all we've got at the moment. We've got more chance of making it to the barn than the front of the house."

Fee nodded and followed him when he took off at a crouching run toward the outbuilding.

They made it in through the side door, out of view of the house. The barn was dark and damp, and smelled of mice droppings. "I don't think Alberta uses this building very much," said Fee.

It was dark, the only light coming in from a high window covered in grime, and neither of them wanted to put on a light.

"Where is it?" whispered Henry.

"Over here somewhere. I don't know exactly." Fee walked to the side of the barn, near the old feeding stations, and poked around. She couldn't see anything, and began to wonder if Geraldine had boarded up the entrance, leaving the tunnel to rot away. Perhaps they wouldn't be able to find it after all.

Henry followed her over and started searching around as well, turning over barrels, and pulling aside old rotten saddles. "What are we looking for? A hatch? Or a door?" he asked.

"I don't know. She just mentioned it in passing. I could be wrong about it being here still." As she poked around the edges of the barn, trying not to be squeamish about the layers of dirt and spider webs, Fee was starting to think she'd misheard Geraldine. They'd have to think of a new way to get into the house. They were closer now; perhaps they could sneak—

"Found it!" said Henry, from where he'd been searching.

Fee grinned and clambered over to where Henry was pulling aside old farm machinery, and lifting bales of hay. While she was busy giving up, he'd been finding what they needed.

"It's well hidden, but I can see a door in the wooden floor," said Henry as he hefted a tool box.

Fee peered over his shoulder and down at the floor. Her heart skipped a beat when she saw the old trap door opening, with a brass handle. She tried not to get too excited. It could be a storage area with no tunnel at all. But it seemed too coincidental. It had to be what Geraldine had told her about.

Henry pulled on the handle, and with a groan of protest, the door swung up and over. Fee flicked a panicked look to the door of the barn, hoping the noise hadn't traveled to whomever was occupying the main house.

When she returned her gaze to the door, she saw a set of stairs leading down into darkness. The stairs looked very old, and they were coated in dusty spider webs. She shivered.

"I'll go first, just in case," said Henry.

"Wait. Here, take him," said Fee, and she handed him Bing. "He has a light."

The little robot obediently lit up the air around them with a dim light.

"He'll glow brighter, just ask," said Fee.

A noise outside the barn made them both jump. Someone had heard the creak of the door opening.

"Hurry," said Henry, and he grabbed her hand, dragging

her behind him. He pulled the door back down over their heads and they crouched on the stairs.

"How do you turn the light off," he whispered. The light went off.

"Do you think they'll notice the stuff we moved around?" whispered Fee into the darkness. She could feel Henry's hand tightening around hers, and took comfort from that.

"I hope not. It's at the back of the barn," he replied quietly. "We should keep going down."

"Okay."

Henry led the way slowly down the steps. Fee's eyes were beginning to adjust to the darkness, and she saw he had one hand on the wooden wall to one side, and put his feet carefully one after the other down the steps.

"I think I'm at the bottom," he said eventually.

"Tell Bing to make a dim light. I think it'll be okay now," said Fee.

As Henry pulled Bing out of his pocket, the tiny bot put out a small light, showing a room filled with old broken barrels and shelves containing empty jars.

"Over there, on the other side." Fee pointed to where she could see another door hiding behind some barrels and a curtain. "If you weren't looking for it, you wouldn't know it was there."

Henry pulled her by the hand across the room. They shoved the barrel aside as quietly as they could and exposed a dusty old door in the wall. Creatures scuttled away from Bing's light, and Fee tried not to think about what might be in the room with them.

There was no handle to this door, so Henry put his fingers along the edge and pulled. It wouldn't come, and he wasted a few minutes pulling and pushing at different angles along the side of the door.

Fee looked around the edge, trying to find a way in that

made sense. Her eyes lit on something in an even darker corner of the room. She left Henry still working on the door, and peered in behind a shelf and another barrel. There was a small circular door close to the ground, this time with a handle. "Henry. Over here. There's another one." She pulled open the door, and knelt down on the ground in front of a very narrow tunnel. They would have to crawl through it on their hands and knees, maybe even their stomachs. She hoped this was the right way, because they wouldn't be able to turn around half way.

Henry came over and crouched down beside her. "Are you sure this is it?" he asked.

"Nope. But it opens, and it's going in the right direction." Movement sounded above them in the barn. "And I think we better keep moving, just to make sure."

Henry pulled on the door, and this time it opened. He took a breath and then crawled into the hole. Fee was trembling just watching Henry's slow progress. She pulled a barrel to hide the door, and then forced herself to follow closely behind Henry, closing the door in the slightly wider entrance area.

It was surprisingly dry inside the tunnel, and regular wooden beams were doing a good job of holding it together. Spiders and other unnamed insects scuttled across her path every now and again, but Fee managed to keep her screams on the inside.

Henry crawled slowly but steadily ahead of her, occasionally glancing back to make sure she was okay. It was hard to tell in their dark little tunnel, but she thought they were heading in the right direction. She wondered what the tunnel was there for. Geraldine had kept it carefully maintained, if its condition was any indication. She'd probably been expecting something from the Witch Hunters.

Fee wished she'd realized how important that was. She'd

have made sure it was maintained as well. Maybe widened it out a little.

Eventually Henry stopped. Fee crawled up close behind him, and he turned to look back at her, his eyes golden in the dim light from Bing.

"A door is just up ahead. Any idea where it's going to put us out?"

"I think it has to be the basement," whispered Fee. She hoped.

"I'll go first and check it out. I'll signal if it's safe. Don't come out before then, just in case."

"Okay." Fee tried to calm the hammering of her heart as she contemplated going into the house filled with unknown people, all of whom were out to kill her.

CHAPTER 31

*H*enry climbed out of the tunnel, and looked up. Fee had been right; it was a basement, cartons everywhere marking it as a storage locker. It had been too much to expect that they'd put Alberta down here, he supposed.

Still, he'd been hoping.

He stood up and looked around, listening for sound over his head. He went to the one exit door he could find and turned the handle. It squeaked as he opened it and he winced. Poking his head out the door, he saw a small landing and then a set of stairs going up. It was all in darkness, so there was probably a door at the top as well. Better for them to hide, if nothing else.

A noise behind him made him spin around, arms up and ready. But it was just Fee, climbing out of the small tunnel.

"I told you to wait there," he said in a low voice.

"You took too long," she replied, her eyes daring him to say something.

He didn't bother. He'd been about to get her anyway.

"There's a set of stairs leading up. Do you know where it goes to?"

"The kitchen," whispered Fee.

"Is there a particular place they might hold Alberta?"

Fee shook her head. "We don't even know who's here, or if they're holding her."

Henry knew there was someone here. He'd always relied on his intuition, and it was beating him over the head right now, telling him this wasn't a safe situation. "Well, let's assume that we know that. Where do you think might be places they'd hide her. The living room? Her bedroom?"

"Sure, both those places. Maybe we need to split up when we get up there?"

"There's no way we're splitting up. It's too dangerous," said Henry more sharply than he'd intended. He already felt nervous about being here, and having Fee with him. He didn't need them splitting up to make it worse. Then he saw the look on her face. "Too dangerous for me," he added with a grin.

"Come on then. Let's get this over with," said Fee.

They crept up the stairs, trying to keep to the outside edge, to avoid the squeaks. At the top, Henry slowly opened the handle and peered out, trying to figure out what he would do if he actually saw someone. They hadn't even talked about their escape plan. "Clear," he said softly.

They tiptoed into the kitchen, a bright sunny room, with flowery curtains, and a big table in the middle.

"Which way?" he whispered.

Fee nodded toward a door to the left, and led the way. Without waiting for him, she opened it and looked around the side. Fear spurted to life inside him, and he strode over.

But nothing out in the corridor either.

Fee pointed to another door across a hallway, and then led the way over to it. She pressed her ear to the door, and stiffened. Henry leaned over her and listened as well. He could hear the sound of male voices, speaking rapidly, as though they were arguing.

Fee backed away from the door, and pointed down the hallway. Henry led the way this time, going as quietly as he possibly could. There was a door down from the kitchen, and again Fee put one ear against the wood.

Before Henry could stop her, she opened it, and peered inside.

A noise indicated she'd surprised someone by her entrance. But Fee pushed the door open wider, and went in, pulling Henry along behind her. He closed the door, and turned, hoping he was about to see Alberta. It was a large bedroom, with an old-fashioned bed taking up a large portion of the space. On the bed, two women were tied up, with gags over their mouths. One was an older woman with grey hair, and the other was a few years younger with long dark hair and a sad expression on her face. Both were staring at Fee like she was a ghost.

Fee was staring right back, her face white.

"Fee? What is it?" he asked coming to stand next to her. He glanced at the women. "Is it Alberta? Who's the other lady?"

"It's my Mom," whispered Fee in a stunned voice.

Henry raised his eyebrows in surprise, and looked back at the women. The younger one did look a little like Fee. "Should we help them?" he asked.

His question seemed to spur Fee into action. She raced over to the older lady, and started by pulling off the gag over her mouth, moving onto the ropes that held her hands and feet.

Henry went to untie her mother, but Fee looked up and shook her head. "Leave her. It's a trap. She's a Witch Hunter."

Henry looked into the panicked eyes of the other woman

on the bed, and shook his head. "I don't think so, Fee. Look. She's terrified."

"Of us. That we're going to get her out of here." Fee's voice was hard.

Henry shook his head. "That makes no sense, Fee," he said. He remembered what she'd said, that this woman had stood by while her father tried to kill her. That must have left a few scars.

"Leave her," she said again.

"Oh, my dear, you can't possibly leave her here. They'll kill her," said Alberta, her gag free. "It was her visits here that tipped them off to how she felt about them. That's why we're here."

"What are you talking about?" said Fee, pausing her untying.

"Your mother has been visiting me. I didn't tell her about you, not at all. But she's been telling me for a long time how she's missed you, and that she regrets what happened. They overheard her."

Fee narrowed her eyes at Alberta. "Did you tell her about me? About our relationship?"

Henry knew why Fee was upset. If Alberta had said anything, then she was the reason the cult had been able to find and target Fee. Instead of being a help, she'd been a terrible hindrance.

But Alberta shook her head emphatically. "Absolutely not. I knew it was too dangerous. But I didn't realize how suspicious they'd become. They've been checking my computer. Watching my emails."

"How? They don't use technology."

"They do when it suits them, my love. I've discovered that the hard way. Now let your nice man here untie your mother. We need to get out of here as soon as we can."

Fee wavered, and Henry could see that it was a tough

decision for her. She'd thought of her mother as the bad guy for so long that the idea she might not be so bad was confusing.

She glanced at Henry, but he had no answer for her, other than her mother was scared.

"Okay, untie her legs and take the gag off. But we leave her hands tied."

Henry went to her mother, and pulled off the gag. She let out a relieved sigh.

"Thank you, Wild Feather," she said quickly. "I promise you I'm not a spy."

Fee glanced her way once, quickly, and then ignored her, finishing off Alberta's legs. Alberta was rubbing her hands and legs, and Henry knew the pain of having the circulation returned would come in a moment or two. He quickly untied Fee's mother's legs, and hesitated over her hands.

"Leave it, Henry. Please." Fee's voice was tortured, and for that alone, Henry left the bonds over her mother's hands. She was going to be a hindrance like that, but perhaps once they were in the tunnel he could persuade Fee to change her mind.

He glanced at Fee, and saw the anguish in her face. She was struggling with this whole thing. He needed to get her out of there quickly.

"Okay, we're going out the same way we came in. Hope-fully, they'll still be in the other room. They sounded like they were arguing, so maybe that will keep them busy."

"An awful lot of maybes and hopefullys are in that plan," said Fee's mother.

"Then you can stay behind," said Fee sharply. "We didn't come here to get you."

"No, thanks. I'll come with you."

Henry went first, peering again out the doorway. It was clear, so he waved them all to follow him. They tiptoed along the corridor, and then Henry held open the door to the kitchen, urging them through faster. Just as he was about to shut the door behind him, he heard the growl of a dog, and turned to see a large rottweiler snarling at him from the other end of the corridor.

"It's their dog. Damn vicious thing it is, too," said Alberta. "Shut that door!"

Henry slammed it shut just as the dog leaped for him, forgetting the need for silence. He heard shouts from the other side of the living room, and swore. "Everyone down those stairs. *Now.*"

They didn't need him to say it twice. Fee led Alberta and her mother down the stairs, as Henry put a chair under the door of the kitchen.

"This isn't going to get us far, Fee," said Alberta. "No exit from the basement."

"Just keep going and let us deal with that," said Fee.

On the other side of the door, Henry could hear the men thundering down the hallway to the room where their captives had been kept.

"They're not here!" came the shout, and the efforts to open the kitchen door doubled.

A big body slammed against it, and the door partially cracked down the side. Henry's eyes widened and he raced after the others through the basement door, grabbing the old key out of the lock on the other side, and managing to get it locked from the inside before he raced down the stairs.

In the basement, he found Fee shoving her mother into the tunnel after Alberta. Up the stairs, the door was being broken down with the same ease that they'd broken down the first door. He locked the second door to the basement, throwing the key to one side. They'd proved that locking a door wasn't going to hold them up for long. He could hear their shouts as they made it through the top door.

"Hurry," said Henry. "We don't have much time."

Fee pushed her mother through, and Henry piled boxes in front of the tunnel door in an attempt to hide from their pursuers. Fee went through the tunnel entrance and Henry was right behind her, pulling boxes in front to hide it, just as the men started to work on the bottom door.

Henry tried to wait patiently as the older women crawled along the tunnel, but it was difficult. He could hear the angry noises behind him and then the unmistakable crack of a gun going off. His whole body jerked in response. They'd be sitting ducks if they found the trapdoor. He looked around him trying to see if there was a way he could block it off.

The wooden beams were holding it in place, along with a fairly solid support structure. Banging at it would only alert their pursuers to where they were.

He tried to calm his heartbeat, just crawl slowly after the others, and not think about getting a bullet in his back. The crawl along the tunnel seemed much further on the way back, the darkness winding ahead of him. Fee kept glancing back, sometimes looking at him, and sometimes trying to see behind him. Henry preferred not to look behind in case he saw something he didn't want to.

Then they were there. He saw the light up ahead as Alberta opened the door to the lower room in the barn. Fee's mother toppled out and then Fee followed. Henry sucked in a noisy breath as he reached the exit, feeling like he was breathing fresh air again for the first time in years.

"That was a nightmare," he gasped out, lying on the floor for a moment. He opened his eyes to see Fee looking down at him, a hand out to help him up.

"We're not finished yet," she said.

CHAPTER 32

$\mathcal{F}$ee crouched at the corner of the barn, looking back at the old wooden house. Their escape had certainly caused a panic among the men who were previously hidden from view. There were currently three men running around the house, guns raised, looking for them.

"They can't have gone far," yelled one man.

"Just make sure we get them back," yelled another. "I don't care how."

She crept to the back entrance of the barn where the others waited. "We have to make a run for it to the corn," said Fee. "And fast." She glanced at Alberta.

"I'll be fine, love. These old legs will get me where we need to go."

"All right, we just have to do it." Fee shivered. How were they going to get them to the corn without being seen?

"You three go. I'll provide a distraction," said Henry, nodding to the gasoline can in the corner.

Fee looked at Henry for a moment. If the barn were on fire at the front, perhaps the men wouldn't notice them making a run for it at the back. It was a good plan. Any yet. "You do it quickly, and then run after us, okay?"

Henry nodded. "Of course. I'm not crazy." He grinned. "Much." He raced back into the barn, and started creating a pile of flammable objects.

Fee watched him for a moment, and then gathered the other two women close to her by the door. "When it's time, we all run as fast as we can across the lawn to the corn. The car is maybe a minute of running through the corn, but we have to be fast. They'll know something is up as soon as the blaze hits the barn. They might not even care enough to stop the fire." She glanced back at Henry to see if he was listening to her. "So we just run and don't look back."

"I'm going to light her up now," said Henry. "Get ready to go."

Fee took a deep breath. The sound of a fire crackling over old dry wood soon became all she could hear. Smoke started to block their vision. It was time. "Okay, one. Two. Three. Go!" They shot out of the barn, Fee holding onto Alberta's arm, dragging her along.

The older woman ran awkwardly, favoring one hip, but they eventually reached the corn. Not daring to stop, they ran a few yards further in. Fee stopped and stood puffing, her hands on her knees. She'd been spending too much time inside these last few years.

Then she remembered Henry, and stood back up, creeping back to the edge of the corn, trying to see what was happening.

"Shouldn't we keep running, dear?" said Alberta. "I don't know how far it is, but I'd like to get to the car before those men find us."

Fee rubbed one hand over her eyes. Henry should have just come with them, and they could have all been out by now. But Alberta was right. Henry could run much faster than either of the older women, so it made sense to get them to the car first. "Okay, let's go." She could always come back and make sure he was okay if he didn't appear quickly.

She led them across the cornfield, following the line of smashed corn that showed their way through. Soon they were at the car.

"How are we all going to get in there?" asked her mother. She was looking at Max's huge body in the back seat. "I think you're going to have to leave that thing behind."

"We'll just have to squash up," said Fee, glancing at her mother. They wouldn't have had a problem if it weren't for her. "You two stay here. I'm going to check on Henry." She raced off before either of them could say anything.

Running through the corn, Fee could hear shouts, and the sound of something exploding. Her heartbeat sped up. Something must have been in the barn that was more explosive than the gasoline. She ran harder.

Reaching the edge of the cornfield, she paused. The three men were running around the outside of the barn. One was trying to put the fire out with the hose from the house. The other two were searching for them.

All of a sudden, Henry erupted from a position near the house, running away from where Fee and the others had gone. One of the men saw him and shouted, raising his gun to shoot.

Fee held her breath, but the shot went wide.

Henry kept zigging and zagging toward the side of the house.

Another shot rang out, and this time, Henry fell to the ground.

Fee gasped. She glanced between the men and Henry. They were running over to Henry, who was lying still on the grass.

Without thinking, Fee yelled. "Hey, scum bags! What

about me?" She waited until they'd seen her and took off at a run behind the back of the barn, away from the worst of the flames.

Heart pounding in her chest, Fee tried to think. What the hell had she been thinking? How was she going to get out of this mess? In front of her, the back door of the barn loomed. Smoke was pouring out and the heat of the flames felt like it was already burning her skin, but she didn't have a choice. Fee opened the door just as the first of the men came running around the corner.

"She's in the barn," she could hear him yelling behind her.

Inside it was dark and smoky. Her first reaction was to cough, which made her inhale even more smoke. She wouldn't survive for long in here. She needed to incapacitate them, and quickly. The only thing Fee could think of was the old gun that Geraldine used to keep in the barn. She raced over to the cabinet, her heart plummeting when she saw the lock. The shouts of the men at the door spurred her into action again.

She grabbed an old steel fence post, and whacked it at the cabinet. Years of disuse had made the wood rotten, and it broke apart like it was cardboard.

She reached into the cabinet, pulling out Geraldine's old double-barreled shotgun. With fumbling fingers, she loaded the shells, and turned around to face her pursuers.

She held it steady in her arms, remembering the feel of the old gun from years before. She'd learned to shoot on it, and she still remembered.

The first of the men smashed through the door and came running in. Fee didn't even think about it; she pulled the trigger on the gun, aiming for his shoulder. He went straight down. She raced over to him, and grabbed his handgun. She held the smaller weapon in her hand and aimed it up at the next man to come through. He came in shooting, but he was aiming too high, and she hit him in the leg from her unexpectedly low angle. He went straight down. She kept the gun trained on the door, and the third man didn't materialize. On a hunch, she turned toward the main door and pulled the trigger again, this time hitting the third man square in the chest, just as he let off a shot. His shot went wide. When she'd turned instinctively, Fee had saved herself from a bullet through the back.

She tried to get her breathing to return to normal, but couldn't. One of the men groaned, and in fright, she whacked him in the head with the barrel of the gun. The second man rolled over away from her, and she forced herself to knock him out with the butt of the gun as well. They had kept Alberta locked up, and they were shooting to kill, she reminded herself as the bile came charging up her throat and into her mouth. She threw up on the ground next to her.

A support timber groaned and then dropped heavily from the ceiling two yards away, landing in a crash of sparks and flames. Fee jumped and realized she needed to get out if she didn't want to die in there. She looked at the men; she couldn't leave them inside.

Dragging the first man by one leg, she managed to pull him outside by some kind of adrenaline surge, and then the second man. The third man was already dead. She tried not to think about it, and raced out the door past the unconscious men. Across the lawn, she saw Henry, trying to get to his feet. Sprinting, she grabbed him just as it seemed he might fall, and put one of his arms over her shoulder.

"Where did you get hit?" she asked.

He was clutching his side and Fee saw before he answered.

"My side. It hurts like a bitch," he gasped out.

"We need to get out of here. Can you walk?"

"I'll do what we have to do," said Henry.

"Hold your hand down on the wound until we can get you something from the car. We have to staunch the blood."

They staggered into the corn, Henry leaning heavily on Fee for support. A couple of times, Fee was sure he'd actually passed out, but it was only a second or two before he'd start walking again. Fee's heart was pumping wildly and her muscles were pushed to their limit as she carried Henry through the field. Dots were starting to appear in her vision, and she slipped a few times on the uneven ground. Just as it seemed like they were going to be lost in the corn forever, they emerged to find the car was just a few yards away. Fee breathed a massive sigh of relief.

The two women were standing next to the car, waiting for them. When she saw them both, Alberta rushed over to help Fee. Between them, they carried Henry to the car, managing to get him onto the bench seat.

"You'll need to staunch the blood on the wound, while I drive," said Fee, grabbing a sweater from the floor on the passenger side and handing it to Alberta as she climbed in after Henry. Fee raced around to the driver's seat, and pulled it forward for her mother to get in the back.

"I don't want to get in the back seat with that thing," said her mother pointing at Max.

"Get in or don't get in. I don't care. He's staying, and we're leaving now."

Her mother stared at Fee for a second, then climbed in the back seat, trying to avoid touching Max.

Fee slammed the front seat down again, and climbed in behind the wheel.

Henry opened his eyes enough to look at her. "Take care of my baby," he said with the ghost of a smile.

"Of course. I drove her yesterday, didn't I?" Fee complained with a forced smile, trying to keep the tears at bay. She didn't know if she'd be able to get Henry to someone who could help in time.

"Where's the nearest hospital?" she asked Alberta.

"No hospital for miles, you know that, Wild Feather. The closest person who could help is the doctor at Jasper." Her mother's voice came from the back seat, and Fee wanted to ignore her, but didn't dare. Henry's life was at stake.

"Okay then, Jasper it is."

She drove in silence the whole way, the only noise Henry's occasional moans of pain. He went in and out of consciousness, and the blood seemed to spread, despite the efforts that Alberta was making to staunch the flow.

Screaming into the doctor's office parking lot, Fee jumped out of the car, impatiently pulling Alberta out of the way. She practically dragged Henry out of the car, and finding strength she didn't know she had, half carried him up the path and into the house.

When she saw the pair of them dripping blood over the wooden floor, the receptionist stood up immediately. "I'll get the doctor," she said. "Is it a bullet wound?"

Fee nodded.

The doctor came rushing out. He was the same man who'd been servicing the area for years, and Fee recognized him from the few times he'd been allowed to help people on her father's farm. He didn't seem to recognize her, his gaze going straight to Henry, his patient.

"Come, we need to stop the bleeding, figure out what's been hit," he said. He stood on Henry's other side and put his arm around his back and between them. They managed to get Henry into the examination room and lifted him onto the table. Lying down it seemed worse, his face pale and his breathing shallow.

"How long has it been since he was shot?" asked the doctor.

"Maybe half an hour," said Fee.

The doctor worked quickly, cutting off Henry's shirt, and examining the wound. He glanced up and saw Fee at one point, and seemed startled that she was still there. "Can you hand me that cloth?" he said.

Fee silently handed it to him, watching as he dug around near the wound, trying to determine the damage, and then patch it up as best he could.

"He needs surgery to remove the bullet, but it doesn't seem to have hit anything vital," he said eventually. "I'm going to call the helicopter to get him to the hospital in Little Rock." He strode out of the room.

Fee nodded, her eyes wide. This was all her fault. Henry had come to Tampa for a nice quiet break from his usual life, and she'd ended up getting him shot in the middle of Arkansas.

The ring of a phone jerked her out of her maudlin thoughts, and she looked around for the source. It was coming from Henry's pocket, and without thinking, she pulled it out and answered it.

"Hello?"

"Who's this? I wanted Henry." Frankie's now familiar voice filled her ears.

"It's Fee," she said, her hands shaking.

"Can I speak to Henry?"

"He's...he's been shot. The doctor is calling an emergency helicopter." Fee said the last word on a sob.

There was silence for a moment. "Don't worry, Fee. I'll get this sorted. I'll get the helicopter there pronto, and I'll talk to Rilla. She'll get Henry better again. Don't worry about it. We're going to get him better." Frankie's voice strangely soothing, and Fee found herself calming down under the continuing affirmations that he was going to look after it.

"Can you tell me what happened?" asked Frankie eventually.

"We were trying to rescue my friend Alberta from the Witch Hunters. We were almost out, but they saw us, and shot Henry."

"You went after the Witch Hunters by yourself?" said Frankie.

Fee winced, knowing it was her fault. "We weren't going after them. We were just going to sneak in and sneak out. But..."

Frankie sighed. "Typical Henry. Thinks it's all going to be fine, and that he'll find a way through it."

"It wasn't his fault. He only agreed to go along because I insisted on going," said Fee.

"Look, Fee, I'm going to get someone to come down and meet you at the hospital in Little Rock. You stay there, and look after him. Keep his phone next to you and let me know how he's doing."

"Okay. I will."

"It's going to be fine," repeated Frankie.

Fee didn't know how he could promise something like that. It all seemed to be pretty damn messed up from her perspective.

But it was comforting to have him say it all the same.

CHAPTER 33

*H*eading outside, Fee was faced with a terrible decision. Alberta and her mother were sitting in the car waiting for her. The doc had said the ambulance to take Henry to the helicopter would be there any moment. They would have to drive to Little Rock to meet him. He'd said they'd take one passenger with Henry; that was it.

Fee looked between Alberta and her mother, whose hands were no longer tied, she noticed.

"I'm going in the helicopter to Little Rock with Henry. I need you to drive the car and meet us there."

Her mother shook her head. "I'm no use. I can't drive a car."

Alberta nodded. "I can drive it, no problem. Been driving all my life. How hard can it be?"

Beside her mother, Max came to life. "I believe it will be within your powers, Alberta," he said. "And I will be here to help you."

Her mother screamed, and pulled away from Max.

"Calm down," said Fee. "His name is Max. He's a robot."

"What...What?"

"What did you think he was? You were sitting next to him this whole time."

"I...I thought he was a strange machine contraption. Not something that could talk." She was still scrunched up against the far side of the car from Max.

Fee sighed. She didn't have time for this right now. "Max will help you, Alberta. He has a comprehensive navigation system, so he'll be able to direct you if you get lost. I've got to go."

Fee headed back into the clinic, hoping she wasn't making a terrible mistake.

WHEN HENRY CAME TO, he was flying. Literally flying, the thrumming of a helicopter making it impossible to hear anything around him. He saw Fee next to him, and something inside him eased.

She'd come back for him, distracted the men, and carried him through the cornfield. She was still with him. A faint tingle of electricity was running through his hand and up his arm. Henry smiled. She was holding his hand. He couldn't mistake that feeling. Luckily, it was faint, or he might have passed out again.

The ache in his side was dulled down to a manageable level. He'd not been able to think clearly earlier with the pain of the wound. He'd never been shot before, and immediately made a resolution never to be shot again after this. It hurt like hell.

The helicopter began its descent, and Henry closed his eyes. He wondered where they were going. Hopefully, to a hospital, because he was fairly certain that even with the healing from the Carnival, he was going to need a bit of medical intervention.

∿

FEE CLIMBED out of the helicopter and followed Henry's gurney through the doors. She just kept following them quietly, until a nurse eventually noticed her.

"You can't be in here, ma'am. You'll need to go to the waiting room. I'll show you where it is."

She bustled Fee away from the operating rooms and into a large waiting room filled with people. Fee sat down to wait on a hard plastic chair.

She had no idea how much time had passed when Henry's phone rang again. Pulling it out of her jacket pocket, Fee answered it.

"What the hell have you two been doing?" demanded Frankie.

"Pardon?"

"You're both listed as persons of interest in an FBI bulletin! And they've been notified that Henry is in the hospital at Little Rock. Police will be knocking on your door any minute now."

"What?"

"You need to get out of there."

Fee shook her head. "No. I'm not leaving Henry."

"They won't keep you together if they catch you. It's better if you get out of there, so we only have to break one person out of jail, not two."

"I can't leave him," whispered Fee.

"You have to. He'll understand. He's at the hospital; they'll take care of him there for the moment, get the bullet out of him. It gives us a bit of time. Get out of there now, Fee."

Fee looked around the hospital waiting room, trying to figure out what to do. A movement in her hair startled her for a second, and then she pulled the tiny creature out. "Go find Henry," she whispered to her kleptomaniac robot. "Find him and look after him." She crouched near the wall and let the little multi-armed robot go. If nothing else, her little creature would be able to unlock some doors for Henry. She watched him race off toward the surgery area, sneaking into the restricted space when a nurse buzzed herself in.

She stood up, and walked to the door, keeping her head down. Going outside, she was walking along the footpath outside, away from the hospital, when two police cars screamed to a halt outside.

She quickened her pace, trying not to burst out into a sprint.

Since when had she become afraid of the police? She hadn't done anything wrong; and now, she was listening to Frankie tell her to run, when she should have stayed and protested her innocence.

Lucas was right. Running just made her seem even guiltier.

Her steps slowed. She stopped and turned around. At the entrance, the policemen were running into the building. Fee tried to make herself go back. But she didn't want to be arrested, and she was afraid of what the Witch Hunters could do. It wasn't as if she could tell the police they were after her because she used magic.

"Wild Feather!" The voice came from beside her, and pulled her out of her reverie.

She looked and realized that Henry's red Charger was sitting next to her, Alberta at the wheel. She leaned over Fee's mother to speak. "What's happening? Where's Henry?"

"He's in surgery. They're operating to get the bullet out."

"What are you doing out here?"

"They're looking for us. I..." She looked back at the entrance. "I was thinking of turning myself in."

Her mom shook her head violently. "You can't do that, Fee. If they know who you are, and where you are, the Witch

Hunters will get to you. Especially in police custody. You can't give yourself up. It would be committing suicide."

"What about Henry?" Fee was suddenly afraid for him.

"Is he on their radar? Does he use magic? If he doesn't, they won't care about him."

Fee bit her lip. No way was she going to tell her mother Henry used magic too. She didn't know her mother's loyalties; and she was still half convinced this was some kind of trap.

"Fee, jump in the car. We need to get out of here." Alberta was again the voice of reason, and her mother got out of the car, climbing into the backseat, so she could get into the front.

"Where are we going?" asked Alberta. "You said something about an apartment?"

Fee nodded. "Just start driving and I'll direct you as we go."

"Is it close?"

"Not far." Fee looked out the back window as the hospital got further and further away. Was she doing the right thing? Would Henry be okay? She didn't know, and it was tearing her apart.

CHAPTER 34

*H*enry woke, feeling groggy. He couldn't remember where he was, and the white walls made him screw up his face. He'd been having the most amazing dream. It had been like another universe, filled with bright lights and warming touches. He'd been surrounded by love and kindness, soft colors that were soothing and calming. Waking up in a sterile white room took a bit of adjusting.

He tried to move his hand, and the chink of metal on metal was accompanied by the inability to bring it to his face. Looking down, he saw a handcuff around his left wrist attaching him to the bar along the side of the bed. If he'd been feeling better, he might have grinned. He could undo a handcuff in a few seconds flat.

But he felt like he'd been hit by a train that had also stopped and reversed back and forth over him a few times just to make sure. His head was pounding, and his side felt like someone had lit it on fire. He glanced down, but all he could see were white bedsheets and blankets.

He tried to remember something, but it was a blank.

The door opened, and a nurse bustled in. She glanced up and noticed he was awake. "Oh, good. I was hoping I'd see you awake," she said. "The operation went very well. They found and removed the bullet." She checked his chart, and the machines at his bedside. "I'll come back in a while with your meds, and something for you to eat."

"Where..." Henry cleared his croaky throat. "Where am I? What happened?" he asked as the nurse walked toward the door again.

She turned around and looked at him in surprise. "You're at the UAMS Medical Center in Little Rock. You were brought in yesterday on the helicopter from a small farming town north of here." She glanced at his hand in cuffs. "Wanted for a bombing down in Florida."

Henry winced, and it all came flooding back to him. Callaghan Technology. Tampa. Fee. The Witch Hunters. Getting shot.

Now getting arrested for the bombing.

"I'll let the officers know you're awake. I think they have some questions for you."

The nurse headed for the door again, and this time Henry let her.

He pulled at the handcuff experimentally, but let it lie. There was no point in getting rid of it yet: he was in no shape to go anywhere. Something moved at his neck, and he jerked back across the pillow, trying to see what it was. A small metal creature was making itself comfortable next to him on the pillow. He grinned. At least he had someone keeping an eye on him. "Try to stay out of sight, will you?" he said to the little metal robot.

He looked around for his mobile phone, but couldn't see it anywhere. He wondered where Fee was and experienced a moment of panic when he realized she had probably been arrested and sent back to Tampa without him. Hence the robot. He pulled his wrist against the handcuff, tempted to break out now anyway. But no. He didn't know for sure where she was.

What he needed was to talk to the police, to find out where Fee was, and what was happening. There was a chance that Fee had escaped before they'd arrested her. He held onto that thought while he waited for someone from the police to visit.

Even as he lay there contemplating nasty retributions on whoever was actually responsible for the bombing, Henry could almost feel himself healing. It was even faster than usual, and he suspected he was getting some kind of boost from the Carnival. He didn't know how; he'd never experienced anything like this before, but it was certainly welcome.

At that moment, the door swung open, and a tall, gangly man with a thatch of blond hair came through the door. He wore a suit, and Henry recognized him from Tampa.

"Agent Franklin," said Henry.

"Mr. Kokkol."

Henry's eyebrows rose. "Nice to see you again. I think."

"Do you understand why you have a handcuff on your arm?" asked Franklin.

Henry glanced at it. "I'm assuming it's something to do with the bombing?"

"You're a person of interest in the case, and you're considered a flight risk."

"Lucas told us, but I didn't believe him at the time." Henry rattled the handcuffs. "I guess he was right."

Franklin's eyes sharpened on Henry. "You've spoken to Mr. Callaghan recently?"

"He was trying to convince us to go back to Tampa. But we weren't convinced it was very safe."

"What does that mean?"

"Fee was the target of that bombing. If she goes back, they'll just try again."

"That remains to be seen," said the Franklin. "We need to speak to Fee to ascertain that."

"You don't have her?" Henry tried to ask casually, but he was pretty certain he sounded as desperate to know as he actually was.

Franklin paused a moment, but seemed to take pity on Henry. "She wasn't here when we arrived."

Henry let out a breath and lay back on his pillows.

"Tell me, Mr. Kokkol, where have you been since the bombing?"

"We've been hiding from the thugs who did it. Plus I'm not entirely sure that Lucas is as innocent as he's making out."

"That's an awfully big accusation, Mr. Kokkol. Do you have anything to back it up?"

Henry stared at the man's face. He wasn't going to start explaining things to some goon who wouldn't listen. But Franklin had a way about him, something that said he was a rare commodity—someone who actually listened rather than assumed.

"We were locked in a room in the lab for most of the night. If the bomb was planted during the night, we'd have had no way to do it."

"Is there any way to prove this?"

Henry thought about it. "Violet would have known. But she's been destroyed."

"Who's Violet?" His voice was censorious.

"She was a robot. A creation of the research team." Henry paused. "I'm probably not even supposed to talk to you about it, but it popped out."

"But she was destroyed in the explosion?"

"Yes."

"That's a bit convenient, wouldn't you say?"

Henry took a deep breath, trying to think. There must be something that would prove their innocence. "Men were at my hotel room. You could check there, see if they left anything."

"We've been to your room, Henry. It's clean."

"What about Fee's apartment? They probably ransacked it when they realized they missed her." Henry hated the thought of someone destroying her cave, but if it helped them prove her innocence...

"Someone did indeed go through her apartment, Mr. Kokkol. But there's no proof that it was anyone or anything to do with the bombing."

Henry tried again. "What's the reasoning behind myself and Fee doing it?"

Franklin shook his head. "I'm not at liberty to say. I'm only here because they've said you can't be moved for at least a week."

Henry didn't like to tell Franklin that he'd probably be ready to leave by the end of the day. "What questions then?"

"Where were you between midnight and seven o'clock on the night in question?"

Henry shrugged. "Fee and I were both locked in a back room of the lab. The power had gone off and scrambled all the systems. We had to wait until the others arrived in the morning to let us out." Henry looked out the window. "But as you say, any hope of proving that is probably buried knee deep in rubble on the lab floor."

"What about cameras? Does the lab have those?"

"I don't know. You'd have to ask Lucas. I'm just a temporary consultant to the team, not a permanent member."

"It's a big coincidence that just when you join the team, the building is bombed, don't you think?"

"I don't know why they chose now to act. Maybe I was a

catalyst." Henry paused to think about it. "You know, you're right; I probably was." He tapped his finger on the side of the bed, thinking it through.

Franklin sighed. "I'll let you rest for now. I'll be back soon to ask you more questions. You're wanted as an accomplice, Mr. Kokkol. It's Ms. Wild Feather who we're trying to find as the main perpetrator."

"Haven't you listened to a word I said? She didn't do any of it and the longer you pin your hopes on Fee, the longer the real bomber is out there."

"Good day, Mr. Kokkol. I'll be back to talk to you if there is any more information I need." Special Agent Franklin nodded his head and left the room as if Henry hadn't even spoken.

CHAPTER 35

The apartment was in the city center, but Fee still didn't know whether she could trust Alberta, and she definitely didn't trust her mother, so she was leading them in a strange circuitous route, which hopefully would confuse them and mean they'd have trouble finding their way back to the hospital. Or to the nearest police station.

"Here. Turn into that drive way," she directed. She pulled out a key card, and gave it to Alberta to push into the little metal box to one side of the entrance. The metal gate moved slowly upwards and Alberta rolled the car forward.

"It's space number 77." Fee loved that number; it had always felt auspicious to her.

Alberta drove the car into the space, and let out a breath as she turned off the motor. "This car is harder to drive than it looks," she said.

"I don't know, it seems pretty hard to me," said Fee's mother with a half-smile. She was still squished up against one side of the car away from Max.

"Come on. We need to get up to the apartment and figure out how we're going to get Henry out of there."

"You're going to get him out? But he's been arrested. You can't do that." Alberta was horrified.

"But he's been arrested for a crime he didn't commit," said Fee, frowning. If Alberta were going to go all moral on her, it would make everything harder.

Before Alberta could answer, Fee's mother put up a hand. "Let's get up to the apartment and discuss it there. Come on."

Fee popped the trunk, and grabbed her bag and Henry's. She helped Max out of the back seat, and then they all headed toward the elevators.

"Wild Feather," said Max. "I believe I will use the stairs. I would like to check our security measures."

Fee nodded absently while Max headed off in the direction of the stairs, his undulating legs strangely quiet on the concrete floor. He closed the door quietly behind him.

Fee's mother shuddered. "I don't know how you can have a creature like that around. It's against nature."

"Keep saying stuff like that, and I'm going to dump you onto the streets to fend for yourself," said Fee grimly. She was too angry to be in the same elevator as her mother. "Get off at the fourth floor. I'll meet you there." She stalked over to the stairs and followed Max through the door.

Fee pounded her way up the stairs in Max's wake, not sure why she was so angry about her mother's reaction to Max. Summer Dawn had given up all technology, even the good stuff like cars and phones. Of course she'd think Max was an abomination. But it still hurt and it wound her up tighter than a drum.

She arrived on the stairwell landing to the fourth floor to find Max waiting beside the door.

"What is it, Max?"

"I believe we may have a problem, Fee." He kept his voice low so she could only just hear what he was saying.

Fee glanced quickly at the door. "Is there someone here?"

"Yes. They have your mother and Alberta."

"Are they inside the apartment?"

"They are currently trying to get in."

Fee pulled her phone from her pocket, and sure enough, the silent alarm was pulsing. Damn silent. She'd forgotten about checking the alarms. She'd been so damn sure her hidey-hole was secure. Where were they getting their information?

"Set up the protection sequence, Max. Make sure you tell the system to protect the two women."

"Yes, Fee. In the meantime, if you would please take a position behind me, so I can better protect you."

Fee snorted and considered not doing what he said, just to be petulant. But he was right. He had a super hard metal outer than she'd designed herself, and if anyone came smashing through that door guns blazing, she'd at least be protected from a bullet.

She crouched down and pulled up the live feed of the cameras in the apartment. The sequence had already started. The lights were out, and two of the five men had been electrocuted by touching something metal in the room. They were lying knocked out on the floor. She'd been careful to make sure the levels weren't fatal. It was the last thing she needed.

The other three men were holding up their guns, looking around in agitation for an enemy to shoot. It was a pity Fee didn't intend to give them an easy target.

The next step was the gas, which smoked out from multiple surfaces around the room, filling the small space. A couple of the men panicked and tried to leave through the front door and the small balcony. Both had been locked. Alberta and her mother fell first, knocked out by the powerful gas. The bigger men took longer, and fought harder against the inevitable ending. When she was sure all five men were completely unconscious, Fee stood up.

"Let's go clean up this mess," she said.

"Indeed," said Max.

CHAPTER 36

*H*enry looked up when another nurse came into his small hospital room. She was younger, had a geometric bob of black hair, and seemed less like a typical nurse than the previous woman.

Henry grinned from ear to ear. "Rilla! What are you doing here?"

"I had to come make sure you were okay. Frankie was going wild back at the Carnival, ranting about saving you. So we decided to send out a rescue party."

She came over and gave Henry a huge hug.

Henry felt tears pricking at his eyes; it was so good to see Rilla. He blinked them away and smiled again when Rilla leaned back and stared at him as if she were trying to make sure he was okay just by looking at him.

"We've been pushing Carnival magic at you, so you should be mostly healed by now," she said. "It helps that I'm so close."

Henry nodded and pulled his arm up and down on the same side where he'd been shot. "I'm almost up for an escape attempt," he said with a grin.

Rilla nodded. "This is just a scouting mission, to make sure you're okay, and to figure out the patterns of the staff and the officers guarding your door." She sat down on the bed beside him.

Henry raised his eyebrows. "I have guards? I feel honored."

"I'm not sure it's an honor to be arrested, Henry. I send you down to Tampa for a simple one-month contract, and you end up in Little Rock, Arkansas with a bullet wound and a police record."

Henry shook his head and grinned. "I'm a little shell shocked myself."

"Frankie said something about a girl called Fee?" Rilla asked softly.

Henry leaned forward. "We have to help her. She's in danger, and not just because the FBI are looking for her."

"Frankie's been doing research. These Witch Hunters are really bad news." Rilla shook her head slightly. "I don't know if we can take them on and win. They're everywhere. We need to stay under their radar." She said the words softly, and Henry felt the stirrings of a chill on his neck.

"You're not trying to say you don't want to help her, are you?" he said.

Rilla shook her head. "Of course not, Henry." She paused. "But once we've made sure she's okay, I don't think she's someone we can allow into the Carnival long term. It's too dangerous. What if the Witch Hunters find out about us through her?" Rilla looked down at Henry. "They're fanatical, Henry. Did Frankie tell you what happened last time? Fifty people died. We can't risk that."

"So you're telling me not to get too close, because we can't keep her?" said Henry, a pain in his stomach, which had nothing to do with the bullet he'd just had removed.

"I'm sorry, Henry. I really am."

∾

FEE LOOKED AROUND THE ROOM. She had the five men all trussed up like Sunday roasts, in a line by the door. Alberta and her mother were lying on the bed. She'd give them the antidote soon, but she'd wanted time to sort out what she was going to do first.

She stood looking down at the biggest of the men. He was brawny with a full beard and a scowl even when he was unconscious. She gave him a sharp kick in the leg just for trying to kidnap her. Again.

"What are we going to do, Max?" she asked.

"We need to get rid of these men, and get out of here, Wild Feather." Max was obviously feeling better. He'd gone back to using her full name.

"And just how are we going to get rid of five large men without anyone noticing?"

"That will be a problem."

"Perhaps we don't need to get rid of them. They obviously know about this place, so it's compromised now. We could just leave them here."

"That would seem to be the best idea. But before we go anywhere, I believe we need to check our other guests for any tracking devices."

Fee glanced over at Max. She'd programmed him well. It was the only way they could have possibly discovered her so fast.

"Have you checked on me?" she asked softly.

"You are clean. I have not had a chance to check the other two yet."

Fee silently followed Max into the bedroom, and stood at the end of the bed looking down at the two unconscious women.

"What will we do if it is one of them?" asked Max.

Fee sighed. "It doesn't necessarily prove they're guilty of anything. Someone could be using them."

"It doesn't seem probable," replied Max, moving closer to one side of the bed. One of his many tentacle arms came out, and waved slowly over Alberta's body.

"Clean," he said.

He moved to the other side of the bed, and the same tentacle waved over her mother. Fee was so tense and stiff she could have been used to build a house. A beeping noise started up around her mother's ankle. "Not clean," said Max. "Low-level tracking device under the skin. It appears to be around a scar and a break in the bone."

"You're saying it could have been done while she had a broken ankle? That maybe she didn't know?"

"I think it's unlikely, but I thought you would want to know there was a chance," replied Max. "You seemed hopeful. What would you like to do?"

"Can we cut it out?"

"Yes."

"Then let's do it now, before she comes to."

Max left the room to gather the essential items. Fee stood staring at her mother for a moment. She looked peaceful, her hair flowing out around her face, even a slight smile on her lips like she was having a good dream while she was under. A small childish part of her wanted her mother to be innocent. But the more rational cynic said there was no way it was true.

Even knowing her mother probably had helped the Witch Hunters track her, Fee couldn't bring herself to leave her behind. What if they hurt her because she failed? What if she really *was* innocent, whispered a taunting voice deep inside.

Max returned to the room, a scalpel, water, towels, and bandages in his many hands.

"We do not have the luxury of time, Fee. She will waken at any moment."

Fee nodded and grabbed the knife. "Where is it?" she asked.

Max showed her where, and after a brief hesitation, Fee cut into the skin. She found the device quickly and then patched up the small wound.

Holding the tiny device between her fingers, Fee took a moment to understand its makeup. It was smaller than half her pinky nail; nothing flashy, it just did a job and that was it. She glanced at Max. No extra quirks or personality disorders in this device.

The buzz of the mobile phone in her pocket made Fee jump, and she fumbled to get at it.

"Hello?" It was Henry's phone, but she was hoping Frankie might ring back and reassure her that she was doing the right thing.

"Hello? Is that Fee?" a woman's voice asked.

Fee paused. "Yes." Had the police found her so quickly?

"This is Rilla. Henry's Ringmaster," she said then paused. "His boss," she amended.

"Oh. Hi. Henry's..."

"I know where he is. He was worried about you."

"Frankie told me to run. So, I ran."

"Frankie was right. If they'd arrested you, I'm not sure how long you would have survived. Where are you now?"

Fee paused. How much should she tell Rilla? She didn't even know if she really was whom she said she was. "We're in a safe place." She looked around at the blood. "Well it used to be safe. Not so much now."

"We can help you, but you have to meet up with us. Tell me where you are, and I'll come get you."

Fee shook her head. "No. I don't know you. I'm not going anywhere with you."

"If you can't trust me, then listen to Henry." There was a rustling as the phone was passed over to someone else.

"Hey, Fee," said Henry softly. "Let Rilla help you." He sounded sad, and Fee was immediately on edge.

"What's the matter?"

"Aside from being shot and arrested?" he said, a smile returning to his voice.

Fee smiled back, even though he couldn't see her. "Well, yes. Aside from that."

"I'm fine, Fee. But you need to meet up with Rilla, let her and the others help you."

"Does she know about my mom and Alberta?"

"Yes. I've told her what happened."

"We were tracked to my apartment," she said softly.

There was a pause at Henry's end. "Are you okay?"

"We're all fine. I had a few things up my sleeve."

"How were you tracked?" he said.

"I just cut a small tracking device out of my mother's ankle. She was leading them to us the whole time. They wanted us to rescue her. Or at least had a contingency plan in place." Fee felt like the pain was in her voice, plain for Henry to hear.

"Then it's even more important to let Rilla help you. Wait. Did you say you cut it out?"

"She's unconscious. One of the security measures in my apartment. I've also got five unconscious men here that I don't know what to do with."

"Geez, Fee. I leave you alone for a couple of hours, and you get yourself into even more trouble." Henry sounded more amused than exasperated.

Fee smiled. It was good to talk to Henry again. "So I should meet with Rilla, huh?"

"Pack everything you need up from your apartment, including your mother and Alberta, and get out of there as soon as you can. Leave the tracking device there and meet Rilla at the Starbucks on Main and third."

"It's not exactly on my way," she said, trying to find a way out of doing what he was saying.

Henry ignored her. "Leave the others in the car, and go meet Rilla. Once you've met with her, you'll feel more comfortable, and you can follow her to the Carnival's place."

"I hope it's better than this one," joked Fee.

"Be there in an hour, Fee. Promise me."

Fee paused, trying to find a reason to do this without his help. "I promise," she whispered.

HENRY LOOKED UP AT RILLA.

"I'm sorry, Henry," she said. "I see I was too late."

"What do you mean?"

"You're already in love with her."

Henry shook his head, rejecting the idea out of hand. "I've only known her a week. I like her, sure. But I'm not in love with her."

Rilla smiled sadly at him. "So I have an hour to get there?"

Henry nodded. "Who else is here?"

Rilla paused. "Your father and Garth. Plus Jason."

"All of them? Just to rescue little old me?"

"We're not just rescuing you, Henry. We have to figure out a way to prove that you're not involved in a bombing."

Henry sobered. "I know. I'm not entirely sure how to do that."

"We'll figure it out. But first, I have to go find this Fee of yours."

"You've already made it clear that she can't be mine," said Henry tightly. He might not be in love with her, but it sure hurt to think of leaving Fee behind.

Rilla nodded sadly, and kissed him on the cheek. Just as she turned to leave the room, Special Agent Franklin came through the door. Henry held his breath and tried not to look at Rilla as she held it open and kept her head down.

"Special Agent," said Henry with a forced joviality.

"Mr. Kokkol."

"How can I help?"

"It's not how you can help me. It's how I can help you." Franklin smiled.

"You'll have to be a little less cryptic," said Henry, finally breathing easy as the door shut behind Rilla.

"The team down in Tampa doesn't believe you had anything to do with the bombing. They're willing to let you go without being charged. All you have to do is tell us what you know about Fee."

"Fee? You still believe she's the prime suspect?"

"She's our main lead. That's all I'm willing to say at this time."

"I'm not going to tell you anything. She's innocent. In fact, she's the target. You should be protecting her, not harassing her."

"You're not protecting her by not telling us anything, Mr. Kokkol. If we had her in custody, we could get the real story. She'd be more likely to be exonerated," Franklin said persuasively.

Henry shook his head. "I'm not telling you anything."

"Then you risk being arrested for aiding and abetting a criminal, Mr. Kokkol."

"I don't know where she is, or what she's doing. I barely know the girl. I only met her a week ago. You'd be better off asking the guys she worked with." Henry looked Franklin in the eyes and dared the agent not to believe him.

"We believe you know more than you're saying. Unless

you're willing to cooperate, you will be charged as an accomplice."

Henry shrugged. There wasn't much more he could say.

"I'll give you time to think about it," said Franklin, before turning and striding out the door.

Henry watched the door for a long time after that, trying to figure out if he was better off telling them what he knew or keeping quiet.

CHAPTER 37

Fee stood in line at Starbucks, trying to figure out which of the women in the coffee house was Rilla. It was busy, most of the tables filled, and no one looked particularly obvious or suspicious.

Until she flicked her gaze over an older man with the same golden eyes as Henry. She locked eyes with him, and knew he was related to Henry. She blinked and looked away, smiling at the young girl in front of her who was asking for her order.

"Tall caramel macchiato, please," she said absently. As she waited for her drink, she kept glancing his way. Every single time, his grizzled stare was fixed in her direction. She ended up tapping her finger nervously as she waited.

When she had her drink, she took a sip and walked over to the table that held a beautiful woman with striking blue eyes, and the older man she'd already noticed. He was solid, had lines of experience over his face, and saw far too much when their eyes met.

"Fee?" said the woman, her face crinkling into a reserved smile as she stood and held out a hand.

Fee nodded, not saying anything. She held out her hand reluctantly, and Rilla shook it.

"I'm Rilla. This is Viktor, Henry's dad."

She nodded. Of course he was. Viktor remained seated and didn't hold out his hand. Fee was relieved. "Nice to meet you both."

"Please sit down."

Fee hesitated and glanced toward the exit.

"Please, Fee. We're here to help."

Fee sighed and sat down. She took a moment to study Rilla and, for the first time, saw the aura of competency that surrounded her. She was more than simply an attractive face. The reason Fee hadn't noticed was her preoccupation with Viktor. She risked another glance at him; he was still staring hard at her, his fuzzy brows beetled down over his eyes. She didn't sense anything menacing, but he was concentrating on her far beyond what was considered polite.

"Can I help you?" she asked him frostily, her annoyance overcoming her nerves.

"I'm just trying to figure you out. My boy's been nothing but sweet dreams and plain sailing all his life, and now, since he met you, he's been blown up, shot at, and arrested. I'm just trying to figure out what you did that turned him wicked."

Fee sat up straighter. "He hasn't turned wicked. And to be fair, he wasn't blown up. We weren't even there when it happened. The rest of it isn't his fault."

"I know it ain't his fault. I'm sayin' it's yours."

"It's not my fault either," said Fee, hotly. "I didn't ask them to become fixated on me. And I could have maybe tried to get rid of them years ago, but I didn't know they were going to find me again or how dangerous they were. Or that they cared that much about getting rid of me." She said the last on a whisper, wishing she'd just kept her mouth shut.

Viktor turned to Rilla. "You understand any of that muddle?"

Rilla smiled. "Somewhat. You were raised by the Witch Hunters?"

Fee nodded. "Although I didn't know they were Witch Hunters."

Viktor snorted. "How could you not know something like that?"

Fee shook her head. "I don't know. I've asked myself that every day since I escaped from them. Why *didn't* I know?" Fee thought of her mother. "I suppose we have someone we could ask now. Summer Dawn is in the car." They looked at her blankly. "My mother."

Rilla leaned forward. "Look, Fee, we have to make some decisions and fast. We have to get Henry out of that hospital and away from the police. We have to figure out how to get the charges dropped for the pair of you and we need to get ourselves away from the Witch Hunters without getting hurt. But I can't do all of that if I'm worried about you trusting us. Will you come with us now, and let us get you out of this situation?"

Fee looked at both of them, a small frown on her face. Could she trust them? Did she have a choice? She sighed. "I'll help you get Henry out of this predicament. I owe him that."

"What will you do once this is resolved?" said Rilla softly. "I don't think you'll be able to go back to Tampa."

Fee gazed back at her. "I don't know," she said. "Go somewhere far away, I guess." Maybe she could go to an island in the Pacific. She'd heard it was nice over there.

But a tiny part of her was thinking she should fight back against the Witch Hunters. Instead of hiding, she should show them that it wasn't nice to pick on people.

One thing she knew was that no matter how she might

feel about him, she couldn't involve Henry in her fight. She'd have to leave him behind, and that stung.

As Fee walked back to the car, she wondered if she'd done the right thing. But Rilla and Viktor had convinced her that they could be trusted—to a point—and she needed help just now. She had too many people depending on her, and she didn't know how she was going to get Henry out of this mess, let alone herself.

"We're following that green pickup truck," she said to Alberta as she climbed back into the Charger. "I need you to keep an eye on it as well, in case I lose it."

"Where are we going now?" asked Alberta. She glanced anxiously back at Fee's mother in the back seat as she said it. "We need somewhere she can rest up."

Fee looked at Alberta. "She brought it on herself. Don't go feeling sorry for her."

"Fee, I promise," said her mother. "I didn't know about it. I broke that ankle a year back. They must have put it in then." Her mother was repeating the mantra she'd been saying since she woke up and found her ankle bandaged.

"If it's any consolation, that matches the time frame I concluded for the break in my assessment," said Max.

Her mother shuddered where she was sitting curled up in the back seat. She still hadn't adjusted to Max.

Fee pulled out into the traffic, trying to keep the pickup in sight. It turned just up ahead of her, and she followed it around the corner. She didn't have time to figure out whether her mother was lying or not. She had to put her full attention into making sure she didn't lose Rilla.

They drove in silence for the next fifteen minutes, sliding in and out of the traffic, and turning unexpectedly a few times. Rilla eventually turned into the driveway of an old three-story house in the outskirts of the city. Fee parked the Charger behind her.

They all climbed out, carrying their few possessions with them. Max was carrying a bag of items including clothes and toiletries they'd deemed useful from the apartment, and Fee had their hurriedly packed bags from Tampa.

"This way," said Rilla, climbing out of the truck. She glanced at Fee's mother. "I'll get someone to come and carry you up." She ran ahead up the stairs.

"That your robot?" asked Viktor, eyeing Max as he came around the back of the truck.

Fee sighed quietly. Another person who was wary of her machines. "Yes. His name is Max."

But Viktor surprised her. "Very nicely designed, young lady. Very nice indeed." He nodded, and Fee felt an unusual warmth flood her cheeks. It felt good to have someone appreciate her work.

She reminded herself Henry had appreciated it from the start, too. She just hadn't always been open to his appreciation.

They walked to the base of the stairs, and another couple of men, both much younger than Viktor, greeted them.

"This is Garth, and Henry's brother, Jason." Rilla directed them to help Alberta and Fee's mother up the stairs. They followed Rilla into a large living room with a view over the city. Fee went to the window and looked out, trying to gather her thoughts.

Once everyone was settled, Rilla turned to Fee's mother. "We need some answers to help us fix this situation, and it occurs to me that you're uniquely placed to answer them."

Fee's mother nodded. "You're going to help Wild Feather and her friend?"

Rilla glanced over at Fee. "Wild Feather?" she said dryly.

Fee rolled her eyes at her mother. "I go by Fee these days, Mom." She turned to Rilla. "And yes, Wild Feather. My mother is Summer Dawn and my father is Falling Leaf. Now that's over with, let's get on, shall we?"

Rilla grinned. "My full name is Amaryllis, so I feel your pain, Fee."

Fee smiled at Rilla. "That makes sense. Henry did say something about strange names at the Carnival as well."

Viktor cleared his throat. "Can we get on with the task at hand?"

Rilla glanced at Viktor then went to sit down beside Fee's mother. "Summer Dawn, we need information on the Witch Hunters. I need you to answer my questions about them."

"Just call me Summer. I will tell you anything I can to help."

"Okay, Summer. How long have you been a part of the Witch Hunters?"

"Ever since I met Fee's father. He was very persuasive on the topic. He convinced me that the world was a bad place, and that by living as we did, without any form of technology, we were absolving ourselves of sin. Hunting magic users was another part of that. He said they were the work of the devil, and sometimes it did seem like that. We came across some very bad people."

"What changed your mind?"

She glanced at Fee. "When he tried to harm Fee, I started to doubt. Over the years after that, I watched closely, and things I hadn't noticed before started to seem glaringly obvious."

She stopped, and seemed to get lost in her own world.

"What do you mean?"

"I mean that magic is often hereditary and I don't have any."

It took a moment for her mother's words to sink in. "You mean my father has magic?"

Summer nodded. "Most true Witch Hunters have a small amount. It's how they track their prey. It's considered a necessary evil, and they pray to be absolved every time they use it. But your father has more than his fair share and he uses it in his quest."

"What kind of magic does he have?"

"Finding magic for a start. Once he knows someone or has a picture, something of that person, he can find them anywhere."

The breath left Fee's body. He could find her anywhere? "Then how come he didn't find me?"

"You seem to have the magic to counter his. He's been going crazy trying to find you Fee."

"How did he manage it in the end?"

"I'm not entirely certain. Some kind of finding spell that he put on another person. I didn't really understand how it worked."

"How come Fee didn't know anything about the Witch Hunters before she left?"

Summer sighed. "The ideals are ingrained in our children, they just don't realize it. Everything we teach is intended to push them toward our ultimate goal of ridding the world of sinners. But they are not truly initiated into the church until they turn eighteen. If they are going to develop magic, it will have happened by then. A long ritual process ensures they are ready. Fee was two months from her eighteenth birthday when she showed us her creatures. Her magic had taken over, and she'd succumbed to the evil inside."

"Is that really what you believe about me? That I'm evil?" asked Fee quietly.

Summer shook her head. "Of course not. But that's what

your father believes. He will do anything for his cause, including kill his own daughter."

Fee knew it. Had known it for a long time, but to hear the words out of her mother's mouth was a whole other kettle of fish. She rocked back in her chair, struggling to stay calm. How was she ever going to get away from them, if her father was a magic-using tracker who was obsessed with killing her? She closed her eyes and tried to breathe normally.

"If he's usin' magic, how come nobody does anythin' about him?" asked Viktor.

"He's got a powerful hold over everyone at the farm," said Summer. "And I think he's fairly powerful in the hierarchy of the Witch Hunters, too."

"How many are there all together?" asked Rilla.

"They are careful to stay under the radar and there are a finite number of positions available. It's considered an honor to be part of the group, and they don't want just anyone. And not everyone who lives at the farm is actually a Witch Hunter. At least, not in the full sense. I was part of it, but I was never a true Witch Hunter."

"But how many?" repeated Rilla.

"There are fifty true Witch Hunters, the warriors who lead us. They're all highly skilled, focused individuals who would do anything for the cause."

Fee breathed in. Fifty? That didn't seem so bad.

Then she thought of fifty men like her father, all of them focused on her, and she shuddered. It was enough to make her run screaming. She managed to stay seated. At least for now.

CHAPTER 38

*H*enry lay on the bed, staring at the ceiling, trying not to feel like his world was gone mad.

He remembered how he'd felt a week and a half ago, standing outside the Callaghan Tech building, not wanting to go in. Maybe he had some kind of previously un-realized pre-cognition talent? He'd certainly been right about this contract.

He wished he'd said no to Rilla and Jack and just stayed home.

But Fee's bright green eyes popped into his head, and he couldn't completely regret it. Maybe she wasn't someone he'd have a long-term relationship with, but he'd enjoyed their time together, and she'd made him realize that he didn't know everything there was to know about the world.

He thought of her little robots and smiled. A movement under his pillow and a little chittering noise told him that his buddy was still with him. It was the kleptomaniac critter, because things kept going missing and appearing in his bedside drawer, and it kept undoing his handcuffs. Henry'd put them back on his wrists at least five times this morning.

"We have to maintain appearances," he'd whispered to the robot. "If they know I can get out, they'll make it harder on me. First rule of gambling. Don't let them know your hand straight away. Frankie would know what I'm talking about."

A noise at the door was his only warning before Special Agent Franklin stormed in through it. "I don't know how you're doing it, but you can stop right now. Give me back my badge."

Henry just stared at Franklin, desperately hoping the badge wasn't in the drawer next to his bed. "I don't know what you're talking about," he said.

"It was my keys earlier—and I know I didn't accidentally leave them on your damn table—and now my badge is gone. If you don't give it back, I'm going to charge you with burglary."

"How is it burglary?" said Henry, bemused.

"All right, theft then. But I'll damn-well throw the book at you."

There was a tiny chittering noise behind him, and Henry closed his eyes for a second. He knew then that he was going to find the badge tucked away in the drawer. "Maybe you left it here by mistake? Again."

"Where the hell is it?" Franklin's voice was menacing, and Henry knew he'd been pushed too far.

"Try the drawer next to my bed," he said.

Franklin stormed over to the table, and pulled open the drawer. Then he stopped. Henry leaned over and looked. "Holy sugar," he said. "I didn't realize..."

Inside the drawer was a huge pile of items, including four police badges still inside their leather wallets, several nurse nametags, a few empty soda cans, and a hair tie.

"You've got four of them?" exploded Franklin. "That's impossible! How did you do it?"

Henry shook his head. He didn't know how the little

creature was doing it, but he suspected it had a touch of Fee's magic working in its favor. No way was he going to be able to explain that one to an FBI agent. He considered giving up his buddy to its fate, but figured they might confiscate him, and then he'd never get him back. He remembered Fee's face when the other two had been crushed at his apartment. She'd never forgive him.

"Uh. It's a special...skill."

"Because you're a carny? I've done some digging on you, Mr. Kokkol. Contracting to a flash technology company was a scam, wasn't it? You're just a carnival worker," Franklin sneered.

Henry widened his eyes. As many times as he experienced it, the prejudice against carnies from outsiders always blindsided him. "They know where I'm from. I'm good with machines, and that's what they needed on the project."

"I'll be checking with Callaghan, and I'm pretty sure I know what I'm going to find." Franklin grabbed the four badges out of the drawer and stalked to the door. "This isn't the last of this," he said before going through the door, and pulling it shut.

"Now look what you've done, you silly little critter. He wasn't so bad at the beginning. Now he's riled up like a chipmunk on acid. That is not what I call lying low."

The little creature came out from under the pillow, chittering away at Henry. He could swear it was being apologetic, waving its little arms around over its head.

"I know you can't help it. I get that. But you need to learn to use your powers for good instead of evil."

The critter seemed to nod its head, and then stopped, as if waiting for Henry's next words.

Henry cleared his throat. He had no idea how to help the little critter steal the right kind of stuff. But he put his head to one side, and stared at it, considering the options.

"Well, you could try to get me some kind of map of this place in case I have to escape on my own. That would be helpful."

It chittered away, nodding its head, and then disappeared down the side of the bed. He watched it closely, and finally managed to catch its point of exit—a little grate down one side of the room, that it speedily unscrewed using previously hidden electric screw drivers on its body. He had to hand it to Fee. She thought of everything.

FEE WAS STRUGGLING NOT to stand up and pace. She was trying to remain calm, to listen, and plan with the others. They were still sitting around in the apartment, trying to get information from Alberta and Summer. Viktor, Garth, and Henry's brother Jason were just watching as Rilla grilled them.

She knew Rilla was right; they needed to gather information before they determined their plan of action. But it was hard, knowing Henry was in there and she was out here.

Again, Rilla had said he was fine, but Fee was sure Henry would have put on a brave face for his Ringmaster. He'd been *shot* for crying out loud. Shot because of her, no less.

Fee stood, and took a casual turn of the room, trying not to be too obviously impatient.

"So what would have happened to Fee if she hadn't been magical? Or had kept it hidden?"

Summer paused. "She would have become a full Witch Hunter. Her father had great hopes for her."

"What?" Fee burst out, horrified. She came to a stop in front of her mother.

Summer looked over at her, sadness in her eyes. "He was very proud of you. Learning that you were magic almost broke him. He's changed since then." She paused. "It hardened him, made him less forgiving."

Jason shook his head. "Great, so we have some hard, unforgiving maniac after my brother, and possibly after us. Just another day at the office." He rolled his eyes at his father and Garth, who both looked sternly back at him.

"I wouldn't have joined the Witch Hunters," said Fee, ignoring Jason's attempt at humor.

"Your father can be very persuasive on the topic. In all my years, I've never seen anyone leave after finding out." Summer looked at her sadly.

"What about Tall Oak? He ran away." Fee still remembered her teenage crush running away.

Summer blinked. "I'd forgotten about him and his girlfriend. Okay, yes, he left. But mostly they didn't and after you left, your father stopped taking chances. He had all the teenagers watched for signs of magic."

"Did he find anyone else?" whispered Fee. This was the very reason she'd installed Alberta at the house.

Summer looked away for a moment. Her eyes, when she looked back, were dark with sorrow. She didn't answer Fee's question.

"Who? What did he do to them?"

"Little Willow," Summer said reluctantly.

"What. Did. He. Do. To. Her?" said Fee.

"He...killed her."

Fee sat down abruptly. She'd known Little Willow, played with her when they were younger. Little Willow had been a couple of years younger than she was, a pretty, blonde girl with big eyes and a shy smile. Fee felt sick.

She'd put Alberta into the house, assuming that the older woman would be able to somehow protect the children. Or at least, tell her so she could get them away. To learn that she'd been kidding herself, and that another child had been harmed... She should have tried to destroy her father when she could.

"Where is he now?" asked Rilla softly.

Summer shook her head, her long hair falling in gentle waves around her head.

Fee put her head in her hands. Would she have agreed to become a Witch Hunter once she'd turned eighteen? She didn't know. It seemed a little farfetched; wouldn't she have seen it for the terrible organization that it was? If she'd seen her father doing anything to Little Willow, she would have known, wouldn't she? A terrible fear was running through her that maybe she wouldn't have.

Fee put her head back up. Of course, she would have. She glanced over at her mother, waiting for the answer to Rilla's question. She'd failed Little Willow, but she wasn't going to fail anyone else.

"I don't know where he is. But he's searching for Fee; that much I know. He won't rest until he finds her."

"Who else is working with him? Who set the bomb in Tampa?" asked Rilla.

"I'm not sure. One of the younger members, that's all I know. He'd been deep under cover for some time, trying to find Wild Feather."

Rilla's mobile phone rang and she dragged it out of her pocket, answering it tersely.

She nodded a couple of times. "Yes. Okay. Thanks, Frankie. We'll get on it." She pressed the end call button. "We have to get Henry out of there. Frankie's found some chatter among the online Witch Hunters that they're making a move against Henry. They think he'll lead them to Fee. We need to get him out now."

Fee was the first to stand up.

Rilla looked at her and shook her head. "I'm sorry, Fee. But you're too recognizable. They'll arrest you immediately, which will basically hand you to the Witch Hunters on a plate. I can't allow that."

"But...I want to help," said Fee lamely. All of Rilla's arguments were sound. But that didn't change the fact that she wanted to come with them. "I could drive the car. I'll wait outside in the car and wait for you."

Rilla opened her mouth, and Fee could see she was going to say no.

"Please? It would mean a lot to me. I feel...responsible for Henry being in there. I need to help get him out."

Rilla glanced over at Viktor, who shrugged. "Couldn't hurt if she stayed in the car, I suppose."

"What do we do about these two," asked Jason, gesturing to Summer and Alberta.

Rilla smiled at Jason. "Glad you asked, Jason. You'll take them with you in Henry's car to the airport. Meet us at the plane."

"Plane?" said Fee.

"We came down in a friend's plane. It was faster and cheaper and there's enough room for all of us to get home."

"Doesn't Henry hate flying? Isn't that why he brought his car down here?"

Rilla sighed. "We don't have the luxury of pandering to his fear of flying. Worst comes to the worst, we'll just dose him up."

"And leave his car here?"

"Yes." Rilla sighed. "He's going to kill me, but we don't have a choice. The Witch Hunters are dangerous."

CHAPTER 39

$\mathcal{F}$ee sat in the truck and watched as Rilla, Viktor, and Garth walked through the hospital front entrance. Everything inside her was coiled tighter than a drum and she wasn't entirely sure why. They had seemed confident they'd be able to break Henry out without much of a problem.

Viktor had even joked about having broken Henry out of far worse places. Fee frowned, remembering the old man's comments about Henry being purer than virgin snow when they first met. She suspected she'd been played.

They'd only just gone inside when multiple police cars started screaming down the street, pulling to a halt outside the hospital doors. Fee counted seven police cars before giving up counting. Her heart was beating wildly as she wrapped sweaty hands around the steering wheel. She leaned forward, squinting into the distance. What the hell was happening?

Did they know what Rilla was planning to do?

The next minute a small blast rocked the bottom floor of the hospital. Glass rattled, but didn't break, which meant it wasn't a massive explosion. Almost immediately, smoke started billowing out the main entrance. Fee squinted, trying to figure out what was happening. The policemen started scurrying around like ants in a disturbed nest. If it hadn't been so serious, Fee might have laughed. As it was, she just sat there worrying about where Rilla, Garth, and Viktor might have been when it went off. Or was this part of their plan?

People started streaming out the doors, coughing, and struggling with the smoke. The more she thought about it, the more she was certain this wasn't supposed to happen. Rilla had talked about something much more subtle than another explosion. Which meant that they were too late. The Witch Hunters were making their move.

Fee spotted Rilla and then Viktor coming out of the building. They were both grabbed and herded to one side by police officers, along with every single other person leaving the building. At first, it seemed like it was because they were checking them for injuries. Then Fee saw them delaying anyone who tried to leave. They were all being detained for questioning. At first, she thought Garth had escaped, but eventually she saw him being directed to the same area. Her breath caught. All of Henry's rescuers were now immobilized.

Except her.

She licked her lips. She'd wanted to help rescue Henry. She just hadn't realized she'd end up being the only person able to do it. Climbing out of the truck, she slammed the door shut. She walked slowly toward the hospital building, trying to figure out where she should go. In front of her, a hospital worker dressed in blue turned briskly down the side of the main building, away from the turmoil at the front. Fee followed the man down a footpath, trying to stay far enough back that he wouldn't notice her.

He strode past the first building then down past another connected building and turned into an entrance at the back that was clearly toward the kitchens. Fee carefully peered through the door. Inside was a busy food preparation area, filled with people in the same blue coats.

She opened the door, and walked in, trying to seem like she belonged there. She needn't have worried. The noise in the room from several large extractor fans, the people talking, and the banging of pots and pans more than covered the sounds of her entry. She saw someone down the far end opening a closet full of the blue tunics. A plan started to form in her head. Walking over, Fee grabbed a tunic, and then hurried through a door on the other side of the room. It led out into a corridor, with doors down each side. Up ahead, she saw a couple of staff pushing delivery carts toward the elevators.

She pulled on the tunic, and walked into the room the others had just left.

"About time. I swear, you guys are hired because of your snail's pace ability rather than your speed," said a large man standing beside a row of metal carts.

"Sorry," mumbled Fee, trying not to look the man in the eyes.

"Here, take this to the third floor. The room numbers are on the sheet. And hurry about it."

Fee nodded, and grabbed the handle of the trolley, pushing it out the door before the man realized there was an alarm going off on the other side of the building.

She pushed it to the elevators, and pressed the button. Her hands were sweaty and she was convinced someone was going to put a hand on her shoulder at any moment and ask who the hell she thought she was.

The elevator pinged to say it was arriving, and she was so wound up, she jumped.

Taking a deep breath, she pushed the trolley into the elevator car, and pressed the button for level four. In the small space of the elevator, Fee felt like her heart was trying to escape from her body. The walls of the elevator car towered over her, and the camera recording the lift's occupants seemed designed to catch her in the act. They'd see her face and know she wasn't a hospital worker.

She didn't know how she'd made it this far.

The elevator pinged for the fourth floor, and Fee steeled her shoulders. She could do this. Henry needed her help, and she was going to give it. It was her fault he was in this mess.

The trolley made a crashing noise as it bumped its way over the exit to the elevator, and several eyes turned in her direction as she walked out into the corridor. But as soon as they saw her blue tunic and the food trolley, everyone went back to what they'd been doing. The nurses at the nurses' station ignored her, and the patients wandering the corridor didn't even seem to notice her.

She wiped one sweaty palm down the side of her borrowed tunic. Rilla had said he was on the fourth floor, but she'd never mentioned the room number. Her heart still racing, Fee tried to make herself walk slowly down the corridor, back toward the main building. There was a connecting tunnel, and she pushed the trolley down it, not looking left or right.

She was just about to turn into the patient's wing, when a large woman in a nurse's uniform stepped in front of her trolley. "Where do you think you're going?" she said.

CHAPTER 40

A chittering sound woke Henry. It was late afternoon, and the sun was glaring through the window next to his bed. His little thieving critter was bouncing around on the pillow beside his face.

"What is your problem?" grumbled Henry and he rubbed his eyes.

Its chittering increased and he looked again. A series of maps lay on the bed just down from his pillow. Another police badge and a gun were on top of it.

A gun.

"Oh, jeez! Now we're in for it. You can't steal a policeman's gun and have him take it calmly," said Henry, exasperation in his voice. "Now I have to figure out how I'm going to get it back to him without him noticing."

The creature seemed to wilt in front of him. It dropped to the pillow like a dog being told off.

Henry sighed. "You did very well to find the maps. I'm sure that can't have been easy." He didn't have the heart to hurt the feelings of the tiny robot.

It perked up again and started gesturing toward the maps and outside the room.

Henry frowned. It almost seemed like the little critter was telling him to get out.

Now that he noticed it, there was some extra noise going on outside his window. He lifted his arm, and saw that the critter had already unlocked his handcuffs. Henry stood and pushed aside his bedcovers, walking cautiously over to the windows. Directly below were more than a dozen police cars, smoke billowing out the main doors, and police officers running around, herding people, and trying to calm the general mayhem. A news helicopter was flying overhead.

"What's happening out there, little fella?" he asked. "I think I'm going to get dressed, just in case."

Henry grabbed his jeans and shirt from the chair next to his bed. He picked up the map, and hesitated over the badge and gun. But in the end, figured they might be useful if he was about to try an escape. He sighed, put the badge in his pocket, and tucked the gun in the back of his jeans. It wasn't comfortable, but it kept it hidden.

His little critter was now gesturing at the ceiling. Henry looked up and saw a tiny manhole above his bed. "You want me to get out through there?" he said. The critter nodded.

"Is it really necessary?"

The critter nodded again, jumping up and down on the bed.

A crash from outside his room galvanized Henry into action. He climbed on his bed, reached up, pushed aside the door to the ceiling vent, and attempted to pull himself up. Something crawled up his leg at the speed of light, and he almost let go, but it was just the critter making its way ahead of him. It strained his weakened muscles, but he managed to haul himself up, and replace the cover. Sometimes a carnival upbringing had its uses.

He was just about to crawl along the tight air vent tunnel, when the door to his room crashed open. Henry stilled, wondering if he'd made the right decision. He was now on the run—albeit for a crime he didn't commit—from the police. It was going to be hard to live that one down.

"He's not here!" said an agitated voice.

"Of course he is. Look under the bed." The second voice chilled Henry's blood. David. There was only one reason Fee's amenable co-worker would be here.

"I have! He's gone. He must have been warned by all the damn sirens." The first voice was now accusatory. "I told you that was too much."

"I didn't know they'd get here so fast. Who the hell knew they were so damn efficient around here," said David. He sounded ruffled, as if he was barely keeping it together.

Henry held himself rock still, not even breathing. The pumping of his blood was so noisy they must hear it.

"What do we do?" asked the other man.

"We search this room, and then we search every damn room on this floor. He has to be around here somewhere. I'm not going to let him or Fee get away from me after all this time."

They searched the room and, finding nothing, they stormed out again.

"Thanks, little buddy. I owe you one," whispered Henry.

His critter chattered in response, although much quieter than usual Henry noted. At least it had a sense of self-preservation.

Henry began to crawl along the vent shaft, wondering which way he should go. Away from his room was his only thought for the moment. He was sure it would occur to them eventually to search the ceiling and ductwork. Henry soon found a rhythm in the dark vents; it wasn't so different from climbing in and out of awkward places to fix carnival rides.

"We're going to have to get out of here sometime," he whispered to his critter. It bounced against his hip, and paper rustled in his pocket. The maps, of course.

Henry pulled them out, and flicked through them until he found one with both the vent system overlaid over the room schematics for the fourth floor. He whistled under his breath and glanced down at his buddy. "Man, you're a lot smarter than I gave you credit for," he whispered.

It bounced and chittered.

He saw a supply room up ahead. "I need something to wear so I'm a bit more anonymous," he whispered. "I'm thinking I'll find it there."

He crawled laboriously along the tunnel, taking his time to ensure he didn't make too much noise, and eventually found the vent hole he wanted. He put his head through and checked out the storeroom. Medical supplies lined the shelves, but in one corner was what he was really looking for, replacement scrubs for the orderlies and nurses. He flipped himself down, using a nearby shelf to make it to the ground then pulled a set of scrubs over his own clothes. They were a little tight, but it would do to get him out of the building.

He peered out around the corridor, but it was clear. Either the Witch Hunters had left, or they were staying out of the way because of the police. Either way was fine with him.

He strode down the corridor toward the exit he'd noticed on the map. He was heading toward the back of the building. No good going out the front entrance and being recognized by a sharp-eyed police officer.

He slowed as he heard voices arguing up ahead.

"I just do what I'm told, and I was told to come here, deliver this food. I'm not arguing. I'm just doing my job."

"Well, I'm telling you this ward isn't due for meals for

another hour. Let alone the fact we're supposed to be locked down because of the scare in the waiting room downstairs. I'm telling you, you've gone to the wrong floor first."

"I don't think so," said the other voice stubbornly.

Henry grinned. Fee was standing her ground, but she was going to lose against a head nurse. He turned the corner, and winked at a startled Fee.

"Look, she's obviously new. Shall I turn her around and take her back downstairs?" he said blithely, already turning Fee around and pointing her in the direction she'd obviously just came from. He pushed out a little persuasion magic at the nurse, hoping it would be enough to confuse her. All they needed was a couple of minutes.

The nurse puffed out her chest. "Just make sure you don't take too long. We have rounds shortly, and I don't want to be down a staff member."

"Absolutely. I'll be back."

Henry strode off, pulling a bemused Fee—and her trolley —beside him.

"How—"

"Shhh," said Henry. "She's probably got super-hearing. Those kinds of women always do. Amazingly organized, hugely efficient, won't bend the rules an inch, and can hear you a mile away."

Fee gave him an amused glance, but otherwise allowed him to lead her back to the bank of elevators.

She was wearing a blue tunic that she'd obviously scavenged from somewhere, and her face was a little flushed from her run in with the nurse, but she'd never looked more beautiful to Henry. He punched the button for the lifts, and managed to avoid the temptation to turn his head and see if the nurse could still see them. The doors opened, and they both entered the elevator, pushing the trolley ahead. He turned and winced when he saw the nurse standing at the end of the corridor still watching them, a frown on her face.

"How did you get into the hospital?" he asked as soon as the doors shut.

"I'm allowed to speak now?" she raised one eyebrow in his direction.

Henry didn't reply, he just pulled her toward him, and kissed her full on the lips. The usual electricity zinged between them, igniting into a fierce passion that pushed Henry over the edge. He hungrily devoured her lips, their tongues clashing desperately against each other. He wrapped her tight against his body, and would have pulled her to the ground and taken her then and there, if a little chittering noise hadn't brought him back to reality. The accompanying pinch on his ear by sharp little metal fingers didn't hurt either.

"Ow!" he said, pulling back and rubbing his ear.

Fee blinked owlishly up at him. "What happened?"

"Your little critter is being bossy. Unfortunately, he's probably right. We have to figure out where we're going. What level did you come in on? Where are the others?"

"Ground floor. Kitchens." Fee paused, and avoided his eyes for a moment.

"What's happened, Fee?" Henry said with a sense of foreboding.

"I think they're okay, but everyone else got caught up in the explosion out the front."

"Explosion!"

"It was only a small one, mostly just smoke I think. A distraction to let the Witch Hunters in."

Henry nodded. "Who's here?"

"Rilla, Viktor, and Garth. How come you're out of your room?"

"I had a hunch I needed to escape." A chittering noise on

his shoulder made him smile. "And it was the right thing to do. *You* were right, Fee. David is here. He's a Witch Hunter."

Fee took a step back and put her hand over her mouth. "He's here? He's really one of them?"

Henry nodded his head grimly. "That's why we need to get out of here as soon as we can."

Fee nodded. "Where do we get out?" She glanced around the elevator as if she was going to find an exit right there.

"First we need to ditch the cart." Henry glanced down at the bulky thing next to them.

Fee glanced down at it. "I don't want them to know I didn't deliver the food. We can't take it back to the kitchen level."

"We can leave it in the elevator. No one will know it was us."

"But not on the ground level. Too many possible people to see us leave it there."

Henry nodded. "We can stop on the first floor, dump the cart, and take the stairs the rest of the way down. Then go out the way you came in."

They still had their uniforms on, so that might also give them a little bit of protection. "I just hope there isn't some kind of rule against fraternization between nurses and kitchen staff."

Fee glanced at him. "There's bound to be. You had better have some kind of excuse ready in case someone questions you. I'll be okay; I'm wearing the kitchen staff uniform."

The door pinged and started to open on the first floor, and Henry moved forward.

The doors spread apart, revealing two police officers in the doorway. Henry cleared his throat, prepared to give some kind of excuse, but they stepped aside, and waved him past. He nodded at them and, heart pounding, walked out of the elevator. Behind him, he could hear the rattling of the trolley as Fee pushed it out of the elevator. He walked a little way down the corridor, not daring to turn around in case it gave them away. He could hear the cart clattering down the hallway behind him. The door of the elevator pinged shut, and he let out an explosive breath, turning to Fee. "Are you okay?" he said.

"That was too close," she replied, her face pale in the fluorescent hospital lighting.

"Come on, let's ditch this thing, and get out of here," said Henry, grabbing one side of the cumbersome contraption.

"Where's the best place?" she said, glancing around. "Maybe a supply closet?"

Henry opened a door along the corridor. Three patients looked up from their beds. "Anyone hungry?" he asked.

"About time," muttered a grumpy voice from the far end of the room. "They said it was all being held up because of some commotion out front. But that doesn't stop us from being hungry back here."

Henry motioned to Fee, and she pushed the cart into the room. He glanced at her, and then at the three older men, and together they handed out the food.

He tucked the trolley to one side of the room, and waved at the men. "Take care," he said, as he shut the door. "Now, where are the stairs?" He grabbed Fee's hand, and followed as she led them to the stairwell.

They were halfway down the stairs when the fire alarm started up.

"Do you think it's a real fire?"

Henry shook his head. "I doubt it. But it's to cover something. Either it's the Witch Hunters, or it's Rilla and the others trying to give us some cover. Hopefully, it's going to help us some," he said.

They raced down the stairs, bursting out of the stairwell, and following the smells of food cooking along the main corridor. Fee was still leading the way, although he couldn't make himself let go of her hand. Electricity charged between them; and for some reason, it calmed him. A little bit of magic was pulsing through their veins, helping speed them along the corridor.

In the kitchen, they found chaos, as the chefs were both trying to turn everything off, to finish what they were cooking so it wasn't ruined, and leave at the same time. They were all running around madly, and had no time to notice two more people sneaking through the room.

Outside, Henry took a deep breath of fresh air—tinged with smoke—and smiled. It felt good to be outside again.

"Come on, we have to go." Fee pulled him and he ran after her, along the side of the building and out onto the main street, where chaos reigned.

They were walking quickly along the street outside the hospital when a figure stepped out of the bushes in front of them.

"Hi, Fee. Hi, Henry. Good to see you again," said David, holding a gun in front of him.

CHAPTER 41

ee came to a crashing halt, and Henry banged up against her back.

"David. What are you doing?" she asked. It hurt to see him again, a gun held at her chest. She hadn't realized it would feel quite this bad to have her suspicions confirmed.

"My job. Ridding the world of people like you," said David, his voice filled with an emotion she couldn't decipher.

"What does that even mean? What did I ever do to you?" Fee's anger was surfacing. "Do you even realize the terrible things Witch Hunters do?"

"I know it's my duty, over everything else, to rid the world of disgusting magic users."

Something clicked in Fee's head. "Your fiancée," she whispered. "That's why you left your old life. It wasn't a choice; it was forced upon you. You turned eighteen and were told you had to give up everything else to become a Witch Hunter." Her voice was soft with compassion.

David's eyes went dark with anger. "Don't you presume to talk about my fiancée." He took a calming breath, as if reminding himself to be rational.

"How did you find me?" Fee asked, trying to stall for time.

"I've been following you for a long time," said David bitterly. "Useless lead after wrong turn for years on end. Even when I arrived at Callaghan, I thought it was another false lead. You didn't match any of the descriptions. I was about to move on." He glanced at Henry. "But then Henry arrived."

"The blue electricity?" whispered Fee.

David nodded. "And your little robots. When Henry mentioned them to us, I knew it was you."

Fee's stomach knotted. "And you planted the bomb?"

"Eugene wasn't supposed to get hurt. Just you." David's hand was shaking as he held the gun. "Come on," he said, gesturing for her to go ahead of him along the footpath. "We don't have time for chit-chat."

Fee glanced back at Henry. He nodded his head forward, indicating she should go where David was pointing.

Just as Henry walked past David, she felt rather than saw him leap at David. Turning quickly, Fee tried to see if she could help Henry. But it was over in seconds; Henry had punched David in the face, knocking him unconscious almost immediately. He grabbed his gun, and then Fee's hand in his and ran. "There are more of them. We have to get out of here."

The truck was down the street a little way. Fee pulled on Henry's hand when they neared it. "The truck," she said.

Henry shook his head. "Leave it for the others. We need to get out of here."

Fee ran after Henry trying not to think too hard about the possibility of someone shooting her in the back. Was that how her father did it? He had always avoided guns on the farm, so she didn't even know if that was allowed with the Witch Hunters. David was clearly a new breed, ready to take arms to make it happen. She thought back to the explosion in Tampa. More than just guns.

Henry ran a zigzagging path along the streets around the hospital, keeping to the smaller alleyways, and not stopping even for a moment. She was gasping for breath by the time he eventually slowed down. Even then, he kept them moving forward.

"Where are we going?" asked Fee.

"Home. We're going to meet the others back home."

Fee thought for a moment. "The Carnival?"

Henry nodded. "The Compound, at least. Where we live during the winter season."

"How are we going to get there?"

Henry glanced back at her. "Don't tell me you destroyed my car already?"

Fee gave a half smile. "Jason took it to the airport with my mother, Alberta, and Max."

"Then we have to get to the airport." Henry paused. "I can't believe you let Jason drive it."

"Rilla will want you to get on the plane with the rest of them," warned Fee.

"Then we'll get in and out of there before she even knows what I'm thinking."

He put up his hand and flagged down a taxi, and next thing Fee knew they were traveling down the freeway toward the airport.

They sat in the back, thighs touching, holding hands. So much had changed in the last two weeks. She had thought she was happy in her little hidey-hole in the back of the lab. If Henry hadn't come along, she would never have known what she was missing in life. She looked down at their clasped hands. Now she would.

"Have you still got my phone?" asked Henry.

Fee felt her jeans pocket, found the device and pulled it

out. "Here you go."

Henry pressed a couple of buttons, and then it was ringing. "Rilla? It's Henry. We're out. I have Fee with me." He listened for a moment. "Sure. We're heading for the airport now. Okay. Bye." Henry put the phone in his pocket, and settled back in the seat. "She's still at the hospital. The police say they're going to let them all go soon."

Fee nodded. She opened her mouth to ask Henry a question, but glanced at the driver in the front seat. They couldn't trust anyone. She closed her mouth, and leaned her head on Henry's shoulder instead.

They were silent the rest of the trip out to the small private airport.

When the taxi pulled up at the curb, Henry paid the driver, and Fee climbed out, looking around for his car. She spotted it down one end of the buildings. They walked toward it hand in hand.

Fee's head was filled with a million thoughts. "What are you going to say to Jason?" was all she asked.

"Not much. He'll understand." Henry sounded pretty certain.

"You're close to your brother?"

He nodded. "To all my brothers. We're a tight family, remember?"

Fee felt something stir inside her. Jealousy. She wanted to be part of Henry's family, to be someone he could talk to anytime. She pushed that thought down and concentrated on their immediate problem.

"What if Rilla has told him not to let you go?"

Henry shook his head. "It's not like that. Don't get me wrong, Rilla will be pissed when we take off in my car and drive home. But she'll get over it."

Fee thought about it for a minute. "Henry, why are we

taking the car?" she said. "We're here now; we can take the plane."

Henry stopped and grabbed both her hands, looking intently into her eyes. "They'll keep following you, no matter where you go, Fee. We have to do something about that. I have a plan and I need you to come with me for that plan to work."

Looking up into his golden eyes, Fee felt herself drowning. She realized she would do whatever he asked of her without question. It was a terrifying thought. She just nodded, unsure if her voice actually worked.

Henry gave her a quick relieved kiss on the lips, and then dragged her at a fast walk toward the car.

The keys were sitting in the driver's seat, and Henry looked down at them frowning.

"I figured you'd be along for them sooner or later, bro," said an amused voice from the shadows.

Henry grinned over to where Jason emerged from his hiding spot. He strode over to his brother and hugged him tightly.

"You gonna drive it home?" asked Jason.

Henry nodded. "Sure. I'm not leaving my baby here, am I?"

"I figured you'd be against that part of the plan. But I'd get out of here quick. Rilla and the others are due any minute."

"Did she call?"

"Yeah. Wanted to make sure everything was ready. I've got the other two on the plane." He cleared his throat. "The, uh, machinery, wanted to wait with the car."

Fee glanced back to where Max was waiting in the back seat. She grinned. He'd guessed what they would be doing. Not bad for 'machinery'.

Henry frowned. "You keep a close watch on Fee's mother, Jase. I'm not entirely certain we can trust her."

Jason shrugged. "She's been swept for bugs by Fee and her metal friend. The Carnival won't let her in if it senses that she means us harm. That's all we can do for now."

"Just keep an eye on her. That's all."

"Will do. Come on, bro, you better get going." Jason clamped him on the back and half-pushed Henry to the car. Fee climbed into the passenger's seat beside him.

Henry waved one arm out the window at his brother and backed his car out of the spot in one smooth motion. Fee waved goodbye from her seat and wondered why, yet again, it felt like such a final farewell.

HENRY'S HEAD was buzzing with ideas and they all focused on how to get Fee out of the bull's eye of her father's manic desire to kill her.

"Where are we going?" asked Fee.

"Back into Little Rock. I'm guessing David is still there. He doesn't know where we are and needs to sniff out another clue."

"I can't believe it was David," she said softly.

Henry clenched his hands around the steering wheel. He'd been the reason Fee had been discovered. "How long had he been on the team?"

Fee paused and took a breath as if trying to remember. "About six or seven months."

A chill went down Henry's spine at the sheer determination and patience involved in that kind of hunt. "He was just sitting there waiting for you to make a mistake."

"I was pretty careful. I didn't really talk much to the others, except about Violet. That trip you took us on was the first time I really interacted with them outside of work."

"I'm sorry," said Henry, his voice raw. "I didn't mean to help them find you." He glanced over at her.

Fee shrugged. "I know you didn't do it on purpose." Her hands were clenched in her lap.

"Still. I want you to know. It was the last thing I would have done."

"Thanks." She glanced over at him. "I appreciate that."

Henry felt his heart constrict at the expression on her face. She'd realized the lengths they'd go to in order to kill her and she was scared. But that wasn't going to happen. "We have to decide how we deal with him," he said.

Fee blinked. "What do you mean?"

Henry sighed. "They won't stop, Fee. That's what we've learned here today. They keep coming after you, using all their resources, forever. It's like having a human Terminator on your tail, except they're a little less dispassionate about why they want to kill you. It's more personal for the Witch Hunters."

Fee shivered and wrapped her arms around herself.

"I'm not trying to upset you, Fee." He put one hand on her shoulder and gave it a squeeze before putting it back on the steering wheel. "I have a plan. A way for you to get them off your tail."

"And what's that?" said Fee, staring out the window.

"We fake our deaths."

Fee's head whipped around to Henry. "What?"

"We make them think that we've died. I figure it's just like a circus act, and I've designed enough of those over the years. We just have to plan and execute it so that it appears that we died—probably in an explosion—and they don't need to chase us anymore."

"Why both of us?"

"They're suspicious of me too. I don't want to lead them to the Carnival, so I need to disappear as well."

"You can't do that! What about the people who love you?"

Henry shrugged. "I wasn't planning on leaving the Carnival. Just rejoining them under a different name."

Fee stared at him for a moment. "How will we do it?"

"David's not the only one who knows a little bit about fires and explosions. I'm sure between us we'll come up with something."

Fee was silent for a while, clearly thinking it over. Henry left her to it.

"Will I be officially dead? Or will I have access to my bank accounts and just be dead to the Witch Hunters?"

"I think, until we know their true reach, you need to be officially dead for a while. You can always go back and tell them it was a mistake later."

Fee nodded slowly, taking it all in. "Then I'd like to go to a bank before we blow ourselves up, and take a bit of money out to tide me over. Maybe buy myself a new persona."

"Sure. That's a good plan. Does that mean you're willing to fake-die with me?" Henry asked, a laugh in his voice.

Fee looked at him, her eyes intent on his face. "Sure. I'll fake-die with you."

CHAPTER 42

"If I'd known how much work went into fake-dying, I might have reconsidered it," muttered Fee as she lugged yet another heavy box of equipment up and down the stairs at the Carnival's house. Turned out Henry knew where the spare key was hidden, and he wasn't above using it, despite the annoyed phone call he'd received from Rilla moments after they'd arrived back in the city.

Fee had been able to hear Rilla blasting him from her place in the passenger seat, and had winced.

But Henry had been unrepentant and completely silent on his plans for a fake-death.

He was clearly trying to protect them, but it would have been easier to have another hand or two helping carry what they needed down to the car. Apparently, the Carnival folk liked to be prepared when they had a bolthole in a particular city.

"Why do you have a place in Little Rock? With all this stuff in it?" asked Fee as she dumped the box next to the boot of the car.

"We have a few places around, mostly in the capital cities of states we pass through regularly during the season. It's helped us out a time or two."

"The Carnival seems to be pretty well off, if you've got properties everywhere."

Henry shook his head. "Kind of the opposite at the moment. These boltholes, they're not owned by the Carnival, as such. There's this weird contract that governs all the property the Carnival bought about a hundred years ago when they were doing particularly well, and it's owned by a Trust corporation. They were paranoid we'd fall on hard times and sell it all I suppose. We can't touch it, and we don't make the decisions over what happens to the properties. They're just here for us to use."

"Who does decide?"

"I'm not entirely certain. Rilla and the bank have more of an idea of the specifics."

Fee looked at the car, now stuffed full of various pieces of equipment, including some explosives that she was particularly nervous about. "Where are we going to do it? Our fake deaths?"

"There's this place..." He hesitated. "An old deserted fairground on the edge of a farm on the outskirts of the city. We used to pass through here pretty regularly when I was a kid, and one of my older brothers showed it to me." Henry paused to lift another box into the trunk of the car. "But now we're going to blow it up."

"Don't we need to have bodies? To prove we're dead?"

"We're going to blow ourselves to smithereens. And we'll be so convincing they will be certain we're dead, and won't try to prove it."

"I'm no good at acting."

"I'll give you a non-speaking role," said Henry with a grin.

"I'm glad you think it's funny," snapped Fee, sudden tears filling her eyes.

Henry was by her side in an instant. He bundled her into a massive hug, smoothing one hand over her hair. The now-familiar zing of the blue electricity skipped along her senses, heating her body.

"I'm sorry. You'll be fine," he said. "We don't need to do much acting; we just need to pretend our plans went wrong, and instead of blowing them up, we accidentally blow ourselves up. It'll make them think they're smart to avoid our evil plots, and it will convince them we're dead. That's all we can ask for."

"Do you think they'll believe it?"

"If we do it well, they will. It's all about showmanship. We need to practice, and we need to have it set up perfectly. Luckily, I'm good at practicing and I'm a perfectionist. We'll be fine."

Fee felt stupid taking comfort in Henry's arms, but it was all so overwhelming. She'd taken twenty thousand dollars in cash out of her account, and it was burning a hole in her purse. She was casually planning her own death. She had a hot guy giving her comforting hugs.

A couple of weeks ago, the most excitement she'd had was trying to decide whether to have sushi or sandwiches for lunch. Now she was trying to stay alive and she'd brought Henry and his family into it as well.

Fee sniffed. "I'm fine," she said. "It just got the better of me for a moment."

"Let's load this lot up and get going," said Henry. "The faster we get there, the faster we can get this over with."

Fee nodded. "What about Max? Do we take him with us?"

Henry shrugged. "I'm not sure. What do you think?"

Fee swallowed. "He might be helpful," she said. "But

maybe we should leave him here? Just in case?" She couldn't bear it if another one of her robotic family got hurt. She had the other two in her pockets and she'd seen the little thief hiding in Henry's jacket pocket. She had a feeling she'd lost one of her robots to him.

She felt Henry's hand on her back, and found comfort from that small touch. They would get through this together, and then she would be able to disappear, maybe work on a plan to take down the Witch Hunters.

Henry would go back to his Carnival under another name, and everything would work out.

HENRY DROVE EXACTLY the speed limit the whole way out to the old fair.

He'd been fascinated with the deserted fairgrounds since he was a kid. He'd even gone in a few times, trying to fix a few of the rides, to bring it back to some semblance of order. A few of them had started working again, but it had never been enough to resuscitate the whole area. He'd realized some time in his teens that it was never going to be more than a graveyard, and had stopped trying.

Now it was going to have a more deadly use.

He rubbed his hands over the soft leather of his steering wheel and pondered his plan. He knew a lot could go wrong. But it seemed like their only shot at convincing the Witch Hunters to leave Fee alone.

The freeway turned into a highway, and then they were there. Henry turned slowly into the old rutted driveway, and looked around. It was still pretty much as he remembered it, just even more overgrown and broken down. Old rides rusted over with vines and grasses growing high over and around them. The paths were dusty and cracked. High above them a small Ferris wheel was frozen in time, its seats rocking gently in the wind, and the sun shining through the crisscrossed metal rungs.

Fee held up one hand to cover her eyes from the sunset. "It's kind of lovely, in a sad deserted sort of way," she said.

Henry nodded. "I'm in two minds about using this place. I've loved it for so long. But it's the only place around here that I know of that has stuff we can use as a distraction, and no other people around."

"So what do we do?"

"We set everything up we need, and then we sleep. Then tomorrow we call David." He strode along the pathway and gestured for Fee to follow him.

He headed for the administration block first. He wanted the plans for this place. They would have to use their combined abilities to set up a few of the rides. He glanced back at the car. Then they would blow everything up and hope David believed them.

Fee ran to catch up, and half trotted beside him. "So how do we hide out and pretend we're dead?"

"Going through the tunnels at Alberta's house reminded me about this place." Henry pointed to a block of buildings off to one side. "That's the sideshows area. It's riddled with secret passages that lead to each side of the booths, but also into the building on the far side."

"How do you know about this place again?" She was looking around as if she was trying to remember as much as possible of this place.

"My brother Daggen showed it to me one year when I was about seven. We traveled through here every year, though generally not into Little Rock. Stopping by and exploring became a kind of tradition. One year, I even started trying to fix a few of the rides."

"Did you ever see it working?"

"Nah, it was closed down long before my time."

"Why's it still here?"

Henry shook his head. "No idea. Maybe the person who owns it doesn't have the money to fix it, but loves it too much to destroy it."

"We're going to destroy it for him," whispered Fee.

"That we are," replied Henry softly.

They walked into the administration building quietly taking in the damp, dirty atmosphere. "Do you really think we'll find a map in here?"

"I even know where it is." Henry walked straight through the foyer and into the main office, heading for the old safe hidden behind a hideous landscape of the surrounding area.

He pulled it off the wall, and handed it to Fee, who screwed up her face. "I know why they left this here," she said.

"I think they left it here for more than just its ugliness. It was hiding the safe."

"Did they leave much in the safe?"

"Nah, not really. But I know I saw some maps one year when I was being particularly nosy." He rummaged through the papers, and then grinned. "Aha," he said, holding up the pages he was after.

Fee craned her neck to see what he was holding, her eyes taking in the blue and red markings on the old schematics.

"Let's go outside to read them. There's nowhere to sit in here." He grabbed her hand, and pulled her outside, heading toward the teacups. They didn't move around anymore, but they provided a seat on either side of a sort of a tiny table. "My lady, your carriage awaits," he said with a flourish and a bow.

Fee smiled, but didn't say anything, simply climbed onto the teacup ride.

Henry stared down at her for a moment, caught by how the late afternoon sun's rays caught her blonde hair and made a halo of light around her head. She was beautiful. He'd been planning to sit across from her but instead slid into the seat next to her and pulled the maps out in front of them. His thigh touched hers and he shivered. The zing of electricity warmed him up and drove him wild at the same time.

Fee looked at him, her emerald eyes wide. Henry put one hand up to her cheek, and softly smoothed the skin, tucking a stray hair behind her ear. He leaned in and kissed her, gently and softly at first, using the growing electricity between them to add a spark to what he was doing.

He curled his tongue against hers, and the kiss deepened. The next minute Henry was consumed by heat, as the electricity zapped and zinged between them, creating a sensation like nothing else he'd ever experienced. He tried to get closer, to wrap himself up in Fee, pulling her against him. She moaned and put her arms around him, her fingers running through his hair.

Henry tried to be reasonable, tried to pull back and say they needed to plan, but something stronger than his resolve was driving him on. He needed to be closer to Fee, to make her his one more time before they did this crazy attempt at fake dying. It seemed imperative, like they needed to make love to ensure it all came out okay.

His hands roamed over her body, and he found her breast, the nipple hard beneath his fingers. He groaned, wishing they had more time, a better place, and more room. Something hard jabbed into his ribs, and he pulled back, trying to get in a better position.

"I don't think this is a good idea," whispered Fee against his cheek. She glanced down at the hard metal. "And this isn't comfortable."

Henry looked down into her eyes, and tried to think

sensibly. Instead, without a word, he picked her up, and carried her to his car, still parked not too far away. Opening the door and pulling the seat forward, he laid her on the back seat, climbing in behind her.

Fee sighed, and put her arms around his neck, pulling him down again to finish what he started.

CHAPTER 43

"So the map says there used to be a haunted house over there," said Fee, pointing to a burned pile of ash. Worry was gnawing at her insides. They'd looked at the plans of the area, talked through what Henry wanted to do, and even had a quick look around last night. Then they'd slept an uncomfortable night in the back of the car. The reality of what they were trying to do had set in sometime this morning as they ate breakfast from the meagre supplies they'd thought to bring with them.

Henry nodded, distracted as he worked a wrench on one of the cars of the bumper car ride. "Burned down a few years ago."

"What if other things on this map are gone too? Like the tunnels you're so certain are still here. What if they've caved in?"

"We'll check them." Henry glanced up and looked at Fee properly. His face relaxed a moment. "We can do it now, if it will make you feel better."

Fee nodded, wishing she could be more blasé about what

they were doing. She didn't feel calm or confident, and she certainly couldn't bring herself to smile.

Henry grabbed her hand, and rubbed his thumb over her palm before taking off toward the sideshow booths. He grabbed a broom with his other hand when he saw it leaning up against a food stand. He caught Fee's raised eyebrows and shrugged. "There might be dirt and cobwebs," he said. "I thought you'd want me to clear them for you."

"It would have been too easy if it had been clean," said Fee. Inside she was berating herself. She was a farm girl for crying out loud. When did she get so soft?

When robots started being your friends over people, she answered for herself.

Henry turned an old rusted door handle that looked like it was about to fall apart in his hands and led Fee into a dark room. "It's just in here. I'll go first, let you know how bad it is down there, and then you can follow me. You'll need to acclimate to make sure you don't freak out when we go in for real."

Fee shook her head. "Before I met you, I'd never been in a tunnel in my entire life. Now, after only two weeks, I'm about to enter my second one."

Henry grinned up at her. "Hey, the first tunnel was nothing to do with me. It just reminded me of these." He opened a small doorway at the back of the room, and ducked his head to enter the narrow hole. A light flicked on and Henry showed her the little thief critter in his palm, a small torch shining out from one of his pincers. "He's full of surprises," he said.

Fee nodded. "I tried to make them useful."

"You know, Fee, he's more than just useful. He's rather ingenious." The robot chittered up at Henry, obviously pleased with the praise.

Fee shook her head, watching the interaction between

Henry and the kleptomaniac. She was never getting that particular robot to come back to her. Not that it mattered; she liked the idea of one of her little robots taking care of Henry if she wasn't around to do it.

"Come on in, Fee. It's dark and damp, but it's okay."

Fee cautiously followed Henry down into the tunnel, wishing they didn't have to be here. When had her life become so crazy? She'd always known that being raised in a cult by murdering farmers wasn't exactly an average way to grow up; but since leaving the farm, she'd gone out of her way to make her life sensible and secure. Uneventful and safe.

Since meeting Henry, she'd gone from knowing exactly what the day was going to hold, to crawling through tunnels with spiders and god knows what else crawling around, trying to plan a fake death.

The only thing that was keeping her from running screaming was Henry's solid form in front of her, leading her along the narrow tunnel, occasionally smiling back at her, and offering encouragement.

Last night in the car had been... magical. She didn't usually use that word, because of her own associations with it. But the electricity that formed between them at the slightest touch was hard to resist. *Henry* was hard to resist. He was smart and creative, but relaxed and funny at the same time. He didn't take himself too seriously, but he grasped the robotics concepts she threw at him with hardly a blink of the eye. She'd never met anyone so agile of mind. Something about Henry made her feel stronger and more powerful on some level that she'd never noticed before. Everything around her seemed clearer and she was thinking faster than she ever had before.

"There's a small cave-in up ahead," said Henry, making Fee blink and draw herself back to the present.

"Is it going to interrupt our plans?"

"We might have to dig it out a little, but no, it's not going to stop us doing what we need to do."

"Good." Fee paused and glanced back behind her. "You know, I think I need to work on my part of our planned maintenance before David gets here. I'll be fine in the tunnels now, as long as you search them to make sure they're okay, and then come help me finish off."

Henry stared at her intently for a moment. "Are you sure you'll be okay down here once it happens? It's an important part of the plan."

"Of course. I'm not claustrophobic or anything." I just need to get out of here for a while, she admitted to herself. Away from Henry and how he made her feel.

It was more than the addiction to being closer to him that made it impossible to resist touching him when she could. It was the feeling that she could do anything, or be anyone she wanted, if she would only open herself up fully to the energy that flowed between them. It just didn't seem possible and it was making her nervous.

He nodded. "Okay, then that's a good idea. We should get it set up as fast as we can."

"I'll see you soon," she said, and turned to go. She stopped when Henry's hand grabbed her wrist. Suddenly he was there right beside her, pulling her into his arms. His lips crushed hers in another electric kiss that left her gasping.

"Take care of yourself," he whispered, then let her go.

She nodded, and turned, blindly heading back out the way she had come. Her feet were unsteady, and she touched a shaking hand to her lips.

How could one kiss affect her like that?

CHAPTER 44

*H*enry was just crawling out of the last tunnel, when his phone rang. He checked the screen. It was Rilla. He sighed, and pressed to answer the call. He wasn't afraid of their Ringmaster, but he knew it was going to be an unpleasant conversation.

"Hey, Rilla."

"What the hell do you think you're doing?" she said, her voice colder than he'd ever heard it.

"I'm driving my car home." He held his breath, wondering if it was going to be that easy.

"No, you're not. I can feel where you are through the Carnival. You're still in Little Rock."

"Then I'm keeping a dangerous group of murderers away from the Carnival," he said calmly. "We wouldn't just lead them to the Compound. That would put everyone's lives in danger."

"You don't just go haring off on your own without discussing it with me."

Henry noticed she didn't argue with his assessment of the Witch Hunters.

"I need to fix this, Rilla. I'm the one who might have connected them to everyone else. I need to fix it."

"You tell me where you are right this minute."

"I thought you could tell where I was?"

"I can tell you're still around. I don't know exactly where. But I will figure it out, and when I do, we will be coming to find you."

Henry shook his head, even though she couldn't see it. "No. Fee and I will handle it. If too many people get involved, they'll suspect something is up. You'll ruin everything."

"We can help, Henry. Let us help," she said softly, her voice almost pleading now.

"You are helping. Take Alberta and Fee's mother to safety. Make sure everyone else in the Carnival is safe and cared for. We'll sort it out here, and be home soon." *Hopefully.*

"Don't do anything stupid, Henry."

"Stupid? Me? When did I ever do anything like that?"

"Every damn day while we were growing up," growled Rilla. "You promise me that you're not doing anything dumb trying to protect the rest of us."

"These people are dangerous, Rilla. I can't let them find the Carnival. And I need to go, in case Dad's trying to track this call."

He heard the small intake of breath on the other end and grinned, knowing that was exactly what they were trying to do. "Tell my brother and father that I love them too much to let them get involved in this. That goes for you too, Rilla. Fee and I can take care of it. You go home."

"You know that's not going to happen, right? And we'll find you. It's just a matter of time."

"You won't find us soon enough, Rilla. Stay away and this will end well for everyone. If you love the Carnival, you'll stay away." He pressed the end button on his phone. They needed to hurry. Rilla wasn't going to stop looking for them.

He strode out of the sideshow room at the end of the tunnel, and into the sunlight outside. He saw Fee immediately, some kind of internal radar catching on her blonde hair. He waved and broke into a jog.

"How's it going?" he asked, looking at what she was doing.

"I think I'm almost done. It's hard to know before I start it up." She stepped back from the small children's rollercoaster ride, frowning down at the small carriage that sat next to the ride mechanicals.

"Let's test it then," he said with a grin. Being with Fee made all his other worries seem insignificant. She focused his energy on what was in front of him and kept him in the moment. He wasn't sure what he thought about it, but they didn't have time for an in depth analysis right now. They just had to get the next few hours over and done with first. He flicked the switch and the small carriage clicked into place then rolled down the tracks, pausing at the first small hill, and then tracking over the edge. They watched silently as it ran the small course, and then came back to settle in front of them.

"That worked well," said Henry.

Fee nodded. "Seemed to."

"I'm going to call David soon. We have about two hours to set everything else up."

"Shouldn't we give ourselves more time to get it all sorted?" Fee frowned at Henry.

Henry shook his head, letting his instincts take over. "We need to get to him as soon as possible. If we wait, he might leave or do something drastic. We need to provide him with hope."

"Rushing isn't going to help."

"It's not rushing; it's giving ourselves a tight deadline. We can do this Fee. But we need to connect with David as soon as possible. We've already delayed too long." He didn't quite understand the sense of urgency that was pulsing through his veins, but he knew to trust it. It had the sweet tang of magic to it.

They worked silently for the next half hour, making sure they had as much set up as they could. Fee walked over to where Henry was crouched over, pulling out weeds from the teacup ride's rails.

"Your phone or mine?"

He got slowly to his feet and stretched. "Mine. You're not supposed to know I'm calling, remember?" He quirked one corner of his mouth, but couldn't bring himself to do more than that. This was the pointy end of their plan.

He pulled out his phone, and dialed David's number.

"Henry. I'm surprised to say the least," answered David. "Why are you calling me, Henry? To beg forgiveness? I have a lump the size of a baseball on my head, thanks to you."

"I have a deal for you." Henry waited.

"Come on then, tell me what you propose," said David.

"You let me go and forget you ever met me, and I'll hand over Fee."

There was silence on the other end of the line. "I don't believe you. You wouldn't give Fee up like that."

"She's not normal. There's something strange about her. I didn't realize until I spent a bit more time with her."

"Then why not just ditch her and move on?"

"She told me a little about the Witch Hunters and what you do. She thought I'd be sympathetic. But I'm not willing to die for her."

"Then tell me where you are," said David softly.

"I want to make it clear that I have nothing to do with her anymore. You need to leave me alone," Henry tried to make his voice sound scared. He looked over at Fee, and rolled his eyes. She watched him with a slight frown between her brows.

David paused, but Henry could hear his excited breathing at the other end of the phone. Even if he didn't truly believe Henry's story, he was going to do what they wanted.

"Where are you Henry?"

"You swear on your honor that you will leave me alone when you come for her."

"I swear I will leave you alone. All I want is the magic user."

"We're at the old Fergusson Farm. The circus graveyard."

"Ah, a fitting spot for a carny like yourself, I suppose."

"We won't be here much longer. Fee is anxious to move on. We're traveling by night, so you have until five o'clock before we leave."

"Why today? Why can't we just catch up at a later date?" asked David suspiciously.

"We could try." Henry tried to sound unconcerned. "But I don't know where we will be... and I might change my mind."

David's breath hitched. "Okay. We will be there soon."

Henry pressed the end-call button.

"I still can't really believe it's him," said Fee. "I wouldn't have thought he was capable of anything like this."

"Isn't that what the neighbors of serial killers always say?"

Fee smiled sadly. "Yeah, I guess. Are you going to make your other phone call now too?"

Henry nodded and made his next phone call.

"Hello, Special Agent Franklin," he said.

"Who is this?"

"Henry Kokkol."

Henry could have sworn that he heard a growl from the other end of the phone line.

"Where the hell are you?" asked Franklin.

"If you want your gun and badge back, you'll need to meet me."

"Tell me where the hell you are and I'll be there to arrest you before you can take another breath."

"I'm not the one who blew up that building in Tampa, and neither is Fee. If you want to know who the real bomber is, you'll meet us with an open mind. And get your gun and badge back at the same time."

"You can't steal an FBI agent's badge and gun, and expect to get away completely free," said Franklin.

"I didn't steal them on purpose. I'll even show you who did it. But you have to meet us out here. The man who did the Tampa bombing will be here soon, and he's after us both. We're not going to survive if we don't have your help."

"Don't talk shit to me, Kokkol. Just tell me where you are, so I can damn well come and arrest you."

Henry sighed. "Just try to keep an open mind, Franklin."

"Where. Are. You?"

"We're at the old circus graveyard. Fergusson Farm."

Franklin hung up the phone without even saying good-bye. Henry looked at the phone. "I don't think we have long. Let's finish the set up."

CHAPTER 45

Fee ducked down behind the metal sign where she was hiding on the roof of a sideshow as the truck turned into the gravel drive.

They were here.

It was about to begin.

Her heart began to pound as she pressed the button on the remote she had fashioned out of bits and pieces found around the old carnival. The first of the rides started up, the teacups circling around slowly. She watched as four men climbed out of the truck. She squinted, trying to see which one was David. He was standing next to the front passenger door, talking to the man who had driven them all out to this isolated spot. Fee froze as she recognized the driver.

It was her father.

She glanced around, looking for an escape route. She couldn't go up against her father. He would see through what they were doing. He'd find and kill them both. She'd thought they could convince David. Her father was older, more experienced.

Her breaths came in short panicked gasps and Fee struggled with the overpowering urge to run. It was Henry's voice in her head, talking over the plan until they knew it inside out, which finally calmed her thoughts.

They had to do this, here, today; otherwise, these people would be chasing Fee for the rest of her life. And Henry's family at the Carnival would be in danger too, if they ever made a connection between Henry and magic. They needed to think he was a duplicitous bystander in the battle between the Witch Hunters and the magic users they so hated.

She took a deep breath and pressed the second button on her remote.

The kid's rollercoaster ride clicked into gear and began the slow ascent to the small hill at the top of the ride.

The reaction from the men was instantaneous. They all pulled out guns from various hidden spots on their bodies and aimed them squarely at the ride. Her father barked instructions, and the other three men spread out, walking slowly toward it.

One of the booths to one side of the children's ride started up, and the clowns began to move back and forth to a tinny tune, their mouths open wide in a perpetual scream. Two of the men turned their guns toward the clowns, but they managed to hold fire.

Fee shivered. It was such a silly little thing to do, having all these rides start up one by one, but Henry had said they needed to amp up the fear and expectation in their audience, so they would be more likely to believe their ultimate con.

Fee shrugged. She was prepared to believe Henry; he seemed to know what he was talking about.

Down from her hiding place, the men were switching their aim between the kids' ride and the clowns, unsure where their targets might be coming from. Her father barked another command, and one of the men approached the clowns, clearly checking for who was there.

Another ride started near the men, and they jumped again. Henry was hiding on the other side of the Carnival space with another remote. They were rattled, but Fee didn't think they were rattled enough. They were still too calm in the face of the creepy carnival rides around them. She pressed her remote, and ghostly sounds came out from the loudspeaker that was now working across the whole area, thanks to Henry's tinkering. She'd found the box of spooky sound recordings in the office.

They were definitely looking more rattled now. But they were used to dealing with people who had magic. If you believed it was the devil's work, you probably had a high level of fear in your daily routine. They would need to amp up the fear factor another notch to get them to the right temperature for their finale.

Fee pressed another button and the Ferris wheel at the back of the carnival started up, its ancient gears shifting slowly, grinding and squeaking through its slow turn. A loud screeching indicated the lack of oil between the metal, something Henry had insisted they leave to give more of an effect. It raised the hairs on the back of Fee's neck, like fingernails down a chalkboard, and she shuddered, trying to keep her own nerves in check.

The men were yelling to each other, back and forth. Her father barked yet another order, and all three of the other men ran over to him. They huddled together, talking and gesturing, clearly making a plan for dealing with the moving parts.

They all stood up, and two of the men headed toward the clowns, while her father and David came toward where Fee was hiding, in the direction of the Ferris wheel. Fee scuttled back from the edge, and held her breath, trying not to make too much noise.

"I know you're here, Wild Feather. I can feel you." Her father's voice rose over the noise of the Ferris wheel.

Fee shuddered, remembering what Summer Dawn had said about her father's magic powers. Little metal feet pattered across the nape of her neck, curling itself into her hair. All she had was some strange ability to make metal creatures out of nothing. Her father apparently had some kind of sensing magic, so he could find her wherever she went.

Fee frowned at that thought. Hadn't her mother said that her father couldn't find her using his own magic? So was it something to do with David, some kind of magic he had that was allowing her father to find her again? Or was he just an excellent showman who knew the right thing to say to freak out the person he was chasing?

As Henry had said, sometimes it's about smoke and mirrors.

"David here is quite eager to see you. You'll be his first sacrifice, you see. He's been waiting for you for so long."

Fee shivered. Why *had* David waited so long? He'd been there six months before Henry arrived. She thought about the nights the two of them had been working in the office, not talking or interacting, just doing their own work on their own part of the project. He could have killed her any number of times. Had he really been unsure it was her?

It made her very glad she'd never invited him back to her house to meet Max, and that she'd kept her robots secret. They were her magic, her creatures outside the normal bounds of reality. She'd changed the color of her eyes, and her hair was longer and blonder. Her appearance was different enough that perhaps he really had been uncertain.

Or maybe he just hadn't wanted to do it. The David she'd known these last few months didn't fit with the Witch

Hunter stories that she'd learned about since leaving her parent's farm.

"Hey! Down here!" Henry's voice called out and she heard the crunch of gravel stop, as the men turned around to look in Henry's direction.

Murmured voices discussed something, and then she heard the sound of her father and David walking back toward Henry.

The next phase of the plan was in play.

CHAPTER 46

*H*enry forced himself to walk down the wide path between the broken-down sideshows and the rusted rides toward the men who would kill him in a heartbeat if he showed any kind of resistance.

Or if he showed any signs of magic use.

Luckily, his magic was less showy than most others. It just meant that he could see things more clearly and build things faster than most other people. Those kinds of skills could just have been because he was smarter than everyone else. In fact, he liked to hassle his brothers that was just what it meant.

In front of him, David and another older man were coming toward him. He slowed to let them come closer to where he wanted them to finish up. He sensed rather than saw the men behind him, and stepped to one side as one of the men charged him, tripping him as he went past. The other man, his partner, simply held up a gun at his face, and Henry held up his hands.

"He attacked me first. I was just defending myself," he said mildly, trying to seem innocuous. Truth be told, he could disarm the other man just as easily if he was so inclined. He glanced over to where David was approaching, trying to decide if it was better to seem like he couldn't get himself out of this situation.

Then David was there, and the point was moot.

"So, Henry, here you are. Finally." David crossed his arms, and glared at Henry.

The older man behind David cleared his throat, and David stepped back, still clearly annoyed.

"Where is Wild Feather?" the older man said, his voice soothing and calm. He smiled at Henry, and his perfect teeth seemed to sparkle in the light.

Henry shook his head slightly. The man was a damn persuasion talent, more powerful than anyone he'd ever come across before. How could he be a Witch Hunter?

Unless...he was doing it cynically, killing off competition, perhaps getting some curse magic from it, making himself more powerful. And keeping the poor, stupid people who he was using appeased by using his persuasion magic.

It made a terrible kind of sense, and suddenly Henry was worried about their plan for the first time. He'd expected David, not some all-powerful wizard.

"She's gone crazy. Started making the rides go all by themselves," said Henry, glancing around as if searching for Fee. He needed to be extra convincing to make this work.

"He's lying! This is a trap," said David urgently from behind the older man.

"I'm not saying it's not a trap, David. But I plan to find out exactly what we're dealing with here instead of stumbling around under assumptions." The calm voice had a way of drawing everyone around him under his spell. David immediately calmed down, and the other two men almost swayed where they stood.

Henry focused all his energy on the man in front of him.

He assumed he would be just as susceptible to his persuasion talent, but there had to be a way to answer but not answer at the same time and he would damn well find it. He did not intend to go out this way.

"Henry, look at me," said the older man.

Henry found himself staring into a pair of the most mesmerizing dark green eyes he'd ever seen. A small part of his brain was yelling and jumping up and down inside his head, but the rest of him was just waiting to see how he could help this man with the hypnotic eyes.

"Henry, is this a trap? Do you really plan to give Wild Feather up?"

"Fee doesn't want to go with you," replied Henry, madly trying not to answer the question.

"Yes, I can understand that on her part. But what about you, Henry? Did you really plan to give her to me?"

Henry managed to keep his head from shaking the negative, but only just. "I said that on the phone, didn't I?" he said.

The compulsion was like a weight pushing down on him, and Henry could feel the sweat running down his back. But he was determined to make his words his own. He could use his own power against this man, however subtle it might be. He wished he could ask about the magic that this man was using against him, but that would give away his own magic, and that would only work against him in the long run.

The older man narrowed his eyes. "Do you know who I am?" he asked.

Henry shook his head, grateful for the easier question.

"I am a Witch Hunter. And not just any Witch Hunter, I am one of only three Great Witch Hunters left in this fine country of ours."

Henry nodded again, not entirely sure what was expected of him.

"But I am also a father. A father who has a terrible duty to perform. Do not make this any harder that it needs to be Henry. Is this a trap? Or are you prepared to give up Wild Feather to us?"

Henry felt like his eyes were as wide as saucers as he looked at the man in front of him, finally realizing who he was. "You're Fee's father?" he said.

"I am." He nodded ceremoniously.

"And you're here to kill your only daughter?" For some reason Henry felt like it was important to spell it out.

"I have that unfortunate duty, yes."

As soon as Fee's father said the words, the swirling persuasion magic seemed to lose its effect on Henry. "That makes you one sick bastard," he said under his breath.

The realization that he was here to kill his own daughter had been shocking enough to ensure that Henry was free of the magic the old man was using on him. "But no, it's not a trap. And yes, I will give your poor, unfortunate daughter to you."

"Excellent. See, David? It's always better to clarify who your actual enemies are."

David still eyed Henry dubiously, but he obviously had either enough experience of Fee's father being correct or was too scared of him to disagree, because he remained silent.

"Then how do we get Wild Feather here? How are you going to hand her over to us?"

"I need to go and talk to her. I'll convince her to come with me to the building just over there, saying that we're going to hide in there. Once we're inside, you just have to come in and get her. Between the four of you, I'm sure you can manage one small woman."

"I'm sure we can."

"Now, if you could stay here and pretend you're searching this area, I will go find her and finish this off."

David glanced at one of the other men, but other than

that, there was no indication they would follow his suggestion.

"If you don't stay here, she will see you, and decide to cause me trouble. I thought you'd want this to be as easy as possible?"

"We will wait here," said Fee's father. "But you only have five minutes before we come get you."

Henry nodded. Fine with him, the faster they got this over with, the better.

CHAPTER 47

*F*ee ducked down when she saw Henry coming out from the dark alley where he'd been talking with the others. She took a deep breath, pressed the last remote control button, and waited for the last toy to start. The carriage of the larger roller coaster started its laborious climb upward, giving Henry and Fee a chance to set up the rest of their con.

She raced down the back steps of the building, trying to make as little noise as possible. Henry met her at the side entrance, pulling her into a quick kiss that had her blood pumping in seconds despite the desperate situation. Lightning surged along their bodies for a second, and then they pulled apart. She gasped for breath, trying to find her rational center again.

"We have to hurry. He's only given me five minutes. You didn't tell me he was a persuasion talent," said Henry all in one breath.

Fee scrunched up her nose. "What's a persuasion talent?"

"That explains that," said Henry taking off at a run, pulling Fee behind him. He entered the building where everything was set up. She crashed into his back seconds later as he came to an abrupt halt.

"You didn't think we'd let you have it all your way, did you Henry?" said David, holding a hand gun directly at Henry's chest.

Fee took a panicked breath, and looked around the small room. Their escape route was blocked by David, but they needed him out of here for the whole plan to work—unless they were going to kill David as well. Fee didn't know if she could have another death on her conscience.

But the gun he was holding directly at Henry hardened her resolve. She would do anything it took to survive this encounter, including killing David. He had tried to hurt them on multiple occasions, hadn't he?

"What are you doing, David? I thought we had a plan?" said Henry, obviously trying to buy them some time.

"You didn't think we believed you, did you? Falling Leaf might be a Great Witch Hunter, but even he knows that sometimes people can be tricked."

"I think you're giving me too much credit." Henry tightened his grip on Fee, and dragged her in front of him, as if he was forcing her to come around. "You can have her, for all I care." He gave her an intent look, trying to tell her something.

Even though Fee knew and understood it was part of some kind of plan he was hatching, she felt a burst of fear. He sounded like he meant it. She'd never realized her father had been a murderer all those years. What made her think she could trust her instincts with Henry?

Henry pushed Fee further out into the middle, toward David and his gun, and she gave a small moan. She didn't know what Henry's plan was, but being in the sights of David's gun was more than she could bear. "What made you do it, David?" she asked, more to distract herself than him. "What did I ever do to you?"

"You stole my life from me, you and your kind."

Fee frowned. "How did I do that?"

"You were right. I had a fiancée. We loved each other, couldn't wait to be together for the rest of our lives. Then I turned eighteen, and everything changed. I was told of my duty to the Witch Hunters. I was given a mission to hunt you down. They placed tracking magic on me, and set me off into the world. All they knew was that you could make robots and that you'd gone to college. I didn't realize how long it would take. Even when I met you at Callaghan, five years into my mission, I wasn't completely sure it was you. Your hair was different, much lighter, your nose not quite the same as the photos I had of you. Your eyes were a different color. You didn't seem to use magic. So I waited."

"You waited all that time to make sure it was me?"

"Yes," spat David. "And while I was waiting, doing my duty for my country, my fiancée found someone else."

"Oh, David. I'm sorry." And Fee really meant it. She could see how it had hurt David, how heartbroken he must have been.

"You should be sorry. It was your fault. I would have married her and had children by now. Instead, I'm here with no one. Nothing." David's face was a mask of anger.

"But can't you see? You've made another life for yourself. You have friends, Nolan and Eugene. You're good at what you do," said Fee desperately, trying to make him understand, when a part of her knew he never would. "It's not my fault you had to leave your fiancée."

"It's your fault, because your evil nature makes it necessary for people like me to hunt you down and kill you."

"I'm not evil, David. Can't you see? That's the point. It's not necessary to hunt me down, because I'm just an ordinary person who wouldn't hurt a fly. You know that, you've worked with me for all these months."

Fee could see David wavering for a split second. Then his face hardened, and he aimed the gun at her face.

"That's exactly the kind of thing you would say. You're just trying to save your skin."

"Did you mean for Eugene to be hurt?" asked Fee quietly. "Did he do something against you as well?"

David blinked and took a step back. "He raced up there before I could stop him. The damn fool was trying to save Violet."

"All that work on Violet. Was that all fake?"

David shook his head. "I enjoy working on computers. That was the one good thing to come out of leaving home. I've been able to learn far more than I would ever have learned if I'd stayed there."

"Doesn't that mean something? That you've expanded your horizons? Do you even still love this girl?" Fee knew the words were a mistake as soon as they left her mouth.

David's eyes hardened again, and he took a step toward them again. "She is the love of my life. Don't you dare speak about her." He levelled the gun at her chest. "Your father wants you alive so he can question you, but I think I might just serve you up cold."

Fee squeezed her hands tight, wondering what would happen if she just whacked the pistol out of his hand. He didn't look like he knew an awful lot about using a gun. But at that moment, Henry crashed a large iron bar around David's head, saving her the trouble.

David crumpled to the floor in front of her, his gun clattering off to one side.

Fee raced over to the gun and picked it up experimentally.

"Don't point that in my direction," said Henry holding up a hand as if to protect himself.

"I'm tempted to shoot you after the way you gave me up to him just then," said Fee, only half joking.

"It was all part of the plan, Fee. I would never give you up." His words were tossed casually over his shoulder as he pulled David's unconscious body over to the exit. Fee didn't know why her heart was beating so fast.

He didn't mean the words in the way she really wanted him to mean them.

HENRY STRUGGLED to get David's body as close to the door as humanly possible, without him actually being outside it. He was going to have to put something over him to protect him from the blast that was about to rock the small room. He didn't want to be responsible for David's death, not when the poor guy was little more than a pawn in a wider game. A stupid pawn, but a pawn nonetheless.

Fee's father, however, was a target he'd like to take out. Henry sighed. Not something he would be able to work on today. Not if they wanted to get out of here alive.

From outside, he heard the sound of more vehicles arriving in a rush. Hopefully, their other visitors had just arrived.

The sound of a loudspeaker confirmed Henry's hopes.

"This is the FBI. Come out with your hands up."

"Is that the agent you called?" asked Fee from where she was waiting for him by the tunnel.

"Sounds like him. He's a bit peeved about the gun and the badge."

"How did you even..." Fee glanced to his shirt pocket as a little mechanical face popped up and chattered at her. "Oh."

"It wasn't exactly my choice. But he did me a favor in the end, and he was the one who saved me from the Witch Hunters at the hospital."

Fee just nodded, her eyes huge in her face. She looked dirty and exhausted... but determined.

"It'll be over soon. Just help me put these shelves in front of David, and then we'll set it all off."

They pushed the small wooden shelves over beside David. "Will it protect him?" asked Fee.

"I think so. And if it doesn't... well he probably deserves it for hurting Eugene."

Fee glanced down at David. "I don't think he's a bad person. I think he's just chosen a bad path."

"Come on. We have to get this done."

Henry went over to the window, and crouched down. He pressed a button on the old tape recorder they'd found, and it started to play the tape inside.

"We'll never give up," yelled Henry's voice from the tape deck.

"Come out with your hands up, and you won't get hurt," said the voice on the loudspeaker, this time recognizably Franklin's voice.

Henry grinned, and his taped answer came back on cue. "You can't make us!"

"Come on, let's go," he whispered, and half pushed Fee into the small opening in the far wall.

They crawled into the tunnel, and Henry shut and locked the heavy door behind them. The critters, the kleptomaniac and Bing lit the way and Fee started crawling along the tunnel ahead of Henry.

He followed, thinking over the next step in their plan. They made it to a crossroads in the tunnel. "Okay, Fee. Stop here a moment. I need to set it off."

She paused, half turning to watch what he was doing.

Henry pulled out the small remote control they'd fashioned earlier, placing one finger on the solitary button. He glanced up at Fee. "There's no going back from here. We're dead from this moment on."

"Do it," she whispered.

CHAPTER 48

The tunnel shuddered around them, and bits of earth dusted their bodies. Fee had a momentary vision of the tunnel collapsing, and her breathing became ragged. She closed her eyes.

"Let's keep moving," said Henry, the same thoughts clearly running through his head.

She nodded, even though he couldn't see her, and started crawling through the tunnel again. It seemed forever before she saw the little wooden door that marked their exit. She let out a sigh of relief, and her movements sped up until she touched the door, hesitating.

"Do you think it's safe?" she asked.

"As it ever will be. The others should still be sifting through the wreckage, helping David and trying to find us."

Fee took a breath and opened the door. Bright sunlight made her scrunch up her eyes for a second and she blindly crawled forward into the small room at the far end of the fairground, in the staff-only section. Opening up her eyes a sliver, she looked around, trying to make sure it was the right room, looking for the supplies they'd stored here earlier.

"Ah, here you are. Finally," said her father, his smooth voice mocking.

Fee jumped back, but it was too late. Falling Leaf grasped her arm in a tight grip, and he pulled her up and out of the tunnel. Henry crawled out and stood beside her.

"You didn't think I would believe you so easily, did you?" asked her father. "Your whole plan was a little too predictable."

"Let go of her," Henry said softly, his voice menacing.

"There's no point in keeping her all neat and tidy. She'll be dead soon anyway."

Henry moved forward with a suddenness that astounded Fee. He punched her father in the face, and had his arm in a stranglehold until he let go of Fee. As soon as she felt her father's grip loosen, she pulled away, turning back to the fight.

It was over before it began. Another man, one of the others who had arrived with her father, stepped out of the shadows with a gun pointed directly at Henry's head.

"Stop now or I will blow your head off," he said.

Henry paused in punching her father, one arm held ready. He glanced back at Fee and she shook her head slightly. She had David's gun, but she didn't know how to use it properly. In this kind of gunfight, she'd lose every time. They needed surprise on their side for them to have a chance.

Stepping back, Henry shook his hand, as if trying to flick away the pain of punching someone in the head. His face was grim, and he was trying to keep an eye on both men at the same time, his gaze flicking between them.

"Not a very well-thought-out plan, I have to say," said her father. He tutted and shook his head. "I thought you might have more in you than this."

Fee's hand tightened into a fist, and she wished she'd

taken more of a look at David's gun. How hard could it be to shoot someone?

"What are you going to do with us?" she asked.

"Thanks to the police who have just turned up, we are going to hide here for a while. Then I am going to take you both with me back to the farm. We have a special ceremony for magic users like you, Wild Feather. Something to get the taint of your bad magic off me."

"You've got your own bad magic all over you," said Fee. She glanced at the man with the gun. "Do your followers know that you use magic? That you're far more powerful than I am?"

"They know magic users often try to cause a rift between Witch Hunters, and they should ignore anything they say at a time like this."

"What if I could prove it?" said Fee, talking directly to the other man now.

His gaze wavered and he glanced over to her father. "How?" he said.

"Silence! You know better than to engage with a magic user," said her father sharply.

"There have been whispers. Talk of your magic use. If she can prove it..." The man shrugged, his eyes sharp on Fee.

"How dare you!" Without warning, Fee's father leaped onto the other man, and smashed his head against a metal pole. He grabbed for the gun, and without hesitation, shot the man in the chest at point blank range. Blood splattered out and hit her father, providing a gruesome spatter across his face and chest.

Fee screamed, immediately putting her hand over her mouth to cover the sound. Henry scrambled over to Fee, and put his hand out. "The gun," he whispered.

She pulled the gun from her jacket pocket and handed it to him, her eyes on her father as he stood over the dead man.

Henry had the gun safely hidden by the time her father turned.

"Now we can talk openly, Wild Feather. Yes, I do have power. I have far more than you will ever know in your paltry life. And killing you will give me more power than I can describe." He smiled, and Fee could almost see the power crackling along his skin.

"You use curse magic?" asked Henry calmly.

"You know of it? Yes, I am able to gather power through the deaths of other magic users. I cannot begin to explain the power I will receive from Wild Feather. She was born with one true purpose—to be the source of my future power."

Fee shuddered. It had been one thing to believe her father had some kind of belief in a higher power, that he was doing what he was doing for the greater good. To learn that he was simply doing it for power was a whole other lesson.

"Don't you have to be related or connected to the people you kill to gather power from them?" asked Henry. Fee glanced at him, trying to see if he was genuinely interested, or if this was another delaying tactic. He was watching her father like a hawk. A hawk waiting for its chance to strike.

"It's true that a greater power is gathered from people I know or am related to. But I have found certain... methods... over the years that have enabled me to gather maximum power from the Witch Hunter experience."

Fee shivered. "Why are you with them, if you don't believe in their purpose?" she asked softly.

"It gives me an excuse to kill," her father answered simply. "Very often they provide the names and places, and all I have to do is turn up." He took a deep breath, as if smelling roses. "It's the most wonderful thing in the world, to have minions gathering your kills for you, and then protecting you from the consequences."

Fee looked at her father as if he was an insect she was

studying under a microscope. How had this man raised her? How had she not seen him for what he was?

She shook her head. They had to remember that this man was very, very clever. He'd been hiding in plain sight all these years.

~

HENRY STOOD as close to Fee as he could, ready to dive in front of her if her father decided to shoot her right then and there. The gun in his pocket felt heavy, but reassuring. They had some means for fighting back against this maniac.

Outside he could hear the police and FBI rushing about, trying to find survivors in the explosion. They'd clearly found David, and from the excited shouts, he was still alive.

He'd underestimated Fee's father, and his abilities. He glanced at Fee. And his desire to get the powerful curse magic from killing his own daughter.

Henry tightened his fist. That wasn't going to happen. They'd taken precautions in case something happened at this end of the tunnel as well.

The room itself was an old storeroom, filled with the kind of things that were magical to him, but considered junk by most other people. Shelves of machine parts, old engines, broken down bits of the rides, cables, and anything else they'd thought to keep, but had no immediate use for. There had obviously been a hoarder in this particular Carnival.

The tiny explosion they'd planted would tip over several of the shelves on one side of the room; therefore, all they needed to do was get Fee's father over there and set off the explosion.

Simple really.

Oh, and once the explosion went off, the police outside would come running to this room, so they had to escape before anyone else saw them. Henry's head was spinning with the many ways this could all go wrong. But they had to try.

"You can stop whatever it is you're planning now, Henry. My magic will hold out over any puny little thing you have in mind. You can't imagine what it is like to be a creature of magic. It is so very much more than the mere mortal experience."

Henry nodded calmly. So he didn't suspect that Henry was a 'creature of magic' as well. Even better. "I wasn't planning anything."

"I can almost see your brain ticking over. You're going so slowly I can watch every little thought."

Henry shrugged. "You got me. I'll never be able to beat you."

Fee's father tipped his head to one side. "You're not terribly worried by your oncoming demise. Why is that I wonder?"

Henry moved to one side, away from Fee. "I don't know what you're talking about," he said. When Fee's father took a step toward him, he crowed on the inside.

"I don't like it when my targets are too confident. It means they're planning something they think will work." He took another step and another toward Henry.

Henry sidestepped away, and across to the other side of the room, as if he was trying to evade capture by Fee's father. The older man followed him, more out of curiosity than any real fear of losing his prey.

They were closer now to where the explosion was hidden. Just a few more steps and Henry would have the other man over the source, and be able to press the button.

"Hey! You in there! Lower your weapons and come out with your hands up!" The voice was coming from outside their building, but it was clearly meant for them. Henry looked to the window, and saw the face of Special Agent Franklin glaring at them.

"Duck!" he yelled to Fee, and leaping to one side, he pressed the button. Nothing happened for a moment, so Henry wondered if he was going to have to try to explain his strange behaviour to the agents outside the room.

A gunshot filled the space and he heard Fee scream. Then the world disintegrated around them, and he forgot about anything other than trying not to die.

CHAPTER 49

ee couldn't see anything except the dust floating down from the skies. She wondered idly if the light hitting the dust motes meant to make a rainbow of colors. Or perhaps it was just nature's way of providing a floorshow for her while she died.

The pain in her chest was almost too much to bear. She wished there was some way she could force herself into unconsciousness. Surely, that would be better than this excruciating madness rolling its way through her body?

She could hear someone else groaning, and tried to raise her head. Was it Henry? Or her father?

Her father had managed to get a shot off, which hit her just as the explosion was going off. If she'd understood the conversation earlier, that meant he'd managed to get extra magic that might have helped him survive the blast.

Henry, on the other hand, didn't have any extra help. He had almost been as much in the firing line for that explosion as her father. The agents outside had forced their hand.

A hand on her shoulder made her jump. She looked up

and saw Henry, and tears she didn't know she had in her, started to fall down her cheeks. "You're okay," she whispered.

"It takes more than that to kill me," he whispered back. He glanced down at her chest, and his face darkened. "We have to get you out of here."

Fee shook her head. "I don't think we can. I can't move."

Henry glanced behind him to where a door was slowly shifting open. "Then we have to take our chances with the FBI," he said.

Fee shook her head. "No. You go hide."

"No. I stay with you."

"They won't let us stay together," said Fee. "You escaped police custody. They won't take that lightly."

"I'm not leaving you." Fee felt his words right at the center of her chest, and she clutched his hand. "I love you," she whispered. The room faded out, and then back in again.

The door opened and three fully armed and vested up FBI agents entered the room slowly. Henry raised his hands. "She's been shot by that man over there. You need to help her."

The first man came straight over to Henry and had him down on the ground with his hands behind his back before he could say anything more. The second man went over to Fee, and the last to Fee's father.

"This one's alive," said the man next to Fee's father.

"This one too," said the man next to Fee.

"Call for a medic," said one of the men to a fourth man at the doorway.

HENRY RELAXED into the grip of the agent on top of him. They would take care of Fee. He wished her father was dead, but perhaps that was asking too much, given how much of their plan had gone completely wrong.

The policeman pulled Henry to his feet, and put handcuffs on his wrists, which were behind his back.

He half-dragged Henry out the door. Henry took one last look back at Fee, who was watching him leave with large eyes. "It'll be fine, Fee. Don't worry," he managed to say before he was dragged outside into the bright sunshine. Henry scrunched up his face.

"Did you really think you could get away?" asked Franklin, coming to stand in front of him.

Henry shrugged. "It was worth a shot. Nothing like being accused of something you didn't do to give you enthusiasm for your escape."

Franklin glanced at the agent holding Henry's arm. "You are excused agent. Go back in and help with the removal of the injured parties."

Henry glanced back at the man still holding his arm "Take care of the woman. Her name is Fee, and she's innocent of all of this. That man, the one who's still alive, he's the one who shot her."

The man didn't reply to Henry, just saluted Franklin, and headed back inside.

"Now, you can damn well tell me where my badge and gun are," said Franklin fiercely.

Henry grinned. "Your badge is in my back pocket." He lifted his arms and turned his hips to give the special agent easier access. "The gun is hidden back there, in our bags in the storage room. It might be a little destroyed now."

Franklin glanced over his shoulder at the chaos behind them. "How the hell am I going to explain that?" he said.

"Don't explain it too much, that's the key to something like this. Just say it was destroyed."

"I don't need your help to fudge the damn details," said Franklin fiercely.

"You need to take care of Fee," said Henry urgently. "She's got nothing to do with any of this. But that man back there, he's dangerous. You'll find the gun he's holding is the one that shot the dead man in the room, and he's an associate of the other man in the first explosion."

"Who we've identified as David Gardner, one of your friend's colleagues."

"And the real person behind the explosion in Tampa."

"That is yet to be determined. Don't think any of this will get you off the charges of assaulting an FBI agent and theft."

"Are you really going to report that you had your badge and gun stolen...twice?" asked Henry.

"You tell me how you did it, and how you escaped at the hospital, and I might consider holding off on those charges."

"I'll tell you anything you want to know, as long as you take care of Fee. And keep her out of the same damn ambulance as that animal in there."

"Deal."

Medical personnel ran past them in that moment, and raced into the old building. Moments later, Fee's father was being carried out on a stretcher.

"How is he?" asked Franklin.

"He's touch and go, sir."

"Keep him under armed guard. He's a suspect."

"Yes, sir."

Two more paramedics came out, this time carrying Fee between them on a stretcher. She had bandages and a compress on her shoulder, and she was horribly pale. She smiled wanly up at Henry when she saw him.

Henry made a move to go to her, but Franklin held him steady. "Say what you have to say from here."

"Fee, it's going to be fine," he said softly. He glanced up at the grim faces of the medics. He didn't ask what the men thought of her chances, he could see it in their faces. The medics kept going.

Franklin grabbed Henry's arm, and led him along after Fee's stretcher.

A thought popped into Henry's head. If he could only touch Fee, he might be able to use their electricity to give her enough magic to help. It was worth a try. "I need to hold her hand. Just for a minute," he said to Franklin.

"You need to tell me what I want to know first, before you're going to be allowed to do anything."

"I promise I'll tell you anything you need to know. Just let me go to her now."

"She'll be fine for a minute or two. The medics need to do their thing first."

Henry looked desperately between Fee's retreating body and Franklin's determined face. "Okay. I'll tell you how I did it." He glanced down at his pocket. "Using him." The little creature hiding in his shirt pocket obediently popped its head up and chittered at Franklin.

Franklin jumped back in fright. "What the hell is that?"

"It's a little critter Fee made. It's what she does. Why the Witch Hunters are after her. He's a bit of a kleptomaniac, so he got into the habit of stealing things from people in the hospital. He also warned me when the Witch Hunters came to the hospital, and helped me get out via the ducting system."

Franklin shook his head. "There's no way you could have gotten up to that vent. We made sure to put you in a high-ceilinged room."

Henry grinned. "There's no way a normal person would have been able to do it. But I was raised in a carnival, and doing tricks like pulling myself up through a vent is nothing to someone like me." He shrugged.

Franklin walked along beside Henry for a moment, absorbing the information. "That's all it was? A funny little robot and your carnival upbringing?"

"Sorry if you thought it might be something different." Henry frowned. "What did you think I was going to say?"

Franklin shrugged. "There have been some funny goings-on recently. You never know what people are going to say."

"What? Did you think I was going to tell you it was magic or something?"

Franklin glanced sharply at Henry. "Or something," he said.

FEE LAY ON THE STRETCHER, trying to remember what was happening. Why there was pain radiating out from her chest. Why these people were carrying her with fast jolting steps that hurt her whole body.

She didn't understand any of it.

Something chittered close to her ear, and she smiled. They were with her, and that was all that mattered. She wondered where Max was. He must be tidying up in the other room or something.

Was there another room here? Wherever here was.

She closed her eyes again and a face popped into her head: blond hair, an infectious grin, and eyes that marked him for what he was: a golden god. She sighed. It was good to know a golden god just once in your life.

There was some shouting, and then she was laid on the ground. She moaned as pain spiralled out through her body.

"We should get her into the ambulance with the other two," a voice said.

"No. One of them is the man who shot her. We have orders to keep them separate."

"I don't know how long she has," warned the other voice.

"The other ambulance is on its way. It'll be here soon."

Fee felt strange, like she was floating away from her body, and she tried to call out. Her body arched, and her eyes rolled back into her head, but she saw it from above, like it was a movie of her death.

"Sir! She's going into shock," said one of the paramedics, as he pushed aside Henry and the agent standing next to him.

"We're going to lose her!"

Fee watched as her body gasped for breath, and the medic worked on her. It was warm where she was, comforting. She was calm, and unafraid. Then she looked at Henry. He had fallen to his knees, on the ground, screaming her name, telling her to come back. She frowned. Where was she going?

Henry touched her hand, and the blue electricity shot between them and up to where she hovered above her body. She shuddered with the feel of it.

She looked down and saw a cloud-like blue chord connected to her body. She pulled on it experimentally. It zinged down her arm like the electricity she'd become so used to when she touched Henry. But it also dragged her closer to her body. She pulled again, and she was a little closer still.

Below her, the people rushed around like ants. The ambulance pulled away, taking her father and David to the hospital. She wondered if her father was sitting outside his body like this.

Pulling again, Fee gathered this second version of herself closer to her body. The paramedic was frantically working over her, trying to save her battered shell. Blood was everywhere.

Fee glanced at Henry. He was staring directly at her. Not at her body, but at the version of herself that was floating over her body. Like he could see her.

His golden eyes were all she could see; there was nothing else. She lifted one hand, and reached out to him. He reached out his hand in response, and they touched. Suddenly the blue lightning flickered between them, up and down her arm, and along his.

With a devastatingly painful thump, Fee returned to her body, and the pain that filled every last crevice. She screamed.

CHAPTER 50

*H*enry scrambled over to Fee. Her mouth was wide open in a scream that sent shudders through his entire body. He grabbed her hand, and held on for dear life when the medic tried to push him away.

"It's going to be okay, Fee," he said. "It's going to be okay." He tried to push magic, healing, whatever he could through whatever the hell kind of link they had. The damn blue lightning had better make itself useful now, when it was really needed.

He knew what he'd seen. She'd been leaving her body. She'd been dying.

He felt the electricity in his body and knew she felt it too. He had to believe it would be enough to keep them both together, to help her body heal itself.

Then he felt a stronger force, a heavy warmth that he recognized, flowing through him and into Fee. He looked around, trying to see if Rilla was there. For the first time, he was relieved that she'd ignored him when he said he could handle things by himself.

He didn't know if the Carnival could heal an outsider

through him but whatever was happening, he was grateful. He felt tears coursing down his cheeks and didn't care. All that mattered was that Fee was alive and had a fighting chance of survival.

"Sir, I need you to step back. I can't work on her properly with you there."

"I'm not letting go of her hand," replied Henry. "So you'll just have to do what you can with me here." He glared at the medic, and something in his eyes must have convinced the man, because he got back to work without another word, moving around to the other side of Fee to continue working on her.

He didn't know how long they sat there, but police cars started leaving, and another ambulance arrived, sirens blazing. The medic talked to the driver, keeping a wary eye on Henry.

"You can't go in the ambulance with her, you know," said Franklin softly to one side of Henry.

Henry glanced up at him. "Why not? You could come too. To make sure I don't do anything silly."

"It's against regulations," replied Franklin.

Henry snorted. "I get the feeling you're the kind of man who isn't too systematic about following regulations."

Franklin's eyebrows shot down, and Henry thought for a moment that the agent was going to deny it. Then he sighed. "Okay, fine. What if I let you go in the ambulance with her? What happens then?"

Henry shrugged. "I just want to make sure she's okay. You can arrest me at the hospital. Take me to your cells. Interrogate me."

"I just want to understand what happened here today. That's all you have to tell me."

Henry glanced at Fee. "She's someone special. Those two you've got in the other ambulance tried to kill her. Once in

Tampa and once here. That's all there is to this story. Fee and I are innocent of anything except trying to save ourselves. You have to believe me." Henry knew he didn't exactly look believable. He was covered in dirt, blood, and tears. He probably looked like a damn monster.

But Franklin saw something that made him pause. Then nod. "Okay, you can go with her in the ambulance. But I'm coming with you, and you're giving me more information."

Henry nodded. Franklin wasn't so bad. He'd take that deal any day.

Their original paramedic came back with the driver. "Excuse me, sir, but we need to put her in the ambulance now. You'll have to let go of her hand." The driver's voice was familiar, and Henry flicked his gaze upward... into the face of his brother Jason. He tried not to react, but it was the hardest thing he'd ever done in his life.

"Uh...sure." He was so surprised he stepped back without thinking. His connection to Fee grew dim. He glanced at the other medic and saw the man watching him with a stunned expression on his face. Glaring, he reached over and grabbed Fee's hand again. "Actually, I'm going to hold her hand while you load her in."

Jason and the other medic glanced at each other and shrugged, loading Fee into the back of the ambulance slowly so Henry could climb inside next to her. Franklin followed close behind. Henry looked around the inside of the ambulance, trying to understand what was happening. How had Jason inserted himself onto the medical team?

Henry was so dazed that he almost didn't notice the small tightening of Fee's hand in his. He looked down and gazed into her green eyes. "Oh, thank the gods," he whispered. "You're here." He leaned down and kissed her cheek.

She smiled weakly. "Of course, I'm here. Where did you think I was going to go?"

CHAPTER 51

The ambulance took off, and Henry and Franklin had to grab at whatever was closest to keep from falling down.

"Not the smoothest ride in town, eh?" said Henry.

"So tell me why Fee is so special that they'd want to kill her," said Franklin.

"They belong to a crazy cult," said Henry carefully. "They believe some strange things about the world and they think Fee is a bad person. So they tried to kill her."

"What makes them think Fee is a bad person?"

"Because she's talented with robots. They think it's magic instead of talent."

Franklin paused. "They think she uses magic?" he said softly.

Henry nodded. "They're crazy. Fee is just really good at what she does."

Franklin nodded, and stared down at Fee, who had closed her eyes again. "So tell me more about them."

"The people hunting Fee?"

"Yes."

"They're called the Witch Hunters. They're some kind of secret organization who hunt people they believe are using magic and kill them. They're essentially serial killers."

"How is it that they get away with these murders?"

Henry shook his head. "I don't know. This is all a new concept to me as well." He tried to decide if he should tell Franklin that the other man was Fee's father. Would it somehow incriminate them further? And would Franklin find out eventually if he was investigating it? He took a breath. "It was her own father who shot her."

Franklin's face remained the same at this revelation.

"You knew that already?" Henry realized.

Franklin's face didn't give anything away. "I've had her investigated. We found out a few interesting things."

"Like what?"

"Her family. Who they are and what they've been doing."

"Mainly, her father, as I understand it," said Henry, thinking of Fee's mother back at the Carnival.

Franklin shook his head. "The mother has been plenty involved. We have evidence of multiple murders where she was present and participating."

Henry froze. "Are you sure about that?" he said, his voice ragged. What had they done? They'd taken Fee's mother to their home. If Rilla hadn't insisted on chasing him, they could have been back at the Compound by now. "I have to call them." He patted at his pockets, trying to find his phone.

Just then, the ambulance came to a screeching halt on the road. Henry crashed into a set of shelves, only just saving himself in time before he fell completely off his seat.

Franklin didn't fare much better, but he recovered quickly and pulled out his gun. "You stay here with Fee. I'll see what's happening."

Henry nodded, thinking of his brother up the front. If it

were something bad, Jason would be backup for Franklin and if it were something of the Carnival's making, they wouldn't harm Franklin. Either way, he was going to stay here and protect Fee

Franklin opened the back door and peered around the door, his gun at the ready.

He stepped down out of the ambulance and looked around. He closed the door slowly, and Henry clasped Fee's hands tightly, his blood pumping at one hundred miles an hour.

He thought of the Witch Hunters. They'd been a step ahead of them the whole time. Had they known she would be in a second ambulance, traveling down a road on the outskirts of the city? It was possible, if her father had been able to send a message before he attacked them.

Henry looked around for something to use as a weapon, his eyes fixing on a fire extinguisher in the corner. He stood up, grabbing the heavy metal canister, and waited by the slightly ajar door, his arms raised in readiness.

Listening at the door, he heard the sound of a scuffle, and the grunts of people fighting hand to hand. His whole body tensed, and he wondered if he should go out and help Franklin, just in case it was the Witch Hunters. He glanced back at Fee. No, he wouldn't leave her vulnerable.

The door to the ambulance was pulled abruptly open. Henry tensed in readiness to slam the extinguisher down into the face of their attacker.

His brother's face grinned up at him. "You a little anxious, bro?" he said.

"What the hell's happening?" asked Henry, releasing the fire extinguisher.

"We're saving your butt, that's what."

"What did you do with Franklin?"

"He's all right, just knocked him around a little."

"He's on our side, Jason. I hope you didn't hurt him too badly," said Henry sternly.

Jason rolled his eyes at his brother. "You're not very grateful, given that we've just saved you from prison."

"I don't think he was going to put me in prison, Jase. He was actually rather interested in the Witch Hunters. I think he wants to investigate them."

A groan sounded from next to the ambulance.

"You knocked him out?" Henry hurried over to where Franklin was lying prone on the grass next to the road.

Franklin groaned again and opened his eyes.

"Are you okay?" asked Henry, his eyes scanning the man's body for injuries.

"Relax, bro, I used a move that knocked him out pretty quick. He had a gun; I had to get him unconscious as soon as I could." Jason flicked his gaze to Franklin. "Sorry about that."

Henry let out a relieved breath and helped Franklin sit up. The man was still groggy, but he seemed to understand what was happening.

Franklin put one hand up to his neck and moved it stiffly. "Whatever you did, it was effective." He glanced around, first at Henry and then Jason. "So what's happening here?" he asked.

Jason glanced at Henry before replying. "We want you to help us. And if you help us, we'll help you."

Franklin raised his eyebrows, his eyes hard. "What makes you think I'll help you? You just knocked out a federal officer. I think you might find you're in a whole crap ton of trouble."

"We'll help you catch the Witch Hunters, or at least give you everything we know on them. Absolutely everything. In return, we need you to say that Fee died here in this ambulance. And Henry escaped, taking her body out of some kind of weird attachment, but that you're not planning to charge him with anything. So no one goes after him."

Franklin narrowed his eyes at Jason. "And what makes you think I would do any of that?"

Henry cleared his throat, catching on to the idea they'd obviously come up with since he and Fee had left them. "Because we can help you catch a group of people who've been systematically murdering innocent people for years. A group of serial killers. Can you imagine the coup that would be for you, and your agency? Fee isn't part of it, but I'm sure we could persuade her to give you information that would lead to their capture. People she knew growing up, lists of the places they lived. But you need to protect her from her father, and the rest of her family. Even her mother." Henry sent a significant glance to Jason. "We're not the bad guys here."

Franklin sighed and looked between Henry and Jason. "This is highly irregular," he said. "How do I know you're not just trying to con me?"

"The people you're trying to catch have been doing this for decades. Maybe longer. Imagine if you caught them. Imagine if you were the one to bring them to justice. Imagine the lives you would save." Henry was irrationally pleased to note that it was the argument for saved lives that seemed to persuade Franklin.

"If I do this,"—he paused, glancing sternly from Henry to Jason—"*If* I do this, I don't know how much I'll be able to cover over. I'll have to speak to my superiors to make sure it's a deal they're prepared to make." He rubbed one hand over his face, as if he was suddenly tired.

"Between Fee and her mother, you'll be able to take down a criminal organization that has been operating for longer than we've been alive. That's not something every FBI agent has the opportunity to be part of."

Franklin looked up. "I believe I can make the case for it," he said. "Now help me up."

Henry grinned, and held out his hand, pulling Franklin up. "You won't regret it. We'll get these bastards." He turned to Jason. "In the meantime, where's Fee's mother?"

"She's back at the airport. It was just me and Rilla who headed out this way."

"She can't know that Fee's okay. We have to tell her that Fee died here tonight. Franklin says she's in on everything as well."

Jason's eyes widened for a moment, and then a look of sympathy crossed his face. "Poor kid. Imagine having both parents trying to kill you. That's rough."

Franklin nodded. "I want the mother."

Henry narrowed his eyes thoughtfully. It wasn't as if they wanted Summer Dawn hanging around the Compound. "I'm sure we can arrange something. You take Fee's mother, and see if she'll talk. As far as everyone else and both her parents know, Fee is dead. You can contact us through me and we'll help you however we can."

"If you try anything, I'll tell them Fee is still alive," Franklin said, his face grim.

"We'll keep our end of the bargain, Franklin. You keep your end, and we'll be fine."

Franklin glanced around the road. "So now what? How do we work this thing?"

Henry grinned at Franklin. "You want us to tie you up?" he said.

Franklin glared at Henry. "No. Being knocked out is sufficient. Where is the other medic? Or is he in on it as well?"

"He's in the front. I gave him a little something to make him sleepy," said Jason.

"I think as there will be no actual evidence, I will write a report swearing that she died before the ambulance was stopped, and you were so distraught you took the body with you to be buried it in an unnamed place. Leave the mother at the airport, and I will send someone to pick her up."

Henry nodded. "Thanks, Franklin. I appreciate this."

"You just make damn sure this is all worth it. I'm risking my career on you."

"It's worth it."

"It better be."

CHAPTER 52

ee opened her eyes and looked around groggily. She was in a hotel room of some kind. Her first thought was panic, and she tried to sit up. The room spun, and she flopped back down to the soft bed.

"She's awake," whispered a woman from the far side of the room. "Go get Henry."

"But we only just convinced him to sleep," murmured another voice, this time male.

"He made me promise."

There was a shuffling noise, and the opening and closing of a door. Fee closed her eyes again. Henry was coming and that was all that mattered. A moment later, the door opened again, and in rushed her golden god.

"Hey, Fee. How you feeling?" he asked softly, as he grasped her hand and sat on the bed next to her. A chattering noise accompanied his arrival, and a small metal creature raced down his arm, and across hers to hide in the crook of her neck.

She cleared her throat. "My head hurts," she whispered.

Henry turned his head. "Rilla, do we have anything for that?" he asked.

Rilla stood up and came over to stand beside Henry. "Hold my hand, and we'll see what the Carnival can do," she said.

Fee watched as Henry put his other hand in Rilla's. Almost immediately, she felt something warm flowing into her body, reaching out to her hands and legs and her head, pushing soothing and cooling feelings through her whole body. She sighed. It felt very good.

"How is it doing that?" Henry whispered to Rilla.

Rilla shook her head. "I think it's something to do with the connection you two have formed. I've never seen it work on someone outside of the Carnival in quite that way before. Even the people inside it are often not affected like that."

"It's like she's already got some kind of connection. Or that her own magic is amplifying it or something," said Henry with a frown, already trying to understand what was happening.

Fee smiled. He'd keep at it until he worked it out. "So we made it out, then?" she asked. "What happened to my father? Where's my mother?"

"Your father is in hospital." Henry paused. "Your mother has been taken into witness protection by the FBI. She's going to help them investigate the Witch Hunters."

Fee's eyes widened. That was the last thing her mother would have wanted. "But... Why? I thought she was on her way to the Compound?"

Henry grasped her hand tighter. "Franklin intimated that your mother might not be as innocent of the deaths as she had suggested. We couldn't take the chance of taking her with us."

Fee felt dizzy for a moment, her world shifting yet again.

Her mother had been part of it? "Was she trying to get to me when she was at the farm?"

Henry shook his head. "I don't know. It's not clear if she really did have a falling out with your father or not. But we couldn't risk it. Franklin promised to take good care of her. She won't be harmed."

Thoughts crashed into each other inside her head, and Fee closed her eyes, unable to process everything. The only thing that seemed real was Henry by her side, holding her hand. She tightened her hand against his, and sent a silent thank you to whoever was listening that they had sent her Henry. "Thank you," she whispered, opening her eyes to look into his golden eyes.

Henry leaned closer and kissed her softly on the cheek. He brushed away a strand of hair from her face, and smiled. "No, thank *you*, Fee," he said. "You mean everything to me. When I thought I'd lost you..." his words trailed away. His hand cupped her cheek. "It was the worst thing I'd ever felt. I don't want to feel like that again. I love you. I want you to come back to the Carnival with me."

Fee smiled up at him, wondering how a golden god had ever come to love her. She put one hand up to touch his cheek. "I love you too, Henry. I'll go anywhere with you," she whispered. "Anywhere at all."

CHAPTER 53

*F*ee looked up from where she was soldering a connection on her latest creature. The door to the lab had opened, and Henry walked in. He grinned at her and walked over, his arms wide.

She dropped her tools, turned off the soldering iron, and stepped into his embrace. "How was it?" she asked as he crushed her to him. The familiar feel of electricity zinged through her body.

"Good, but I missed you. Four days was a long time."

"What did Lucas say?"

"He paid me the full amount for my contract. Wants me back later in the year."

"You're not thinking of going are you?"

"I'm not sure. I did make a new friend while I was back there. Wanda gave me a hug and thanked me for fixing her glasses."

"That old battle-axe. She didn't like anyone."

"She likes me," said Henry smugly. "They're devastated by your death, by the way. But Eugene and Nolan were determined to get the project up and running again. They were talking about naming her Fee in your honor and they even had Pelgrim in to help them out."

"How did Pelgrim take that?"

Henry grinned. "Surprisingly well, apparently. The other two have mastered the art of telling him off if he steps out of line."

"And they really think I'm…?"

"Dead? Yes. They even held a memorial service while I was there. It was rather sad." Henry looked down at her.

Fee blinked. "Really? What did they say about me?"

Henry laughed. "I'm not going to tell you. It'll just feed your ego."

Fee smacked him lightly on the arm. "You're one to talk about ego," she said. "What about Max?"

The door to the lab opened at that point and a familiar metal face poked through. "Do you wish to have coffee served in here or on the veranda?" Max asked, as if he'd been living there all his life, and not just the five minutes since he'd arrived.

"He's happy to be back with you." Henry leaned down and kissed her. "As am I."

Fee leaned to one side. "It's good to see you, Max."

"It's good to see you too, Fee," said Max. "I'll put it out on the veranda… In half an hour." He closed the door, leaving her alone with Henry.

"Did you hear him? He just called me Fee."

"He's getting soft in his old age," smiled Henry, pulling her closer again.

"I love you," whispered Fee against his lips.

"I love you, too."

Thank you for reading *Hidden Magic*!

Check out the next installment in the series, **Shadow Prophecy**, below.

Celestine has a certain... *reputation*. She's the worst fortune teller the Carnival has ever seen.

It's a reputation she's worked hard to create.

Truth is, Celestine's a liar. She's actually a powerful fortune teller who hasn't gotten a fortune wrong since she was a kid.

But her survival depends on keeping her secret, and she's not about to break it now. Except... what if she sees a future where someone she knows dies? What if she sees a future where the carnival is destroyed and everyone in it ends up destitute and homeless?

What then?

Even worse, if she decides to break her vow of silence, how's she going to convince the people of the carnival that instead of being the world's most incompetent oracle, she's actually the one person who could save them all?

Turn the page for an excerpt of Shadow Prophecy.

EXCERPT FROM SHADOW PROPHECY

Celestine knew she was in trouble.

The morning sun was starting to heat up the rocks where she had fallen, and it would only get hotter as the day wore on.

Reaching out with shaking fingers, she tried to touch her swollen ankle, just above the brown sandal. A bright burst of pain shot out from her foot, right up her leg; she jerked back, bumping against the rocks behind her. Her hand landed against the rough surface, and yet more stinging pain launched its way up her arms. The world started to spin, and her vision blurred.

Panting, she lay still for what seemed like hours until the pain ebbed away and the landscape settled back into place. Celestine tried to pull herself to sitting, but her long skirts were tangled and twisted around her legs; she couldn't drag herself up without moving her ankle, and she was afraid she might pass out if she did that again.

She cursed. When she got home, she vowed she was going to change into pants. It was just that skirts were so much lighter and cooler in the summer months. It also fit nicely with her image as the Carnival's fortune-teller.

Celestine looked down at her hands and sighed. The thin cotton gloves covering them were ripped, and blood pulsed out over the material. Her palms stung from the rather large gash on her right hand, and the smaller grazes on the left. Much good they were going to do her now. She eased the gloves off, wincing as she caught the edge of the wound.

She gently ran a finger over a graze, trying to find the little pieces of rock and dirt so she could pull them out. She had long elegant fingers, and often used her hands to create an aura of mystery during the readings she gave. Punters remembered her hands more than anything else, and now hers were all cut up. What kind of impression would scabby, grazed hands give?

Celestine snorted to herself. Some fortune-teller she was. She should have looked into her own future and avoided this whole mess from the start. She sighed and laid her hands against her chest. If only it worked that way, she would have led a much simpler life.

Not that it mattered, now anyway. She was going to die out here quite alone.

Panic rose in her chest and Celestine flicked her gaze left and right, as if a solution would pop out from behind one of the trees grouped on the far side of the rocky ravine where she'd been climbing. She was in the middle of nowhere, up some godforsaken mountain with a broken ankle and no way to get home. She'd done a fair bit of climbing over large rocks to get to this point, and there was no way she could get back down again on her own.

Even worse, she hadn't told anyone where she was going.

Even Artemis had disappeared on her. She glanced around, trying to make out her distinctive spotted fur hiding in the terrain. Usually her cat—more like a behemoth given her Savannah heritage—could be trusted to stay by her side when trouble hit. If she could have had her large comforting presence cuddled up next to her right now, she would have felt better. A rogue tear escaped down her cheek, and she angrily wiped it away.

She wasn't a quitter. This wasn't going to get the better of her.

She pulled out her mobile phone again. Zero reception. She shoved it back in the pocket of her leather jacket. At least she'd been wearing the thick leather; it had protected the top half of her body somewhat—except her hands.

Celestine lifted her skirt and looked down at her leg. The ankle was definitely swollen, and the long graze down her leg was starting to really hurt. She'd slipped on shale, then tumbled down over a large boulder and into a dried-up creek bed. Lifting one hand to the side of her head, she touched the large lump that was forming, and felt something sticky on her fingertips. She pulled her hand away; congealing blood dripped down from her fingers. For a moment, she felt woozy, and the world swayed around her.

Celestine blinked, trying to get her focus back. Her body felt heavy, and she wanted to just lay her head down and close her eyes. But despite the sick feeling in her stomach, and the way the world was ever so slightly blurry, she knew she had to stay awake.

Just at the edge of the rocks, there were flowers growing in a patch of grass under the trees. It would be lovely to lie in the shade rather than here on the rocks. Several stones were poking into her butt and it was as hard as... well, rock.

Perhaps she could crawl. Rolling over onto her stomach, she tried to come up on all fours. Pain tore up her leg, and she cried out. Waves of agony crashed over her, and she fell back to earth.

She must have passed out for a moment or two because

suddenly Artemis was there, licking her face. Reaching up, she gathered her cat to her, the creature's large body offering comfort where before she'd had none. Artemis gave a warning meow, and pulled herself away from Celestine, melting back into the shadows of the trees nearby.

"Come back, Artemis," called Celestine. Tears pushed their way up her throat again, and she struggled to hold them back. She didn't know why it was so important that she didn't cry. It wasn't as if anyone else was around. But she hadn't cried when she'd run away from her home and family; she hadn't cried through all the lonely months when she'd struggled to make her way, or even after she'd arrived at the Jolly Knight Carnival and discovered she would have to hide herself away to survive.

She'd be damned if she would cry now.

This was nothing. A mere blip on the screen. She would figure a way out of this. As soon as her head stopped hurting, and she could think clearly again.

"Artemis," she called again.

A figure loomed overhead, on top of the very boulder she'd tumbled over. He was silhouetted against the rising sun, so all she could see was a large black outline.

He looked like Death come to gather her up.

But where was his scythe?

"Are you okay?" asked Death.

Celestine shook her head.

"Stay where you are, I'll be right there."

Celestine looked down at her ankle, and the wounds on her hands and leg. It seemed Death didn't know everything, if he thought she could go anywhere.

The landscape blurred even further, and she wondered if this was what death was really like. A gradual blurring of the focus until there was nothing more than whiteness—or perhaps blackness?—everywhere. The good thing was that the pain in her ankle and hands was losing its force. Every-thing seemed to be moving away, and for some reason she didn't mind. What did it matter anyway? She was alone in the world.

And then Death was there with her. At first she flinched away, her instinctual reaction when someone attempted to touch or hold her.

But then, this was Death, wasn't it? What did it matter if Death touched her?

And so she let his soothing voice calm her. Instead of immediately gathering her up against his chest—as she'd halfway expected—Death crouched down by her ankle.

"Is it just your ankle that's hurt?" he asked.

Celestine frowned. Surely he must know? He was Death. She shook her head. Held up her bleeding hands. Pulled up her skirt to show the gash on her leg, just under her knee. The grazes over her legs. Tears started to fall as she bowed her head and showed the bloodied lump that had formed in her hair.

Death frowned, and Celestine noticed he was rather attractive, in a shaggy, unshaven kind of way. Not the skull head she'd seen in pictures at all.

"You're bleeding from that head wound. You probably feel a little light headed."

Again she nodded. Talking seemed pointless when you were dealing with Death.

"I'm going to check out your ankle first. I'll try not to hurt you."

Then he touched her leg.

Celestine screamed, and immediately everything around them went still. The world froze, like they were hanging, waiting for the next moment in time to load. Then lights sparkled across her vision, a rainbow of colors that shone as if the gods had created them. It was so beautiful, and every time Celestine saw them, she wanted to stay just here, in this place, forever.

But she never did.

She was always jerked into the next place.

She felt her body shuddering, and for a moment, pain from her ankle warred with the on-coming vision, and she thought it might not happen. Her heart leaped. This was it. The one time when the visions didn't rule her over everything else.

But then she was dragged under, and her hope died.

There was so much thick, oozing blood; it was spreading like a virus, covering the ground. There was someone talking, muttering, laughing in the background. A woman. An older woman, wearing a stained and dirty suit, holding a sleek handgun.

Celestine's heart started racing.

There was a body lying face down on the ground, at the center of that stain. Celestine knew he was dead, but she didn't know who he was, even though his face was directed toward her. The body was lying in a large warehouse space.

A train running past blocked out all sound for a moment, and time stilled. The overhead bulb shuddered with the reflected vibration.

The bulb swayed toward the corners, and Celestine saw that there were others in the room; she recognized the Ringmasters Rilla and Jack. She knew their faces because she went out of her way to avoid them in the Carnival. There was also another younger woman, and the little girl who'd joined the Carnival in the last week or so. She had an idea they were sisters. In the few times they'd met, the little girl had watched Celestine with a knowledge beyond her years.

She'd made a point of staying away from her as well.

All four of them were huddled down together at the edge of the room. Rilla had her arms around the other two younger women. They were all dusty and dirty, indicating they'd been in the large space for a while. Celestine looked around the room, trying to understand where they were. Boxes were piled high around her.

"I've been waiting a long time for this," the woman said. A gunshot rang out in the darkened room, and Celestine jerked.

Across the room, Rilla fell to the ground, a red stain spreading across her shirt.

"No!" yelled Jack.

Another shot sounded, and Jack grunted in pain as he fell forward. He didn't move.

The remaining woman screamed.

"This is what happens when you disobey me, Tilly. When you try to take what is mine away from me," the woman whispered, her voice hard.

Tears welled in the other woman's eyes—she must be Tilly. She held tight to the little girl, who didn't seem as upset. She was staring hard at the older woman holding the gun, her face a mask of determination.

"They didn't deserve to die, Veronica," said Tilly. "None of them did, not even Sam. They didn't kill Marco. I did."

"You all killed him. Every last one of you," said the woman—Veronica—her voice rising to a fevered pitch. The whites of her eyes were almost glowing in the dark room. "I will not rest until every single person in the Carnival pays for what they have done. And you and your sister are going to watch every one of them die."

The gun-toting kidnapper walked forward. "And then, when I kill you both, you will understand how I feel, the pain I must live with every day," she said. "Everything I ever did in my life was for my brother, and you took him from me."

Tilly cowered back, glancing from the crazed woman in front of her, to the little girl in her arms.

As the vision faded away, Celestine looked down at the dead man lying in a pool of his own blood. His bearded face was visible, as was the green hooded sweatshirt he wore. She didn't recognize him, but she could see his face.

She would know him if she saw him again.

To find out what happens next, check out *Shadow Prophecy* at your favorite retailer!

Want to find out how the Carnival *really* started? Or learn more about where the wishes and curses came from?

Apply to join Trudi Jaye's Secret Society to get free access to the highly classified **Shadow Archives** to find out *more…*

You'll also get the top secret, highly hush-hush weekly Trudi Jaye Secret Society bulletin with inside information on characters, ongoing stories, and early notification about sales and new releases.

Visit www.trudijayewrites.com/shadow-archives to apply to join the secret society today!

Other Books by Trudi Jaye

Dragon Rising Series
Lost Dragon (Prequel Novella available via the Trudi Jaye
Secret Society)
Hidden Dragon
Searching Dragon
Fighting Dragon
Cursed Dragon
Warrior Dragon (coming soon)

Demon Hunter in Hiding Series
Dreams & Demons (Prequel Novella available via the Trudi
Jaye Secret Society)
Secrets & Demons
Agents & Demons
Magic & Demons
Dragons & Demons
Spells & Demons

Elemental Witch Series (With Tania Hutley)
The Trouble with Magic
The Problem with Witches
The Danger with Demons

Firecaller Series
Salt (Prequel Novella available via the Trudi Jaye Secret
Society)
Subtle Knife (Prequel Novella available via the Trudi Jaye
Secret Society)
Fire Mage
Royal Mage (due out soon)

Dark Carnival Series
The First Wish (Prequel Novella available via the Trudi Jaye
Secret Society)
If Magic Were Wishes
The Gift
Magic for Lost Souls (available via the Trudi Jaye Secret
Society)
High Flyer
Hidden Magic
Shadow Prophecy

Hi! I'm Trudi Jaye, and I'm the author of this book. I live on a rural property in New Zealand, surrounded by horses (not mine!) with my lovely husband and cheeky tween (not quite a teenager, but thinks she's a teenager) daughter.

For a long time I was a magazine writer and editor, and wrote articles on everything from cruise ships and movie stars to chainsaws and architecture. Now I write novels full time.

I enjoy yoga, although I'm not very bendy, and karate, although I don't like the idea of hitting anyone.

www.trudijayewrites.com